Beautiful Beloved

The Howard Saga

Chrisna Kruger

Red Heart Publishing

All you need is love

ISBN: 978-0-620-99273-2

For everyone who has loved and lost,
For everyone who has never loved at all.

Preface

Is it better to have loved and lost,
than never to have loved at all?

Alice Browning discovers her fiancé, Robert Everton, stood her up on the night of her graduation, to spend the night with another girl. She also finds out Robert was only interested in her for her money. From now on she will be much more discerning when it comes to choosing a groom. No man will again know about her inheritance – she is merely nurse Browning. Alice breaks away on a holiday with her aunt to the small town of Arundel, West Sussex where she once again encounters the handsome stranger she briefly met in the city.

The handsome Oliver Howard is the adopted son of Sir and Lady Howard of Stanton Estate in Arundel. He is a young, attractive, and very successful cardiologist. But Oliver will never open his heart to love, because Stanton Manor and the people living in this glorious mansion still hides the secret of his lineage – and some secrets of their own. Aunt Emily hates Oliver and she had banned Oliver from the manor. Oliver has not been back to Stanton Estate in twelve years. Uncle William is dying of cancer, and Oliver's chances to find the answers to his lineage are getting slimmer with each passing day as he tries to get his answers hidden inside the manor which he may not enter.

The sparks immediately fly between Oliver and Alice. Oliver

thinks of Alice as a pretty, empty-headed form of entertainment, and Alice is tired of men treating her like a fool.

Oliver can never offer his love to a girl when he doesn't even know who he is... He is a man without a name.

Alice learns the most unexpected thing that can happen in life is love... and it is very possible to love that one wrong person.

Is love enough to unite two broken hearts or will it always be about money?

Chapter 1

Alice Browning's green eyes flash. She shakes her head making her blonde hair swing around her shoulders. "I can't believe it!" She says angrily, trying to keep her voice controlled. "There I was the entire night, all dressed up, waiting just for you, and that is where you were! Visiting Stephanie Simms in the nurses' quarters."

"Please, Alice, don't be so dramatic," Robert tries to calm her down.

"Dramatic? One night, Robert, I needed you with me just this one night, and I'm being dramatic?"

They are sitting in a little street café waiting for their breakfast. It would've been their usual lazy Sunday breakfast outing, but today is not another usual Sunday for them, Alice thinks to herself. She glances outside through the window next to her and sees the storm-clouds gathering. A few of the other people are already turning their heads in curiosity, and others in amusement, in their direction. How much longer is she going to allow Robert to treat her this way? All four years of her studies have been the same story with him. And studying nursing and living in the nurses' quarters didn't give her much leisure time to take his behaviour too seriously, she was always working or preparing for exams. When he asked her to get married, she told herself that he knew how important her studies were to her and he would change once she was a qualified nurse and they got married. Afterall, he was already twenty-six years old; he has finished his studies and he was making a good name for himself in the architecture world. All his business dinners and late nights out have always been about his career and his future, and she had always been supportive. He wants to further his studies but has maintained these past four years that her studies were their first priority. But last night at her graduation function and being named the top student of her group, the one night she wanted him by her side, this one night, he didn't even bother to show up. Alice looks down at her engagement ring on her left hand. How happy was she when he proposed to her, she wonders to herself? And now, trying to remember that moment on her twenty-first birthday, she doesn't even know the answer to her own question. Was she even happy about it? Or was she just going through the motions of what everyone expected of them after dating for three years? What she expected of them? Everyone dates for two to three years, then everyone is engaged for two to three years, then married for two to three years, and then start a family. Everyone blissfully happy and successful by the time they are thirty.

Alice slips the sparkling ring off her finger and puts it down on the table in front of Robert.

Robert grabs her hand. "Alice, be reasonable. Consider the fact that I had the decency to tell you the truth. Nine out of ten other men would've lied about having a flat tire or a car that wouldn't start," he says muffled.

"You did lie. If one of the junior students didn't see you sneak out of the nurses' quarters late last night you would've gotten away with your clandestine visit Scot-free. If I were any other girl, I might've forgiven you. Again. But everyone knows that men visit Stephanie Simms for only one reason. And you do thát on the one night I asked you to reserve for my graduation function. One night, Robert. You couldn't even use your usual excuses of a business dinner or a late meeting with your boss. No, you spent the night with Stephanie Simms. It is over."

"My dear Alice," he chuckles, "Don't be silly, you carry on as if we will never see each other again, and yet, we are going to Greece with your father in two weeks. We have a wedding to plan and our move to Italy. The next six months will cement our entire future."

"Let go, Robert. Let go of my hand." She pulls her hand free, "You mean yóur future will be cemented in the next six months. My father knows the truth about last night. In fact, he knows more about the truth than I apparently ever did. We are not going with my father, I am not going with my father, I already cancelled with him last night. There will be no wedding to plan. I wish you all the best with your further studies in Italy next year. You are a fantastic architect, and you will have a highly successful career. All I ask of you now is to forget that you ever knew me, Robert Everton, I don't want to see you ever again," she pushes her chair back and gets up. She tries to remain dignified as she quickly makes her way between the little tables in the small café and walks out the door.

Alice comes to a grinding halt a few feet from her small red car and glares at the expensive gray car parked just a few centimeters from hers. The dreaded thing parked there, so broad and shiny like something that belongs in a space movie. She rushes the last few steps to her car, stops the grocery trolley and swings to face the metallic-gray car. Great, this weekend is turning into a total nightmare, she thinks, fighting her tears of frustration. "Idiot! Rude and ignorant man! I hope you crash into a tree and end this beast's existence!" She curses the car and its owner to her heart's content unaware of the people passing by looking at her with expressions of both bafflement and amazement.

"Can I maybe be of help, Miss?" asks a gallant male voice behind her. Alice swings around to the man's words as if she were stung by a bee. She is only half aware that the stranger is extremely tall and broad shouldered, has black slightly ruffled hair, extremely blue eyes, and a strong dimpled chin.

"Can you pick up that car and move it out of my way?" she asks ready for a fight. For a moment he doesn't understand what she is saying but then he chuckles in amusement. This girl in front of him is slim, and small enough to fit under his chin. Long blonde hair and a porcelain fine face gives her the appearance of a child - until you look into her stormy green eyes. Her eyes remind him of the sun-drenched green hills of Scotland, and he wonders just for a second if she is wearing green colored contact lenses because blond-haired people usually have blue eyes.

"Oh, no... no, if I were Superman, yes, but I am just a normal man." he answers with forced seriousness, "but if you have his telephone number, then I will phone Superman for you."

"Funny!" she retorts and then turns back to the metallic gray car. "I feel like I can kick this thing! Maybe I should knock out its windscreen!" She swings back to the man. "Do you see a stone anywhere that I can use?"

Obediently the man looks around him in the parking lot of the shopping center and then he sighs "No, sorry miss, I don't see any stones. If I were Superman, I could probably pull out on of those lamp poles for you, but..." he says with his hands in the air.

"Yes, you already said, you are just a normal man." Alice glares at him and he wonders whether she might kick him instead.

"If you could maybe tell me what the problem is..." he starts adding.

"Don't you have eyes in your head?" she asks sarcastically. "The red car is mine. I am really in a rush to get home, but how can I open my car door if this gleaming monster is parked only a few centimeters from mine?"

The man moves closer, he aims with his left eye pretending to measure the distance between the two cars, and then he shakes his head at a loss. "No, you are right again, it is definitely impossible. I actually doubt if there is enough space for your shadow to fit in between the two motor cars."

"Exactly! Men are so selfish and inconsiderate!"

"And idiots," he somberly agrees with her.

Alice looks at him suspiciously. "Are you making fun of me?"

His eyes widen in pure innocence. "Oh, no, miss. To tell you the truth I have absolute sympathy with your situation. But there is a quite simple solution to your problem: open the right-side door and slide over to the driver's seat."

She stares at him as if he is the embodiment of total stupidity. "And you don't think I would already have done that if it were actually possible?"

"Well, why haven't you?"

"Because you poor… e … Because mister, the lock on the right-hand side doesn't work. I cannot unlock the door from the outside."

He instantly looks even more dejected. "Then there is only one solution: you and I can go and have a cup of tea to drink while we wait for the … e … idiot to show up and move his car," he suggests with a smile.

Alice looks at the man in front of her with more interest. He definitely is very handsome, she decides. If she were not so upset, she would even find him rather irresistible. But as it seemingly is a man responsible for her current predicament she is certainly not giving in to any man's invitation at this moment.

"That is very friendly of you, mister, but…"

"Oliver," he quickly interrupts her.

She frowns irritated. "That's friendly of you, Mr. Oliver, but it just so happens I'm actually quite in a hurry. I was supposed to be home half an hour ago already."

He quickly glances at her hands before asking: "Are your husband and children waiting for you at home?"

"I am not married, but my aunt and I are going on holiday," she unwillingly shares with him and looks around her indignantly. "How long must I still stand around and wait here? Aunt Helen told me to be quick."

"What about a taxi?" he offers enthusiastically.

Her eyes flash again with a noticeably clear message to him about what she really thinks of his limited intellect. "I need my car for us to go on holiday. And we want to leave early enough to avoid driving at night."

Oliver sighs in surrender and looks at her small red car with more intense interest. "You know, the idiot is not really responsible for the predicament that you find yourself in, miss ... e ..." he falls silent waiting for her in anticipation.

"Browning - Alice Browning," she gives him the information reluctantly.

"Alice! A small name for a small lady. Nice to meet you, Alice. I am Oliver..."

"I already know, Mr. Oliver," she crisply interrupts him. "And as I also should have known you are partial to the idiot who parked his car almost on top of mine'"

"Oh, no, I am not, but it is only fair to the idiot to point out that you did park your car over the parking line. If you had parked correctly then you wouldn't have this problem right now."

"I had to park so skew, because the car to my right was parked so skew."

"Oh ..." Oliver rubs his right hand over his mouth and chin, he looks obviously uncomfortable and takes out his car keys. "If you promise not to physically attack me and do me bodily harm, dear Alice, I will now immediately move my car. Goodbye, Alice. Or do you want to have a cup of tea with me first?" he asks hopeful.

He sees the different shades of red flashing across her face with her mouth opening and closing as she is searching for the words, and he hastily turns to the metallic gray car.

"You ... you insolent, selfish man..." she starts, but then the car door already slams close behind him.

He presses the hooter of the car once, waves, smiles, and drives away fast.

"Men are idiots," Alice informs her small red car infuriated and unlocks the door.

Alice uses her chin to press the doorbell at Helen Upton's house. She hears how the front door is pulled open next to her, but she doesn't lift her chin from the doorbell.

"Alice! What in the world are you doing?" asks Helen alarmed. "Come in, my girl, come in. We are already running late. I thought you were leaving for Greece in two weeks."

Alice moves her eyes towards Aunt Helen, but she keeps her chin on the doorbell. "Please help me with these grocery bags Aunt Helen. If I move now, all of this will fall on the stairs."

"Clumsy girl," chides Helen chuckling. "I told you last night we would get everything we needed when we got to Arundel. When will you learn not to do everything at once?" she asks and takes three of the bags from Alice.

"Goodness, that's better! Aunt Helen, please, I don't have the strength now for another lecture: an idiot of a man is responsible for me being so late, two idiots in actual fact," she explains as she follows Helen down the passage to the kitchen.

Helen comes to such an instant stop that Alice bumps into her. "Ouch! Aunt Helen, are you trying to break my nose?" she asks, taking a step back and rubbing her nose .

"Sometimes, my dear Alice girl, I wish I could break your neck," says Helen, but she sounds more worried than angry. "I understand that you were without a mother's touch since you were five years old, but I cannot believe that your father and three brothers had never taught you to behave and talk like a lady."

"In a house full of men, a girl can't afford to act like a Lady, Aunt Helen," answers Alice and follows Helen into the kitchen.

She places the grocery bags on top of the kitchen table and then explains: "If Aunt Helen should ever hear my three brothers ... I know strings of curses, and I can kick and bite harder than any of them."

"My dear girl ..." Helen just shakes her head. "You make it sound like you grew up in a circus. Your father is a respected man, a medical doctor, and young David is now also a doctor and a married man."

"Maybe, but David has always been part of the Three D's - the three devils: David, Donald, and Dane. The three of them did a decent job of roughing me up since I was small. David was never too bad because he's also older than I am, but Donald and Dane... They could never understand that I was a girl, and when I didn't want to do as they commanded, well, then they would simply make me do it. Do you not remember all my blue marks, Aunt Helen?"

Helen smiles unwillingly. "Your blue marks and their bite marks ... No, Alice, I have not forgotten. but you are now grown up - already twenty-two - and now a girl with a degree in nursing. Surely you don't call your patients idiots ...?"

"Only in my mind and if they really deserve it," says Alice while she helps Helen to pack the food cans in the box. She quickly looks up. "That's why I don't want to work in a hospital, Aunt Helen. There is always a matron looking over your shoulder. And I hate the routine ... I will do private nursing and choose my patients - preferably female patients."

Helen stares at her in shock, a bottle of dishwashing liquid forgotten in her hands. "What are you saying, child?"

Alice hesitates, until this very morning she was engaged, she thinks somberly. And then the image of a tall dark man with extremely blue eyes flashes before her, and her anger simmers. His eyes were bluer then blue - almost black - with long black lashes. It's unfair that a man should have such beautiful eyes, she thinks to herself. For a second, she believed he was trying to help her, but he was just another insolent idiot, and he misled her on purpose. Just like Robert. She is the laughingstock of the year. At this very moment he is probably laughing himself to death because she did not realise that he was the owner of the metallic gray car.

"Let it out, Alice, what's going on? Why your late phone call last night to say you were coming to Arundel with me? You and Robert were going to Greece in two weeks, and you have your wedding to plan," says Helen worried.

"Please, Aunt Helen, stop with the lecture! I broke off the engagement with Robert this morning. My father and I had a long discussion last night. You can be sure to know from hereon in I will choose my groom much more carefully. He must respect women and treat me like a valuable piece of crystal. I want to be his queen, not his slave."

"You are the one, my girl, looking for a loyal slave, not a man. I can tell you this now: no women with self-respect will be satisfied with a man that plays the role of a slave," says Helen, a worried frown on her forehead.

"Don't start, Aunt Helen," says Alice bitingly, turns her head away and sighs deeply. She puts her hand on aunt Helen's arm, her eyes pleadingly on her face. "I'm sorry I am so quick to bite, Aunt Helen, it's been a long night. Why must people lie and deceive? I have been working so hard these four years. It is in these four years that I have met Robert and we have planned our future together and last night was supposed to be the start of everything. Must I now just forget what he did and pretend nothing has changed? That I can't trust him? This isn't the type of marriage, the type of husband I want."

"Absolutely true, child. But keeping busy is usually exactly the remedy to forget," says Helen calmly.

"Maybe I shouldn't forget," she says angrily, her face stern. "Maybe I will learn my lesson better if I remember every day that my very attractive, charming fiancé decided on the threshold of our future to spend a night with another girl – that will prevent me from repeating my foolishness again."

"Foolishness?" asks aunt Helen confused.

"To believe and accept excuses, to not see the truth that is right under one's nose. That there is something like respect and loyalty. It is all nonsense, Aunt Helen. Any man can marry any girl, as long as the circumstances suit both. It suited Robert to plan a future with me because I own the old family farm in Greece. He waited until my twenty-first birthday to get engaged – and started with his plans to further his studies next year in Italy. We would not have had any financial problems ever again once I sold the farm."

Helen shakes her head in shock. "What do you mean sell the

farm? Is that why you broke off the engagement?"

"I knew nothing about it, but my father told me about Robert's plans last night," answers Alice and sighs tired. "That is why Robert made such a huge fuss last year to get engaged on my twenty-first birthday, and why he was so adamant we get married now after my graduation and then move to Italy. Robert visited my father about a month ago, and discussed the possibility of me selling the farm, with him. Father obviously explained to him that the farm cannot be sold under any circumstances as it is the family farm of the Browning's." Alice falls silent and pulls up her shoulders. "Well, that was the end of Robert's endless love for me, and last night he spent the night with another girl whose parents does have enough money to fund his studies and his lifestyle in Italy."

"The low-life..." Helen keeps quiet and looks at Alice sympathetically. "I am sorry, Alice. I have always thought of Robert as hard working and charming, but now... You were in a relationship for four years, and I was convinced he genuinely loved you. I... I don't know what to say."

"What else than that Robert obviously loved his future with my money, not with me?" She laughs bitterly. "I actually need to thank my father. If he didn't see through Robert's plan, I would have married a man who never actually loved me. But my father isn't as easily fooled as I am. When Robert started talking about selling the farm, he quicky realised Robert needed the money for his further studies in Italy. That is why he didn't mention the rest of my inheritance I get now upon my graduation. Thank heavens for common sense... I should be grateful I escaped Robert's plan," she smiles wryly, and Helen sees the tears in her eyes just before she turns her head away.

She takes a tissue from her handbag and holds it out to Alice. "Here, dear child, cry your tears and then you remember that you are Alice Browning, newly qualified nurse and top student of your group. You have earned everything you have worked for. You are not just beautiful, Alice, you also have a kind heart. You deserve the undying love you have always dreamed of."

"You are wonderful, Aunt Helen. You don't know how ugly I feel and … repulsive – I was nothing more to Robert than just a little rich girl with money to fulfil his ambitions. Undying love. Does that even exist?" Alice walks to the kettle and switches it on. "Never again will a man treat me like a nitwit again. If I am too particular, then I will remain single - like you, Aunt Helen," answers Alice, shrugging her shoulders matter-of-factly.

Why did Aunt Helen never get married, she wonders like so many times before?

Helen is already fifty-five years old, but she is tall and slender, with a slight red shimmer in her blonde hair, and with intelligent brown eyes. Her face bears the signs of a great beauty in her youth which even time could not erase. Is it her inbred, snobbish way that has kept men at a distance? No … there has always been men in Helen's life. During her career as a lecturer in psychology at the university she would often have dinner parties and then she would invite male friends as well, and more than one of them always looked at her with clear admiration.

"Why did you retire at fifty-five, Aunt Helen? I always thought you would marry one of your colleagues and retire then … and I have always quite liked Professor Winthorp," asks Alice curiously while she sets the teacups for them.

"I liked all of my colleagues," answers Helen impassively, "but somewhere during my youth I heard that love was a non-negotiable condition for a happy marriage."

Alice looks at her totally baffled. "How can one get to such an old … e… fifty-five years old, without ever falling in love with even just one man?" she asks in pure disbelief.

"I would agree that it is impossible, but it can happen that one falls in love with the wrong man," answers Helen without looking up.

"Aunt Helen, is there someone that you are in love with?" asks Alice curiously.

Helen gives a slight laugh, "No Miss Curiosity. But a long time ago, before I was so old and fifty-five, I did love a man. But unfortunately, he did not love me. And by the time I got to accept it I was so focused on my career that I just never got to finding someone else."

"Did it take you a long time to get over him?" asks Alice impressed.

"No, Alice. For a lot of years, I buried myself in books and in my work, so I did not have the time to miss him. And then, one day, I realised I was now a spinster and a career-woman, with no husband or children. That is what happens when one waits too long: you become selfish with your own lifestyle and your time." A smile reaches her eyes, "But I found the consolation prize: you."

Alice feels how she becomes part of the warmth of Helen's smile. She walks over to her aunt and gives her a long hug. "If I had to be honest, I must say I am glad you never got married, Aunt Helen. When I was younger, I could never have shared my aunt with a man and a house full of children."

"As long as you make sure that I have grandchildren one day," teases Helen and pours their tea. "I already made us some sandwiches. You are probably just as eager as I am to get to Arundel."

"Too eager and too excited to eat anything now," agrees Alice while quickly drinking her tea. "How far is Arundel from Stanton Estate?"

"Stanton Estate isn't just a house. It is the entire land that belongs to the Howards. Stanton Manor is their house, their castle, which stands on a cliff overlooking the entire valley of Arundel. Sir George Howard had the manor built when he realised that Arundel made the perfect stop between the coast and the city for transporting goods. The town of Arundel flourished, and so did the Howards. I remember as a child ..." Helen falls silent as if she got lost within her own memories.

"I remember you told me that my grandfather was the doctor in Arundel," attempts Alice to bring her back to the present.

Helen sighs. "Yes ... yes, those were wonderful years. I know West Sussex is known for its winter rains and strong coastal winds, but when I think of my youth in Arundel, then I only remember sunny days and playing on the riverbank," she recalls, with the nostalgia truly clear in her voice.

"Then why have you waited so long to go back to Arundel? We have often gone to the beach at Littlehampton in Decembers, but …"

"I have my beach house at Littlehampton," Helen interrupts her quickly. "You did enjoy your holidays there, didn't you?"

"Yes, except that time when my brothers came with."

Helen chuckles with the memory. "Now that was a disaster which I will never repeat again."

"But why have you never gone back to Arundel?" repeats Alice her question.

"There wasn't a reason for me to ever go back. I told you your grandfather was already in his fifties when I was born. He passed away when I was still a student. There was nothing to go back to," answers Helen, but she avoids Alice's eyes.

"But now you have a reason to go back again…"

Helen hesitates, a slight frown on her forehead.

"Why not? I have retired from my career and when Doctor Howard – "

"Doctor Howard?" surprised Alice interrupts her. "Then you know the people of Stanton Estate!"

"Child, give me a chance to finish," says Helen angrily. "Obviously, I have known the people of Stanton Estate, but I am now talking of at least thirty-five, maybe forty years ago. In those days, old Sir George Howard's son, Edward, still crowed king in our small town, but in the meantime he and his wife had also passed away."

"Then Doctor Howard is now the owner of Stanton Estate?"

"No. Edward had two sons. Henry and William. Henry died in the war. So, William became the owner of Stanton Estate."

"And Doctor Howard then?"

"He is not a real Howard. Doctor Howard is my cardiologist. And because I grew up so close to this surname, I asked him once whether he was related to the Howards of Stanton Estate. He told me that William Howard and his wife, Emily, had adopted him, but later they also had a son of their own, Richard," explains Helen, her voice strangely tense.

"Is Richard then the sole heir of Stanton Estate?" asks Alice mesmerized.

Helen keeps quiet, memories swimming before her mind's eye. She sighs impatiently. "I suppose so, yes, but we have nothing to do with the Howards. I told you we were going to visit my old friend, Aunt Eleanor, who lives in Tortington."

"Tortington. Where on earth is Tortington?"

"It used to be part of the Stanton Estate. I remember the place: Edward Howard had a house built there when Henry got engaged to Annabelle Montgomery. Edward's wife, Lady Caroline, did not want to live under the same roof as her would-be daughter-in-law. Already then, Edward's health was failing and the possibility that Lady Caroline would survive him was great. The house was built, and after Edward's passing, Lady Caroline lived there. Aunt Eleanor was her care-giver, and her friend, until her passing and she then received life-long right on the house."

"Oh, it sounds wonderful! I would bet that Aunt Eleanor could tell us everything about the Howards," says Alice quite excited with the intrigues of the Howards.

Helen looks at her with uncharacteristic sternness. "Under no circumstances are you going to place Aunt Eleanor under interrogation, girl. She is an old Lady of seventy-eight – an old Lady who needs peace and quiet. It was extremely gracious of Dr Howard to invite us to Stanton Estate to visit her, but I don't want us to be a burden to her."

"What does Stanton Estate have to do with Dr Howard? If he is just an adopted son, then he ..."

"He inherited Tortington from Lady Caroline, his grandmother. And that is now enough questions, Alice. If we are planning to still leave here today, then we should get our things packed in my car," says Helen, suddenly in a rush, and gets up from the kitchen table.

"Your car, Aunt Helen?" Alice jumps up dismayed. "I am driving with my own car, Aunt Helen. I especially had new tyres fitted and had my car serviced. I know by now Aunt Helen: you are just going to want to walk by the river, while I will have to phone a taxi when I want to go anywhere."

"But Alice-child, you know my car is always at your disposal," says Helen calmingly.

"And you know I don't want to drive that huge old car, Aunt Helen." Alice places her hand beggingly on Helen's arm. "Please Aunt Helen, I am independent, and I do have my driver's license. And I have been driving my own car for more than three years now. I promise I won't race or be irresponsible."

"If that is a promise … I will drive in front, and if you pass me, I turn around immediately and come home. I, unfortunately, have experience of your driving skills."

"That was when I was still learning to drive," says Alice offended.

"We will have to stop somewhere and sleep over in a hotel. I am not driving after dark," sets Helen another condition.

"Yes, Aunt Helen. Good, Aunt Helen. As long as we get to Arundel before Christmas, Aunt Helen" answers Alice and walks out of the kitchen to fetch her luggage.

"Smarty pants!" Helen calls out to her, but then her expression sombers. Why does she want to go back to Stanton Estate? The people who mattered, aren't there anymore – except Eleanor Wallace. And memories. Such sad memories, which had her fleeing her entire life. Maybe that is why she had to go back: to find a grave for her memories; to lay to rest her lost dreams for good. And still: she can dig a grave, but she will stand next to that grave with empty hands, because memories live in your heart.

Alice stops her car in front of the entrance to Stanton Estate and stares in amazement at the granite walls with the name Stanton Estate in wrought iron letters fastened onto it. Her eyes search further, and then she sees the castle-like mansion on a high cliff, rising dark and gray against the ice blue sky. A mansion of secrets, she thinks to herself, and she feels a shiver of excitement mixed with a little bit of fear running cold down her spine.

"I knew your car was going to fail you," says Helen unhappy through the open car window next to hers. "Let's push your car out of the way, Alice. Look, there you can see Tortington, on that hill right next to the river."

"Don't you have a soul, Aunt Helen?" asks Alice insulted. "There is absolutely nothing the matter with my car. I only stopped to admire Stanton Estate." She forgets about her slight upset and continues enthusiastically: "The mansion looks like a castle from a fairy tale! All those towers and chimneys, and that huge clock-tower … The dark granite makes it look haunted. Are the ghosts of the Howards still haunting this old mansion, Aunt Helen?" For a while Helen stares at her totally speechless, and then her irritation kicks in. "I am dead tired and hungry and thirsty, and you waste our time staring at that old mansion! For goodness' sake, child, remember that you are now an adult, and to behave as such. Now, come!"

"Aunt Helen, you have the romantic inclination of a hungry bed-bug!" calls Alice tauntingly after her and starts her car again. She will have to work on Eleanor Wallace, because if it depends on Aunt Helen, she will never even see the inside of Stanton Manor, Alice thinks to herself as she follows in the twisting road to Tortington. Maybe she kan befriend late Sir William's son, Richard. Is he married? Well, then she can become friends with his wife. She is definitely not visiting in Tortington for six weeks, and not visiting Stanton Manor even once.

She brings her car to a stop next to Helen's in front of the white house, gets out en stares in surprise at the flower garden surrounding the house. Tortington is exceeding all her expectations, she thinks, and smiles impressed.

"Come closer! Come closer!" invites a clear, youthful voice.

Alice turns her head and stares surprised at the large, stocky woman with snow white, curly hair; big, friendly gray-blue eyes and the warm summer sun in her smile. She comes at a strong gate walking towards them and opens the garden gate.

If this is Aunt Eleanor Wallace … Alice shakes her head in disbelief. Too many summers have carved deep lines into Eleanor's face and the burdens of the years has come to lay as a hump on her shoulders pushing her neck forwards, but a laughter as bright as a summer's morning shines in her eyes and reflects in the youthfulness of her smile.

"Aunt Eleanor! It has been too long. You look wonderful," says Helen heartily and kisses her old friend.

"Wonderful or wonderfully old?" teases Eleanor and turns to Alice who walks closer hesitantly. "And you are Alice. Welcome at Tortington, dearie. I am so delighted to have some young company again."

"Hallo, Aunt Eleanor,' greets Alice and receives a spontaneous hug and a kiss on her cheek.

"Forget about your luggage. You both look warm and tired. Let's first go find something to drink and to eat," invites Eleanor hospitable, hooks into Helen's arm en starts walking to the house.

Alice lingers in the front garden, overwhelmed by the variety of flowers and plants. She had already noticed the dark green of a natural forest just left of Stanton Estate, but she never expected to see so many flowers grow so close to the coast.

She searches further and then she sees the stonewall on the southside of Tortington. The wall shields this magnificent garden from the cold south-easterly winds, she realizes.

The sound of a rumbling car engine catches her attention. She sees a luxurious metal-gray car getting closer extremely fast, she is still wondering if she recognizes the driver, and then she storms closer angrily just as the car stops only a few centimeters from her own. The driver gets out of his car and Alice chokes on her anger as her eyes meet the black-blue eyes of the tall, broad-shouldered man.

"You … you …" stammers Alice, out of breath from anger.

"Idiot or selfish?" he asks and smiles mockingly.

"I know some terrible curse words, I have three brothers," she warns and feels like a total fool as he just continues to smile at her. She glares at him. "Why do you do it? Why do you park so close to my car? You know very well that I can't get in from the right side."

"It was a precaution. When I invited you the last time to join me for a cup of tea, you refused. Now you don't have a choice: we first go have a cup of tea together and then you can have your car back. All right, Alice?"

"Why?" she asks obstinately. She knows men. She knows how they look at a girl when they are interested in her. But Mr. Oliver is definitely not interested in her … except that he finds her very amusing. No man has ever treated her like she was a clown, she thinks angrily. If Mr. Oliver thinks he has discovered a new plaything, he is sorely mistaken.

"Shall we say I want to make amends for the inconvenience I caused you when I parked you in at the shopping centre?" he asks gallantly, the laughter still dancing in his eyes.

"That is impossible. Aunt Helen and I arrived just now, literally as we speak. Aunt Eleanor is making us tea," she answers with a cold superiority. She sees the surprise on his face and continues in triumph: "I am visiting here. If you want to drink a cup of tea – there are coffee shops in the town. Goodbye, Mr. Oliver."

That's it, now she had properly put him in his place, she thinks very impressed with herself and gets even more furious when he just smiles even broader and starts walking towards her. "Fantastic! Aunt Eleanor is the best baker in the district. Come, little firecracker, I am looking forward to that cup of tea and all of Aunt Eleanor's forbidden treats."

He takes her by the arm, but she pulls away confused. "Do you know Aunt Eleanor?" she asks baffled.

"Better than my own mother, because she raised me." His eyes search involuntary for the dark building on the cliff.

"Richard and I. Because Aunt Emily's … e… health, was never really the best."

"Richard Howard?" she asks, her voice faint.

He frowns. "Don't tell me my adoptive brother already met you. He has a reputation of …"

"I don't know him," she interrupts him, "I know of him. But if he is your adoptive brother, then why are you Mr. Oliver?" she asks suspiciously.

He pulls up his shoulders. "Because you decided to call me Mr. Oliver, little Alice. I am Oliver Howard."

"Doctor Oliver Howard?" she asks breathless.

"When I work, yes, but my friends call me Oliver. Do you think we could be friends if I promise to never park so close to your car ever again?"

How can she be friends with a man who is so spiteful and inconsiderate, a man who gets her so angry, she wonders, and she is aware of an uneasiness within herself. She isn't angry, she realizes, but she feels humiliated as Oliver continuously taunts her and laughs at her. She knows she is pretty – even her hyper-critical brothers say so – but Oliver Howard makes her feel as if she is a total joke.

"I choose my ..." she starts with an ice-cold disdain and swallow her words when Helen and Eleanor walk out onto the front porch.

"Oliver!" Helen calls out in surprise. "What are you doing here, child? I'm not sick."

He laughs heartily and gives Helen a hug. "That is only proof of how good a doctor I am, Aunt Helen. Welcome at Tortington. I know you are really going to enjoy your visit here." He turns to Eleanor, who is standing there wringing her hands. "Hallo Aunt Eleanor. Are the nerves acting up again?"

"Yes, yes, Oliver, no need to play doctor-doctor with me, my dear boy. It is on behalf of your Uncle William that I asked you to come home urgently, but the question is: will they allow you to talk with him?"

Chapter 2

The smile disappears from Oliver's eyes and gives them the look of cold, black crystals. He tensely stares at Eleanor and then asks bluntly: "Did Aunt Emily and Richard say that I was not welcome at Stanton Manor to visit Uncle William?"

"How could I say, Oliver?" asks Eleanor evasive and looks away. "Since William got so sick, I suggested on several occasions that they should tell you about it, but Emily told me quite straightforwardly that I should not bother myself with the Howard's affairs."

"Aunt Eleanor, you are not answering my question. Did Aunt Emily say, in so many words, that she did not want me at her house?" asks Oliver again.

Alice notices the little muscle on his cheek jumping and she wonders about his level of stress. Aunt Helen did say that he was William and Emily's adopted son, yet he calls them Uncle and

Aunt. Why is he not welcome at Stanton Manor? Is it possible that they might be jealous because his grandmother Caroline left Tortington to him, and not to their own son, Richard? She actually wishes he would leave now, so she could ask Aunt Eleanor about the people of Stanton Manor.

"You know your Aunt Emily, Oliver. She is ... e ... as quick to change as the weather. You see, I did offer to write to you to inform you of the severity of your Uncle William's illness, but Emily ... well, she got quite upset with me," answers Aunt Eleanor and blushes at her own incapability of hiding the truth.

"Aunt Eleanor, you probably mean that she went crazy," he says angry. "How serious is Uncle William's condition, Aunt Eleanor?"

"Cancer ... stomach cancer. That is why he came back home. There is nothing more that the doctors can do for him," she says almost in a whisper while her eyes wordlessly beg him for forgiveness.

"Cancer!" He stares at her upset. "My goodness, Aunt Eleanor! You should have told me months ago! If there is one person in Stanton Manor who never treated me like an intruder, then it is Uncle William. And he never asked that I should come home to see him?"

"Not initially, no Oliver, but when Beatrice told me that William wanted to talk to you ... I could not postpone any longer, that is why I phoned you." She guiltily looks at him. "Don't resent me too much, Oliver. You know I never set foot at Stanton Manor since dear Caroline gave me lifelong rights to Tortington. Emily has never been able to forgive me for that. She is totally convinced that I plotted with Caroline, which is why you, an adopted child, inherited Tortington."

Oliver smiles compassionately and puts his hand on her shoulder. "I realise that Aunt Eleanor. I also know that Miss Beatrice Crompton and all the household staff have been forbidden to have any contact with you. That is after all the reason why we decided that you could house tourists, otherwise you would've been too lonely."

"Beatrice did come over, but it was so late, and I was already in bed. But she had to come to tell me. She could not bear William's pleas any longer. Fweh, child, it is as if he realised that Emily had forbidden you the house as well, because Beatrice says he whispers when he talks about you. Whispers and pleads ... pleads continuously that there are things which he must say to you."

He frowns surprised and then pulls up his shoulders, "I shouldn't get too excited just yet, but I really want to belief that he wants to tell me about my own parents. Aunt Eleanor, you for one, know very well how that has haunted me my entire life – the fact that I don't even know who my own parents are, where I come from. Should Uncle William pass away, I will never know." His eyes search for the granite manor on the cliff. "I am going there right now."

He looks at Alice and Helen and a self-conscious smile lifts the right corner of his mouth. "I am very sorry that you had to become part of our family feud but hopefully I can get this all sorted out today still. I you would please excuse me ..."

"Do not drive there, Oliver. If Emily sees you coming, she will have all the doors and windows bolted," warns Aunt Eleanor.

"I was planning to walk, Aunt Eleanor. I know my dearest Aunt Emily too well," he answers with a bitter smile and walks towards the garden gate.

Alice watches him walk away with a feeling of disappointment, wishing he had invited her with, and then becomes annoyed with her own thoughts. Oliver Howard is a stranger to her – an arrogant man who most probably realises how attractive he is and who never wants for female companionship. That is why he treats her like she is a clown, she thinks insulted and gets angry all over again. Why would she bother with him? What does it matter if he never finds out who his biological parents were? And still ... she wishes she could help him, because if the tables were turned, she would also not have been able to rest without knowing the truth.

"But Alice-child, do you not have ears?" forces Aunt Helen's inpatient voice her back from her thoughts. "Aunt Eleanor has gone to pour us some tea. Let's go inside."

"I knew Stanton Manor was a house full of secrets," says Alice very intrigued while she walks with Helen to the front door. "Just think about it, Aunt Helen: generations of Howards have lived in that old house. I want to know everything about their lives, their loves, and …"

"Curiosity killed the cat, my girl. Be careful what you wish for, getting involved in some situations in life are not worth the heartache it will cause you," interrupts Helen her angrily. "Remember: we are here on a holiday, not to play detective."

"But don't you also wonder who Oliver's real parents are, Aunt Helen?" asks Alice as they walk into the dining room where Eleanor is already sitting at the head of the table and busy pouring tea from an antique silver teapot.

"That is actually something I wanted to ask Aunt Eleanor."

"What, dear?" asks Eleanor while she is handing a cup of tea to Helen.

"The child is just nosy, Aunt Eleanor." I have already warned her not to pester you with questions. The Howards – and the past – has got nothing to do with her," says Helen strictly.

A smile glides like a misty hand of youth over Eleanor's expression. "In that case: we are not going to give your Aunt Helen heartburn, Alice. Here, have some tea. I hope you both have a good appetite because I started baking before sunrise."

"Am I supposed to only eat and not say anything, Aunt Helen?" asks Alice annoyed.

"That is correct, child. Aunt Eleanor and I will talk, and you can just listen. I knew all the people from Stanton Estate, and I would very much like to know what has happened to them all," answers Helen cheerful.

"Luckily, you won't always be eating, right dear?" Eleanor smiles and winks unnoticed at Alice.

Alice smiles gratefully, reassured that she has found a co-conspirator in Aunt Eleanor. She must just be patient: Aunt Helen likes to take long walks and then she will use her chance to find out everything about the Howards.

Beatrice Crompton hears the backdoor opening, turns away from the passage door and walks with the very distinguished gate of a plump woman trying to maintain her balance, straight towards Oliver. Her crystal blue eyes disappear as a wide smile wrinkle around her eyes, but she holds her chubby finger warningly in front of her lips. "To the pantry, Oliver. It is safer there," she whispers.

Oliver waits until she closes the pantry door behind them and greets in a muffled voice: "Hallo, Miss Crompton. Is all this secrecy really necessary?"

Beatrice tries to frown worriedly, but only manages to look sad. "It is the test of all tests, my child. You know Emily: I believe the poor soul has two personalities, and both personalities are equally unstable."

"But Uncle William's illness far outweighs her wants."

"Exactly, Oliver, but his illness is "very testing" on Emily's "fragile system"", she answers mockingly quoting Emily with her fingers in the air. "And rightly so. William knows his time is getting short and there is an injustice he must rectify, before he meets his Creator," says Beatrice quietly and sighs sadly.

"What injustice, Miss Crompton?"

Beatrice's piousness disappears as her anger boils up again. "Now, how should I know that, Oliver? Did Eleanor not say anything to you? William pleaded with me that he needed to talk to you. I told Emily about it … and then all hell broke loose. Such a cursing and yelling I heard the last time was the day when William brought you here years ago. I had to pamper her for a weeklong and had to make sure she drank her medicine regularly, otherwise the poor soul might have committed a murder. But what else was to be expected? She was a newly-wed and she thought you were William's child out of wedlock. You know, to be honest, the thought also crossed my mind, although only fleetingly. But on the other hand: William had loved Emily for so many years, that it was quite unbelievable that there could ever have been any other woman in his life."

"Uncle William has assured me that I was not his biological son," says Oliver curt.

"That's what he assured all of us, but he wanted for you to call him "Father"... And that, Emily could never accept. It was humiliating for her that a foundling child ..." Beatrice pulls her breath in sharp and claps her hand over her mouth. "I am so sorry, child. I am a stupid old woman of sixty, and I have been looking after Emily since I was twenty. Sometimes I forget who I am and then I speak as she does."

Oliver's lips pull into a bitter grin. "Nothing can hurt me or shock me after having gone under Aunt Emily's sharp tongue in Stanton Manor for sixteen years, Miss Crompton. But we are wasting time. Is it at all possible for me to speak to Uncle William?"

Beatrice pulls nervously at her white apron, her eyes wide. "Maybe now, Oliver, because Emily just took her medicine, and she is resting for a while. But, please, walk on your toes, and talk very softly ... I find it most wonderful how fine of hearing a sick person like Emily is."

Mentally ill, Oliver thinks to himself grimly and opens the pantry door. He looks over his shoulder at Beatrice. "I will use the kitchen stairs to go up to his room. Is Richard in the vicinity?"

"No ... no, he has gone to Chichester. Be careful, child!" warns Beatrice with a hoarse goose voice and chews with the speed of a starving field-mouse on a ginger biscuit trying to calm her own nerves.

Oliver stares upset at the yellow, pale, skin, the sunken eyes, and hollow cheeks of Uncle William who lays motionless under the white sheet. At a time, Uncle William was a big, forcefully built man, but the sheet does not succeed in hiding his now emaciated body.

He should've returned a long time ago, Oliver thinks guiltily. Uncle William has never treated him as a step-child. What does it matter that Richard continuously tries to humiliate him, or that Aunt Emily was so open about the fact that she hated him?

Uncle William was his hero, even if he never had the courage to protect him from the animosity from Richard and Aunt Emily.

Pride. He was young and proud and after grandmother Caroline left Tortington to him, he no longer wanted to impose on the people of Stanton Manor. And, by then, he was already a doctor and busy specializing as a cardiologist. It is hard to believe that twelve years had gone by so fast. He didn't want to put up with Richard's and Aunt Emily's insults anymore, that is why he never returned to Stanton Manor. But it was Uncle William who paid for his studies and bought him his medical practice. He owed it to Uncle William to at least have kept some contact with him, he thinks to himself. And now? Is he too late?

As if he became aware of the presence of another person in the room, William opens his eyes and stares at Oliver. "Oliver?" rasps his voice over his white lips.

"Uncle William, you recognise me..." Oliver smiles past the lump in his throat. He takes a seat on the chair next to the bed, and takes William's one boney, cold hand in his. He got here just in time, he thinks, because the only sign of life in William is the dim light in his blue eyes which lay deeply sunken in their sockets.

"You came," continues William while his boney fingers grab Oliver's hand with an unexpected strength. I cannot explain – she will hear. But it is there ... there in the old hiding place. Righteousness must prevail, otherwise ..."

"You!" The word is high and shrill, filled with hate, as if a dark curse is screamed over him.

Oliver jumps up, his eyes on the tall, skeleton-like body of the woman with wild, gray-black hair and wide, dark eyes wearing a loose-fitting long white nightdress who has appeared in the bedroom door. Her lips jump away from her teeth, her face pulls in madness as she storms into the room, grabs a scissor from the dressing table and lifts it threateningly up in the air.

"Cursed intruder! Today you will die!" She screams and steps with prowling, animal-like movements towards him.

"Aunt Emily, please ..." attempts Oliver to calm her down, and keeps his eye on her hand holding the scissors up in the air.

She stops moving, throws her head backwards, and laughs long and shrill. Her laughing breaks off at once, but then she sees the fear and concern on Oliver's face and her victory laugh of revenge splinters through the tension in the room.

"Emily … Emily …" mutter Uncle William and lifts his hand. "My beautiful Emily … my lovely bride … It is our wedding day, Emily … and I am the luckiest man on earth. Do you hear the church bells, Emily? Do you hear the wedding march playing? We are getting married, my only Emily …"

Oliver sees how the madness leaves Emily's eyes to be replaced by a cunning smile. "The poor fool! He is delirious again. That's what he does most of the time: talks for hours about our wedding day!" Her eyes are black of suspicion. "What did he say to you, Oliver?"

"Your bouquet … Don't forget your bouquet," says Uncle William, his voice in a monotone. "Where is the ring? Such a lovely ring. You like the ring, right, Emily?"

"Shut up, William!" snarls Emily and steps closer to Oliver. "I asked you a question, intruder: what did this crazy, old man say to you?"

"He was delirious, Aunt Emily," answers Oliver gruff.

"Emily!" Beatrice rolls into the room and quivers to a halt next to Emily. "You again didn't drink you calming medication. I am phoning Doctor Graham this instant."

Fear makes Emily shrink away from Beatrice. "No! No, Beatrice, you cannot. I borrowed Richard's binoculars, and I just wanted to look around a little bit … see what old Eleanor was doing there at Tortington. She always has visitors … holiday makers. I watch them through the binoculars. It is something to do. You always leave me alone, since William got sick … I don't want to be alone, Beatrice. If you come with me – I will drink my medicine, as long as you promise not to phone Doctor Graham," pleads Emily with the desperate fear of a child.

"You don't want to listen to me, Emily," says Beatrice accusingly. "I told you we must get a nurse to help with taking care of

William. I cannot be everywhere at once." She falls silent and presses her lips together in a thin line of disapproval. "If Doctor Graham hears that you are walking around with scissors in your hand, and threatening our visitors …"

"This foundling child is not a visitor!" interrupts Emily gruffly. "He plotted with my mother-in-law and inherited Tortington. Now he wants to plot with William and run off with Richard's inheritance. I will kill …"

"Emily!" cuts Beatrice her off. "Give me the scissors. Now!"

"Such a beautiful bride … the prettiest girl in the district," mutters William and smiles at Emily.

"William is delirious again," says Beatrice matter-of-factly. "Now, give me the scissors and come with me to your room, Emily."

"Not before this intruder doesn't leave," says Emily stubbornly, and holds on to the scissors with both hands.

"What does it matter if he sits here for a while with William? William is in any case not at his full senses," says Beatrice impatient.

"I will go when he goes," maintains Emily.

Oliver turns his back on Emily and bends over William. He holds William's right hand for a moment tight in his. "Goodbye, Uncle. I am grateful I could see you again."

William looks him straight in his eyes and winks slowly, before he says: "Do you hear the church bells, Emily? It is our wedding day …"

"You are exhausting him, Oliver," says Beatrice worried. "If you will go now …"

"I am already on my way, Miss Crompton, but you are right: Uncle William does need a full-time nurse. It is impossible for you to take care of two patients," he says in his clinical tone.

"Listen to the learned foundling child!" sneers Emily. "I am no-one's patient. "Beatrice is my Lady in waiting who was still hired by my own parents. Tell him, Beatrice. We were the rich Montgomery's of Chichester. My mother also had a Lady in waiting. I never shared my school seat with the workers' children. I had my own Governess and Beatrice," she proudly tells him.

"I had forgotten you were one of the royals, Aunt Emily," teases Oliver, his face taut with no expression, and he walks out of the room.

He walks slowly down the kitchen stairs and stands waiting in the backdoor, his eyes fixed on the passage door. Why did Uncle William wink at him? Was he really delirious, or does he just use it as a weapon against Aunt Emily? Maybe Miss Crompton would be able to answer his questions, he thinks to himself, and looks up relieved when he hears the stairs creak.

Beatrice wipes her face with her lace handkerchief and thuds down gratefully in a chair, her eyes dumb-struck on Oliver.

This is how he remembers Miss Crompton, he thinks: a round lady with a round face, buried between soft lace and frills; a lady with chubby hands holding a fine lace handkerchief, as if she secretly believed that the soft lace and fine frills would hide the size of her round body.

"I am glad you waited, Oliver," says Beatrice when she at last catches her breath. "But Emily can be difficult ... extremely difficult. And it is true what you said: I now have two patients. I have more than enough staff to help with the chores around this huge, old manor, but William and Emily need my personal attention. Maybe I should have a talk with Doctor Graham ..."

"I have known Doctor Norman Graham since my student days, Miss Crompton. We studied medicine together. I will phone him and explain the situation to him. He will insist that Uncle William needs a full-time nurse to take care of him."

"Will you, child? That would be such a huge burden lifted off my shoulders, I do not feel very confident to speak to a doctor. And then there is Emily: she keeps an eye on me like a hawk when Doctor Graham is here, because her biggest fear is that she will also end up in a mental institute like her mother."

"I remember, Miss Crompton." He looks at her sharply. "How often does Uncle William become delirious?"

Beatrice's shoulders start shaking, her laughter inaudible, as if the sound is smothered under layers of fat. "William is a dying man, but he didn't survive thirty years of Emily's unreasonable demands and unpredictable outbursts per chance. William is only delirious when Emily gets uncontrollable."

He stares at her amused. "Miss Crompton, do you mean Uncle William only fakes his delirious episodes?"

"Not always, no. Sometimes the pain gets too much and that can cause an episode. But the moment he starts talking about his beautiful bride, then I know it is just an act. You see, Emily has this cunning streak to sneak to his room – and usually in the middle of the night – to start a fight with him. Always about you, the foundling child … Forgive me, Oliver. But, yes, he and I then agreed that he will fake an episode when she starts arguing with him. And that is what he also did today."

"Then he was totally conscious when I spoke with him?" he asks hopeful.

"I believe so, Oliver. What did he say?"

He frowns confused. "Not much. Just that he couldn't explain, because Aunt Emily would hear him. But something is in the old hiding place. Do you know what he was referring to, Miss Crompton?"

"Hiding place … hiding place…" she repeats deep in thought and sighs. "No, child, I would lie if I said I knew." She notices his disappointment and continues excitedly: "But Richard might know. I will try to find out from him and let you know."

"If Richard knows about this hiding place, then he will destroy anything he finds there before I could ever lay my eyes on it," he says bitterly. "No, rather say nothing to him, Miss Crompton. Maybe Aunt Eleanor could know something."

Alright then, Oliver. Please remember to speak to Doctor Graham. Goodbye, child," Beatrice gets up to give him a hug, she wipes her face again with the damp lace handkerchief.

"Goodbye, Miss Crompton, and thank you for your help," he says, and walks out of the kitchen.

His entire future is in the hands of a dying man … and a crazy, old woman, he thinks to himself with a feeling of despair bordering on anger. If he doesn't find the hiding place and Uncle

William passes away, the secret of his lineage will be buried with Uncle William. He needs an ally in Stanton Estate … but who?

Frances Leighton smiles. She can't wait for tomorrow. doctor Norman Graham is bringing doctor Oliver Howard to the clinic. She can't wait to see him again. They saw each other twelve years ago when they finished school and then he left to study in London. Now he returns as a successful cardiologist. She wonders if he is returning for good, and if that were the case, whether he would be taking over from doctor Graham as the new superintendent.

His family, the Howards, all but own Arundel and they built the clinic thirty years ago in tribute to their oldest son, Henry Howard who died in the war. It will only be fitting that a Howard now also run the clinic, she thinks to herself, lost in her own dreamworld. And yes, she dreams on, now that she has been the matron for almost three years, he will see in her a woman very capable of taking the clinic under her wing and to manage the personnel with a very strict regime. Together they will make this clinic hugely successful. Well, even more than it currently is.

Just like Oliver Howard she is very particular about etiquette. She likes people she can rely on. She doesn't tolerate any laziness. Negligence makes her eyes spew fire and dishonesty awakens the wrath in her. People must always put their best foot forward if they don't want her to get angry and upset!

"Oliver is a Howard through and through, albeit not in blood," she heard Miss Crompton say to one of her friends earlier this week. They were having tea in the café on the riverbank, the two old ladies didn't notice her. "He is a man of black or white. He doesn't waste his time with people who keep secrets and play games, especially not with other peoples' lives."

But of course! she decides in the silence of her office, she hates it just as much. Any of her personnel will attest to that.

She smiles to herself while she gets up and walks out of her office to the staff canteen. She has taken it upon herself to arrange a big welcoming tea for doctor Howard. A few of the junior staff helped her to clear the canteen of all the excess furniture and to set two large tables for a very formal high tea to welcome their esteemed guest.

The young matron smiles contently as she glances over the canteen on last time. It looks smart enough for her standards. Now doctor Howard must only arrive tomorrow. She asked doctor Graham to bring him directly to the canteen.

The occasion will obviously not last too long, because some of the staff is still on duty. Some of the night-shift personnel will also attend. Everyone is very excited to meet doctor Howard. Most of the personnel moved to Arundel during the past thirty years since the hospital opened the first time and very few of them knew or would remember Oliver Howard as a child or as a teenager.

She will be at her absolute best performance tomorrow for doctor Oliver Howard. He impressed her in school with his work ethic and his intellect. He was always the top scholar and not to forget how handsome he was. She plans on getting to know him better. A whole lot better!

Alice keeps her eye closed and breaths evenly until Helen closes her bedroom door softly. She lays perfectly still and listens to Helen's footsteps creaking away in the passage, she hears the front door open and close and then she jumps up in a hurry. "You clever girl," she says to herself in the mirror as she quickly pulls a hairbrush through her hair. She slips on her sandals and trots out of her room.

Eleanor turns away from the stove in surprise as Alice walks into the kitchen seconds later, pulls out a kitchen chair from underneath the table and sits down. "And now, dear? Did you not go for a walk with Helen along the river?"

"I was still fast asleep when she peeped into my room, Aunt Eleanor," answers Alice with a mischievous smile which totally contradicts the piousness in her voice.

"H'm. I wondered when you were going to start questioning me about Oliver," says Eleanor, pours herself a cup of coffee and takes a place next to Alice. "Oh goodness, where are my manners, Alice? Would you like a cup of coffee?"

"I am so curious, I would probably choke if I drank anything right now, Aunt Eleanor. Oliver … Why does he not know who his biological parents are? And why does he refer to his adoptive parents as Uncle and Aunt? Why does his adoptive mother hate him so much?"

Eleanor chuckles. "If I knew who Oliver's biological parents were, then he would be a happy, married man by now. Or, no, now I am lying I never had much time for Charlotte Hastings. There are girls who are pretty and good hearted, but then there are those girls who use their beauty to get up to nothing good. Charlotte was one of those girls."

"But did Oliver love her?" asks Alice and feels an inexplicable tinge of disappointment. She believes she will never be able to fall in love with Oliver, but just the thought of him loving someone else, fills her with a feeling of loss.

"That is what he said to me, and because he is not a man to easily talk about his feelings, I believed him. He really wanted to marry her, but he is an adopted child. I still remember how he begged William to tell him the truth about his biological parents. But William just snubbed him off, and Richard taunted him... Emily made sure that Richard never forgot that he was a real full-blooded Howard, and the sole heir to Stanton Estate," remembers Eleanor bitter.

"But if Charlotte loved Oliver..."

"She didn't. She loved money, which is why she married a man almost thirty years older than herself. Oliver was heartbroken, but he had one consolation: he never asked Charlotte for her hand."

"Because he didn't know who his parent was?"

"Exactly, my dear. He was only a year or so old when William brought him here to Stanton Estate – it is now twenty-nine years later. Emily was beside herself with anger because she initially thought that Oliver was William's illegitimate son. I don't know what William said to her, but she eventually calmed down and she and William adopted Oliver." Eleanor shakes her head in unbelieve. "This is something I just never understood: Emily could not stand the sight of Oliver, even as a small toddler, and yet she agreed to the adoption."

"And Lady Caroline Howard, Uncle William's mother? Did she not know the truth?"

"No, child, she was also in the dark, just like I was. But she and I were then already living here in Tortington, and we had little Oliver over regularly to visit with us." A smile lets the love in Eleanor's eyes light up. "Those were happy days, then. Our lives revolved around little Oliver's visits, because with him here, we both could forget that we weren't young anymore.

"But did Lady Caroline not ask Uncle William about Oliver?" continues Alice with her interrogation.

"Obviously. We all had questions about Oliver and then William told all of us that Oliver was the child of two of his old student friends. But he adamantly refused to tell anyone who they were, because he intended to raise Oliver as his own son."

"And did you believe him, Aunt Eleanor? Lady Caroline was his own mother, did she believe him?"

Eleanor smiles guiltily. "How shall I put it, Alice? We wanted to believe William's story, but he was quite the Lady's man in his day. I have always had the suspicion through all these years, that Oliver is indeed William's own son."

"And is Richard younger that Oliver?" Alice wants to know eagerly.

"Two years younger, yes."

"But the Oliver is the heir to Stanton Estate, Aunt Eleanor! I would bet everything I have that Aunt Emily's animosity and hate stems from that fact, because her own son can't inherit Stanton Estate if he has an older half-brother."

Eleanor shakes head, her expression grim. "That all depends on William's will and testament, and … Oliver doesn't look like a Howard. Both the Howard brothers, Henry and William, were blond with blue eyes. Richard has dark hair, like Emily, but then he looks almost like his younger father's twin. Oliver is the outsider … the one who has never fitted in." She notices the disappointment on Alice's face and continues sympathetically: "Believe me, my dear, I would give anything to see Oliver in Stanton Manor, but we have absolutely no evidence that there is even one drop of Howard-blood running through his veins."

"A firecracker and nosy," suddenly comes dissatisfied from Oliver who appeared in the back door. He comes closer, the well-known glimmer of his teasing in his eyes. "From where your sudden interest in me, little Alice? Are you going to perhaps ask for my hand the moment you discover that I am the actual heir to Stanton Estate?"

"No, I'll safe you the anticipation, and just ask you to get married right now. How does Saturday suit you?" she answers back, immediately angry and ready for a fight.

Eleanor chuckles. "You tell him, dear! Since he finished his studies and had become a real know-it-all Doctor, it is hard to put him in his place."

Oliver walks in silence to the fridge and takes out a cold beer before he also takes a seat at the kitchen table.

"You are quiet, Oliver," worries Eleanor. "Don't tell me Emily suspected you were talking to William."

"I had a few minutes alone with him, but Aunt Emily quickly put an end to our short talk." Oliver takes a sip of his beer and asks with tense seriousness: "Aunt Eleanor, do you perhaps know anything about a hiding place? Uncle William said there was something in the hiding place – all the evidence, everything I want to know. What was he referring to?"

Eleanor frowns in thought and then shakes her head. "I truly don't know, Oliver." She gently pulls in her breath. "Yes, wait, something does ring a bell."

"Yes, Aunt Eleanor?" he asks tensely.

"Your late Uncle Henry, and your Uncle William had this secret hiding place when they were still young boys. But where that was no-one could ever find out," she recalls.

"Somewhere in Stanton Manor?" he asks excited.

"I believe so, child."

"A nurse ... Uncle William needs a full-time nurse. If the full-time nurse is willing to help me search for this hiding place ..."

"I am a nurse," says Alice, and gives him a challenging look.

Chapter 3

Oliver places his can of beer down slowly on the kitchen table, his gaze grim on Alice, who is looking at him in anticipation. "There is a time and a place for everything, Alice. I enjoy our arguments because you amuse me. But my lineage is to me a profoundly serious matter. Who so ever is appointed as Uncle William's full-time nurse should be a responsible and mature person because she will hold my future and my happiness in both her hands," he says with a cold emphasis.

"And?" she asks pulling up her shoulders. "Is it then your opinion that I am not capable enough to nurse your old, dying Uncle?"

"What do you know about nursing?" he asks bluntly. "You can't be much older than eighteen. Do you really believe for one second that I will place my entire future in the hands of a frivolous student?"

"You … you insulting, chauvinistic … e… man!" she starts and jumps up angry and upset. "It is so typical of you men: you just look at a girl and make your own assumptions. You took one look at me and decided I was a flippant eighteen-year-old teenager with a pretty face and nothing between my ears – and that, Doctor Howard, is only proof of how little you have between your ears!"

"That is a huge improvement, Alice-child," says Helen who enters the kitchen from the passage. "I am so grateful for the fact that you called Oliver a man and not a pig."

"If you knew what I was calling him in my head, Aunt Helen, we would both cringe of embarrassment," says Alice angrily and glares at Oliver with naked hostility on her face.

"You are back, Helen," says Eleanor calmly. "I warned you the weather was a bit windy. But you know yourself: the mornings are usually so pleasant, but around lunch time the coastal winds pick up."

"I didn't forget, that's why I only walked up to the border wall and enjoyed the view over the river." Helen looks questioningly at Oliver who is staring out in front of him. "What is the argument about, Oliver? Did you insult my niece?"

"It seems I did. But she drove me to it, Aunt Helen. I believe I do have a sense of humour, but when someone jokes around with matters which are of life and death importance to me ..." he answers, straining to contain himself, and falls silent.

"I wasn't joking around," Alice throws back, her temper still simmering. She turns to Helen. "Oliver said that his Uncle William needed a full-time nurse to take care of him. I offered to help and then he said I was a frivolous eighteen-year-old student without the sense of responsibility to hold his future and happiness in my hands."

"Excuse me?" asks Helen baffled.

An amused chuckle escapes from Eleanor's lips. "Let me explain, Helen, Oliver is way too angry to open his mouth."

"I am not," he says quickly. "Uncle William needs a full-time nurse, Aunt Helen, but I will phone one of my old university friends, Doctor Norman Graham, to ask him to send the right person. He is also Uncle William's personal physician."

"Well, that suits me perfectly," replies Helen content. "Alice and I are here for a holiday, and this girl has worked more than hard enough these past four years during her training as a nurse and to receive her degree as a registered nurse."

Oliver's head jerks in Alice's direction, disbelief on every line of his expression, and he looks straight into her triumphant smiling face. "You – a qualified registered nurse?"

"And a cum laude-student, dear know-it-all Doctor Howard. On top of that, both my father and my oldest brother are doctors. If there is someone who does know the responsibilities of a nurse taking care of patients, well, then that is me." Alice sits down on her chair, leans back, and folds her arms across her chest. "You don't have to kiss my feet, but you may kneel before me and ask me for forgiveness for your insulting comments."

"Little wiseacre," he says gruffly and continues grudgingly: "All right, I did make an error in judgement, and I am sorry, but I still don't belief that you are the right person to help me."

"What do you mean, Oliver?" asks Helen confused. "Is this nurse not supposed to help your Uncle William?"

"Yes, Aunt Helen, but I am hoping she can also help me at the same time. I was with my uncle this morning to ask him about my own biological parents, but all he said was that I will find all the evidence in the old hiding place."

"Which old hiding place?" asks Helen interested.

Eleanor leans forward. "I believe it is Henry and William's old hiding place. When they were children, they often spoke about their secret hiding place. Unfortunately, none of us adults ever bothered with the two young boys' chattering. So, I can't help Oliver."

"But I can," says Alice full of confidence. "I bet in a huge castle-like building like Stanton Manor there would be dozens of secret rooms and passages."

"There aren't," says Oliver bluntly. "There is one secret room behind the bookcase in the study, but everyone in the house knows about it. Uncle William always used it as his hunting room."

"When last have you been inside this hunting room?" asks Alice quickly.

"More than ten years ago, but it could not have been Uncle William's secret hiding place, because it has always been used to store his hunting rifles. And besides, even the household staff know about this room, because they clean it regularly."

"Then there must be another hiding place," says Alice deep in thought, and then continues, her eyes urging on those of Oliver: "If I were Uncle William's private nurse, I would have the opportunity to ask him about it. And if I were living in Stanton Manor I could search for this hiding place."

"Over my dead body!" says Helen with a fierce finality.

"Aunt Helen, please, I don't want you to die," says Alice mockingly. "I know the story and I am dying of curiosity to see the inside of Stanton Manor." She looks at Oliver, "Even though you think of me as a huge joke, you should know that you can trust me. Should you get any other nurse from the town or even the city, everyone will know very soon that she is looking for a secret hiding place."

"What Alice says makes perfect sense, Oliver," says Eleanor seriously. "We often have functions and markets to keep our small clinic going, I know the nursing personnel. The married nurses will not be willing to live in the manor on a full-time basis, and the unmarried ones … They are all head over heels in love with Richard."

"Is nobody listening to me?" asks Helen terribly upset.

Alice gives a long, exaggerated sigh. "Must we really listen, Aunt Helen?"

"You are going to give a heart attack one of these days, girl! I know you: you consider this a huge adventure to go and live in Stanton Manor, but you are very uninformed about the real situation in that place. Emily Howard has been a mental patient her entire life. She is extremely unstable and regularly gets totally out of control. Even when I was still young and lived here in Arundel all the people used to say that it was only her parents' money and Beatrice Crompton which kept Emily from being admitted into a clinic for the mentally disturbed," recounts Helen upset.

"But I am not going to be Aunt Emily's nurse, Aunt Helen. I will make sure to stay out of her way."

Oliver clears his throat uncomfortably. "It is not that simple, Alice. Aunt Emily comes and goes as she pleases, because Miss Crompton can't keep an eye on her and Uncle William."

"That is why I am going to take care of Uncle William, and the Miss Crompton is freed up to give all of her attention to Aunt Emily."

"As long as Emily drinks her medication she is as tame as a little lamb," says Eleanor calm. "Miss Crompton will not allow any harm to come to Alice, Helen, and like the girl says: who else can we trust?"

Helen looks pleadingly at Oliver. "You know I never got married, Oliver. Alice is all I've got. Do you believe she will be safe in Stanton Manor?"

He gives an uncomfortable dry cough, his gaze uncertain on Alice. "That will all depend on her, Aunt Helen. She will have to be extremely careful in this undertaking and she will also have to tell Miss Crompton when she decides to look around for the hiding place."

"I will! I will!" promises Alice enthusiastically.

Eleanor lays a calming hand on Helen's arm. "We can always phone her at Stanton Manor, Helen. Alice knows we are here. While Beatrice is there to keep an eye on Emily you don't have to worry about Alice."

"We have to decide very quickly, Aunt Helen," says Oliver tense. Nobody knows Alice is here as a visitor, but if Richard should come here unannounced ... I don't want under any circumstances for any of the residents of Stanton Estate to know that I know Alice."

"I haven't unpacked my suitcases yet," says Alice and gets up. "When must I go?"

Helen looks at her concerned. "Alice-child, are you sure what you are getting yourself into?" she asks with a feint glimmer of criticism.

"I already told you, Aunt Helen: I want to do private nursing," she answers stubbornly, reconsiders, and puts her arm around Helen's shoulders. "I promise you, Aunt Helen: I will not do anything to put my life in danger. But I am able to defend myself – have you forgotten about my three brothers?"

"If this is the only way … " Helen sighs dismayed. "I can only pray that I will never regret this day."

"You won't, Aunt Helen. And I will come over regularly," promises Alice, gives her aunt a kiss on the cheek, and turns to Oliver. "I am ready for your instructions, Doctor Howard," she says formally.

"Follow me, nurse Browning," he replies with just a hint of a smile on his lips and walks out of the kitchen.

Alice follows Oliver in his metallic gray car with her small red car, sees the town down below them and steps hard on the brakes when Oliver suddenly swings out of the road and turns left between some trees. She frowns surprised, and then she sees the dim tracks of a road twisting through the trees, and she follows him again. A few hundred meters further he brings his car to a stop and gets out. She parks next to him, switches off the car and frowns in question as he walks towards her.

"Get out, Alice. We need to talk first," he says in an even tone.

She tries to read the expression on his face, but his lashes hide his eyes as he holds the door open and helps her out.

"You sound very serious," she says worried. "Did you not tell me the entire truth?"

"I didn't, but that was on Aunt Helen's behalf." He presses his lips together and then starts talking extremely fast: "I didn't tell you what happened this morning when I visited Uncle William. I had hardly spoken to him when Aunt Emily stormed into the room."

"But I already know about that."

"Not everything. She grabbed a pair of scissors, and she would've attacked me if Uncle William hadn't pretended to be delirious.

I wasn't really worried, because physically I am much stronger than she is, but on the other hand: a crazy person usually has more strength – and cunning – than a normal person."

"Is she then aggressive? Has she ever hurt anyone?" asks Alice worried.

"No ...no, not as far as I know. Miss Crompton makes sure that she takes her medication and then she is totally controllable, but Aunt Emily can be very sly. She apparently only pretended to drink her medication this morning. Miss Crompton was under the impression that she was sleeping, but she was using Richard's binoculars to spy on Aunt Eleanor. She probably saw me coming to the manor."

"But then she already knows about me!" says Alice upset.

He smiles reassuringly. "That is impossible. Aunt Eleanor's house in a double story. She can't see any cars parked in front of Aunt Eleanor's house from Stanton Manor.'

"Oh ... But if she tries to attack me with scissors ..."

"That is why I'm telling you about the incident. She mustn't know under any circumstances that you know me or Aunt Eleanor. You will have one day off every week and then you can meet Aunt Helen per chance. But under no circumstances ever talk about me." He looks at her intently. "Do we drive forward, or do we turn back?"

She isn't the joke to him anymore, she is now his ally, thinks Alice and realises that a special feeling for this tall, broad-shouldered man with the black-blue eyes has taken hold in the warm darkness of her heart where love is born and nurtured. There is nothing she will not do for him. But he can never know that, because then she will again see the taunting laughter in his eyes, she decides and turns away from him.

"If you are scared ... I will understand, Alice," he says with understanding.

"I am not scared. I want to help you," she answers muffled.

"Even after all my insults?" he asks guiltily.

She smiles with a forced carelessness. "That is why I became a nurse: I feel sorry for people. Or maybe I just like people because

I like to help people."

"I'm not sick. You don't have a reason to feel sorry for me."

"No, but you need help, or you will never know who your parents were. And that is a challenge … almost an adventure."

"A very dangerous adventure," he warns.

"You already warned me."

"Yes, but … there is Richard."

She looks at him surprised. "The sole heir of Stanton Estate? My word, Oliver, are you going to tell me he is also mentally unstable?"

His lips pull grimly. "Definitely not, but Richard has always had an eye for the pretty ladies. And Aunt Emily has never let him forget that he is the sole heir of Stanton Estate. I believe he thinks of himself as a prince who can just snap his fingers to get whatever he wants. Girls are in general quite keen to comply to his whims without him even having to snap his fingers."

"No!" She stares at him, not sure if she should be angry at him or if she should laugh at him. "Doctor Howard, you have already misjudged me once: I am not a frivolous eighteen-year-old student. Come, let me release you of your concerns: I grew up with three brothers and all their friends. I assure you I am more than capable to keep even the most obtrusive man at a distance."

"You don't know Richard." He sees her offended frown and continues quickly: "As long as you are warned. Please, don't let Richard suspect that you are trying to help me. We have been sworn enemies for several years now."

"Weren't you even friends as children?" she asks surprised.

He smiles cynically. "The prince and the slave – that was Richard and me. A child usually follows the example of his parents and Richard saw from very young how Aunt Emily treated me. Uncle William was always the peace-maker, the man who always told me to never lift my hand to Richard because I was older and stronger than he was. That is why I visited grandmother Caroline and Aunt Eleanor so regularly at Tortington, I might have retaliated."

"And as you got older?"

"Aunt Emily could never forgive me for also out-performing Richard in school. And then when I inherited Tortington ... After grandmother Caroline's funeral I never returned to Stanton Manor."

"I don't blame you. Thank you for telling me about you and Richard."

He looks at her with something like astonishment in his eyes. A few days ago, she was just a pretty girl – no, a breathtakingly beautiful girl – whom he met per chance in a parking lot at a shopping centre, but now she was his ally.

"You are a kind and beautiful woman, Alice," he says, a hoarseness in his voice, "I'm glad I've met you. Thank you, again, for helping me to find some answers." He rests his strong hand on her shoulder. "Friends and allies?" he asks, and holds out his hand to her.

They shake hands and smile in each other's eyes.

He steps away from her, open her car door, and helps her back in her car.

Oh, goodness, she feels so light-headed. Never before has a man had such an effect on her. Not even the attractive Robert with all his charm. She suddenly wonders how many women here in Arundel will lose their hearts to doctor Howard.

"Thank you for that warm welcome, Norman. You should've warned me," says Oliver, smiling at his old acquaintance.

"No, no," Norman holds both his hands up in the air. "That was all matron Frances' doing. I was just commanded to bring you to the canteen the moment you arrived. And matron Frances isn't someone to argue with, as you'll come to find out yourself soon enough."

"On that point, I want to make it clear that I have no intention of moving back to Arundel. My visit is purely for personal reasons, and as you are well aware of, only because of my uncle's deteriorating health."

"Noted and accepted, Oliver. You said over the phone you had an urgent matter to discuss with me regarding your uncle. What can I do for you?"

Doctor Norman Graham listens intently to Oliver but can't keep his eyes off of Alice. He decided years ago to follow in his wise father's footsteps and only get married when he turned thirty-six years old, but that was before he met Alice.

He hopes that there isn't already a relationship between her and Oliver.

She likes Norman Graham, thinks Alice. He has auburn-red hair, a short nose giving his face a boyish quality, and a broad, friendly smile. He is shorter than Oliver, and he is stocky, and the warmth in his voice will reassure any patient of his.

"Do you hear me, Norman?" asks Oliver irritated, suddenly furious that Norman is so blatantly interested in Alice. The exact reason why he and Norman were such good friends when they were students was because Norman was more interested in his studies than in girls. Has Norman suddenly undergone a personality change? Why is he looking at Alice as if she is the first pretty girl to ever enter his office?

"Every word, old friend," says Norman with a wide smile and turns reluctantly back to Oliver. "And I have already thought of a very agreeable lie: Alice is the daughter of one of my mother's friends. Alice and I have known each other for years and ... e ... she wanted to be closer to me, that is why she asked me to find her a position in our clinic. Unfortunately, there aren't any positions available right now, but she really wants to specialize in private nursing. How does that sound to you?"

"Fantastic!" says Alice approvingly.

"Nonsense! It sounds like Alice is trapsing after you," says Oliver dissatisfied. "Alice, you love the countryside and the sea, and here you have both. That is why you came here to Arundel."

"But what is my role then?" asks Norman dejected.

"I know you because our parents are friends. I knew you had a practice in Arundel, which is why I came here, in the hope that you could have a position for me," suggests Alice.

Norman nods his head in agreement and smiles happy with himself. "That works for me. What is our next step?"

"Phone Miss Crompton and explain the situation to her. Miss Crompton can tell Aunt Emily that she asked you to find a full-time nurse for Uncle William. And then Alice can go to Stanton Manor," says Oliver business-like.

Norman looks at his watch. "I have a better suggestion: if you can wait an hour or so, Alice, I will drive with you to Stanton Manor and introduce you to its people."

"That won't be necessary, as long as you just phone Miss Crompton," says Oliver decidedly and gets up. "Alice and I will drink a cup of tea in the coffee shop in the meantime and after that she can immediately go to Stanton Manor."

"No, Oliver. Someone in town could see us together and Aunt Emily could hear about it. I agree it is better if I go with Norman," objects Alice.

A deep frown carves between Oliver's brows, but he realises the truth in Alice's words and says reluctantly: "Yes, let's do that. And ask Miss Crompton to phone me the moment you are safe in Stanton Manor."

"Yes, I will. Goodbye, Oliver," she greets him, but secretly wishes she could think of one more reason to stay with him just a while longer.

"Goodbye Alice," he says gruffly, nods his head at Norman and walks out of the office.

Helen stirs her cup of tea lost in her thoughts, a worried frown on her forehead, staring into nothingness.

"Helen?" Eleanor lightly touches her arm. "If you keep stirring there won't be a bottom left in that cup."

Helen smiles. "Sorry, Aunt Eleanor. It isn't my intention to be so uncompanionable, but ..." Fear fills her eyes, and she continues tense: "After my father's death you were my only contact with the happenings in Arundel. I remember how shocked we all were to hear about the engagement between Henry and Annabelle because everyone had already been whispering that something wasn't right, that the Montgomery's were hiding something."

"Have you forgotten, Helen? Late Caroline was against the marriage between Henry and Annabelle … bitterly against it. That is why Henry decided to go to Ireland and rather finish his studies there in Dublin. There were arguments from dusk till dawn inside these walls when Henry suddenly announced that he was leaving to study in Ireland. And then the war started…" She drifts away in her memories and shaking her head goes on: "Not that any of the rumours ever made any sense to me. Henry was a young man of twenty-five or twenty-six. If he really wanted to marry Annabelle nothing would've been able to stop him."

"Is it possible that he believed all the whispered rumours?"

"Henry would not have paid any attention to any rumours. No … no, I believe there was another reason – like Annabelle's secret meetings with Henry's friend, Grayson."

"Aunt Eleanor!" Helen stares at her in surprise. "You never said anything about that in your letters to me."

"I didn't want to because …" Eleanor falls silent and her eyes ask Helen for forgiveness when she speaks again: "You were still so young, Helen. It is difficult for a young girl to hide her feelings. I knew you loved Henry."

Helen looks down at her hands, draws invisible pictures with her finger on the tablecloth and then looks up, with a wide smile. "It is a lifetime ago, but I suppose one never forgets one's first love – especially also if it were your only love."

"No, one doesn't forget, but that is the reason why I didn't want to tell you about Annabelle's unfaithfulness. You would've had new hope that Grayson and Annabelle would get married and that Henry would come back and fall in love with you."

"No, Aunt Eleanor. I was still in school when Henry and Annabelle had their relationship. I already knew then Henry would never show any interest in me, and hence my reason to decide to study in London."

"That is what you say now, but then … In your letters you always asked about the people of Stanton Manor, but you never mentioned Henry's name. I knew then that you had not yet gotten over him, that is why I kept quiet."

A smile wipes a sliver of pain from Helen's eyes. "Does one ever forget, Aunt Eleanor? My studies helped, but when you wrote to me that Henry had died in that bomb attack … I also wanted to die, but death knows no mercy. I lived, I kept on living, and I just emersed myself deeper into my studies. And then one day I realised I could think about Henry without wishing I was dead as well. Then I knew, my time of grieve was over."

"And yet, you could never find love again?" asks Eleanor sympathetically.

"No – and it wasn't due to lack of trying. Maybe, had Henry and Annabelle gotten married, it would've been easier. But Henry's death made me a widow without him ever loving me."

"If Annabelle could only love like that … After that Spring Day she never heard from or saw Grayson Lumley ever again. We could never figure out what had become of him. He was just gone. And when Annabelle heard about Henry's death, she packed her bags and … William was now the sole heir of Stanton Estate, and Emily and William didn't wait even three months to marry," recalls Eleanor with an expression of pure contempt on her face.

"Emily was a rich girl and her parent's youngest child. Why was it so important for her to marry a rich husband?" asks Helen in wonder.

"Money seeks money, Helen. Unfortunately, Richard takes after his stingy mother. Oh, he flirts with every pretty little face, but Beatrice tells me he has basically moved to Chichester since Charlotte Hastings became a widow – and the woman is two years older than him!"

"Did Charlotte's husband pass away?" asks Oliver from the passage door.

Eleanor blushes bloodred like a teenager caught in the act. "So sad, yes, Oliver. You must remember: Thomas Hastings was almost thirty years older than Charlotte. He had a heart attack a month or three ago and collapsed on the golf course."

Oliver walks closer, his movements shaky, and he sits down at the table. "You never let me know, Aunt Eleanor," he says grimly. She looks at him intensely. "Did you really want to know, child?"

He quickly looks up, and then he looks down again. "Charlotte and I went to school together. We finished school together. We were always together, Aunt Eleanor."

"I remember, yes, but she never wore your engagement ring. There are people who say you are the reason why she married an older man," says Eleanor, watching him closely.

"You know that is not the truth, Aunt Eleanor. I was a dirt-poor student with no prospects to ever inherit any riches. But that was not all: I was also a man without a lineage. How could I ask any girl to be my bride when I could not even tell her who my parents are?" he asks bluntly.

"If your bank account were fat enough Charlotte wouldn't have cared about your parentage. But things have changed now, Oliver … You are now a successful cardiologist and the owner of Tortington. I heard Charlotte inherited the entire fortune from Thomas. You know where to find her. Nothing is stopping you from contacting her," her voice scraping with disapproval.

"Did I not hear you right, Aunt Eleanor, Richard has already set his sights on Charlotte?"

"That is true, but you have never before really cared at all about what Richard was up to."

"And I still don't care, but … " he leaves his sentence unfinished and turns to Helen. "Doctor Norman Graham has agreed to take Alice to Stanton Manor, Aunt Helen. Norman will pretend that Alice is the daughter of one of his mother's friend's and that she is keen to live and work in the countryside close to the coast."

Helen looks at him, searching his face. "Are you certain my niece will be safe in Stanton Estate, Oliver?"

"As long as Alice doesn't take any unnecessary risks …"

"That is exactly what my concern is. Alice considers her visit to Stanton Manor as one big adventure, but I could never have a peaceful night's rest until she is back safely under my roof," answers Helen and accuses him with her eyes.

Matron Frances Leighton hangs up the phone for the umpteenth time. She has tried several times now to reach doctor Howard, but the receptionist at the hotel keeps saying he isn't available. She forgot to ask him his pager number when they had his welcoming tea at the clinic. They also had such an interesting chat in the short while that he was at the clinic, she didn't even think about it.

She would really have wanted to entertain the man tonight; it is also nothing short of expectation that she as the matron should make sure that the visiting doctor is taken care of. He must see and know that she is a woman who thinks of everything and everyone. Yes, he must be very well aware of her exceptional characteristics which he won't easily find in any other woman. She must be an absolute rarity to him – someone not to be taken for granted and also someone who stands out head and shoulders above all other women. She smiles self-assured. But of course, she is one of a kind. And thát, doctor Howard will find out soon enough!

Her face suddenly tightens. She won't make a mistake again. Her short-lived marriage to doctor Peter Sutton was a mistake. Specifically, because he had one flaw that affected her which was that he was always flirting with other girls.

That made her jealous and furious, and to top it off she started to feel insecure because he taunted her with the other girls. But to be honest, she should've gotten to know the man better before she fell head-over-heels in love him and married him so quickly. "You made a mistake to marry Peter Sutton," her mother said to her that night when she went home and cried on her mother's shoulder over her failed marriage. "Peter is not the marrying type, my child. He will never be satisfied with just one woman. I told you to wait and to make very sure before you decided to marry him."

Yes, she remembers very well. And she had thought that she was certain about Peter's love for her. But it didn't take long for him to show his true colours. He didn't even have the courtesy to wait until after their honeymoon on the French Riviera. She had started to think he was only trying to make her jealous. But she quickly found out that was not the case, especially when she saw him in the restaurant with another girl, kissing her like he was resuscitating her.

She shakes her head. That won't happen ever again, she decides. There will never be a second Peter Sutton in her life to hurt and humiliate her like that.

And, luckily, she has grown older and wiser, and her eyes will be wide open this time. Doctor Oliver Howard is definitely not a man one will find behind every bush. His type is rare, and that fact alone has convinced her that he is the right and the only man for her. After him she will never allow any other man into her life ever again. She will fight for him, because she knows with a man like him by her side, she can only have a happy and wonderful life!

Emily opens her eyes, sees Beatrice sitting on the chair next to her bed and shoots up in a sitting position in her bed. "Why are you babysitting me, Beatrice? Did I do something under the influence of all that medication again? I have said to you time, and time again: those pills make my head spin and then I don't know what I'm doing. Is the bedroom door locked? Speak, Beatrice! What have I done this time? What?" her words follow in an increasing crescendo and ends in a shrill fearful scream.

For goodness's sake, calm down Emily," Eleanor says impatiently. "The medicine is prescribed by Doctor Graham. It is when you refuse to take your medicine that you act irresponsibly and uncontrollably. Don't you remember? You drank your medicine, and you were sleeping peacefully until now."

"Then why are you babysitting me? Why is my bedroom door closed?" asks Emily, her eyes wild with suspicion.

"Because I wanted to tell you about Nurse Browning. You see, I phoned Doctor Graham and I told him that I was neglecting you because of all the time and attention William requires from me. He personally brought nurse Browning here and gave her specific instructions on taking care of William," relates Beatrice calmly.

"Browning? One of the villagers' daughters?" asks Emily insulting.

"Oh, no. This girl has a degree in nursing, and she is very capable. Doctor Graham's and her parents are well acquainted."

"A degree, right? Then I must meet her immediately," says Emily and gets out of her bed.

"Your nightgown and slippers, Emily. You do want to make a good impression on the nurse, don't you?"

Emily sticks her nose in the air. "You forget who you speaking to, Beatrice. I am Emily Howard of Stanton Estate. In my house I will not be dictated what to do," she answers with her cold haughtiness, she opens her bedroom door, and walks in her long, white nightdress to William's room.

Alice stares in fear into the dark, glowing eyes who appears in the bedroom door, glaring at her without even blinking. She looks like a character from a horror movie, thinks Alice nervously: long, unbrushed hair, a pale-yellow face with thin sneering lips, an aristocratic nose, and the light of madness in her dark eyes. Alice opens her mouth in a greeting, but she falls silent when a hand

some, dark young man appears next to the woman and his eyes slide slowly up and down over her.

"Now, this is a pleasant surprise, Mother," says Richard Howard pleased. "Did you hire this pretty little thing for my entertainment?"

Chapter 4

Emily pulls her back straight, and her shoulders back, unaware of the extreme contrast between her attempted regal stance and her mad appearance, and she says with cold disdain: "How many times must I remind you of your position as sole heir to Stanton Estate, Richard? Us Howards only associate with people of our own class. This nurse is just another paid help."

Richard blushes in anger. "Please, mother, we don't live in the Middle Ages anymore. I won't be dictated to by ..."

"Quiet, Richard!" cuts Emily him off in a pitched voice. "Have you forgotten that you have your inheritance thanks to me?"

Alice steps closer quickly and says firmly, but in a muffled voice: "If this conversation is going to become a family argument: I have a patient to take care of. He is sleeping peacefully, and sleep is especially important to him right now, then he escapes from the pain. I would appreciate it if you could take your argument elsewhere."

Richard smiles in approval. "A feisty little thing, are you? How did you know that is just how I like them, nursy?"

Emily pushes Richard out of her way with her elbow and she glares at Alice from the cold heights of her haughtiness. "I am Lady Emily Howard, nurse. Do not forget that I am your employer, and I am paying your salary, or you might just be leaving faster than you arrived."

"I am here to give you a professional service, Lady Howard. If you make that impossible for me to do, it won't be necessary for you to ask me to pack my bags," answers Alice with a coldness equal to Emily's.

Emily wildly looks around her, as if she is searching for a weapon, and she grabs Alice's shoulder with a claw-like hand. "How dare you prescribe to me, you miserable pauper! If my money id good enough for you then you will treat me with the due respect, do you understand me?"

"Let the girl go, Emily!" says Beatrice and swings Emily around as if she were a paper doll. "And you, Richard, remove yourself from this room, before you also need medical care. Maybe you think of me as the dedicated servant who is too loyal to speak the truth about you, but body and soul can take only so much! Remember I still have a mouth and I can still speak."

"Calm down, Miss Crompton. I only wanted to welcome the nursy," says Richard apologetically and skulks out to the passage.

"You are my Lady-in-waiting, not my servant, Beatrice," says Emily hurt. "This nurse is in my employment, but she imagines she can boss me around in my own house."

"Because it is for William's sake, Emily. Let's go back to your room," says Beatrice calmingly.

Emily grasps on to the doorsill with both hands. "Not before this ungrateful creature has apologised to me. If I pay her salary, I expect submission."

Emily is acting like a spoiled rich-kid, thinks Alice and stares at her in silence. But Emily isn't a child anymore: she is a sick woman who can be unpredictable and uncontrollable. Oliver isn't really her friend, they hardly just met each other; she is also just a means to an end for him. What is preventing her from packing her bags in her car and going back to Tortington?

"You were unreasonable, Emily, not nurse Browning," says Beatrice without hesitation. "Now, come with me. It is almost time for your dinner. We will get you all dressed up in your finest, and then I will formally introduce you to nurse Browning."

"She has to apologise to me," maintains Emily. Her eyes are glowing with madness as she looks at Alice, who returns her gaze in silence. "Speak, girl! Apologise to me for not treating me with the expected respect."

Alice turns her head silently to Beatrice. "I will pack my bags in my car and leave now, Miss Crompton. I am sorry, but I am not prepared to take care of Sir Howard under these circumstances."

"I understand, Alice, but don't just leave yet. I just want to get my things packed and then I'll be coming with you," says Beatrice and starts to turn to the passage.

"No!" shrieks Emily. She lets go of the doorsill and starts following Beatrice. "You can't do that, Beatrice! I need you. You know I can't do anything without you. Beatrice, please, don't go," she pleads whimpering.

Beatrice stops, her expression uncompromising. "Will you let nurse Browning be, Emily?"

"Yes, yes, I will do anything, as long as you stay with me," begs Emily with the desperation of a child.

"Remember then: I have had it with your tantrums and antics. If you do not listen to me, or if you bother nurse Browning, I will leave with her."

Alice sighs in relieve as she hears their footsteps fading down the passage, and she slowly walks back to Sir William's bed. She looks at his hollow face with the sunken eyes in their dark sockets and she smiles impulsively when he opens his eyes. "I am nurse Alice Browning, Sir Howard. Doctor Graham sent me to take care of you."

His lips pull shakily in an attempt to smile and brings a warm sparkle to his dull eyes. "I heard. Nurse Browning. I will call you Alice because nurses only make me feel sick."

"That is why I am nor wearing a uniform," she answers, and ask in wonder: "Did you hear the argument between myself and Lady Howard, Sir Howard?"

"Uncle William … call me Uncle William." A dark shadow wipes the warmth from his eyes. "I never was a Sir. I was …I was…" he tightly closes his eyes and his mouth twists in pain.

"Is the pain awfully bad, Uncle William? If you want an injection for the pain …" she watches him worried, but he opens his eyes and shakes his head.

"There is pain… and there is pain. It is the injustice … the injustice I did to the child. I should've told him about them a long time ago … a long time ago." His breathing becomes faster. "And I would have, but she stopped me. She threatened to kill Richard – her own child! She wanted to murder my son!"

"Calm down, Uncle William, I am here now. Richard is a grown man. No one will murder him," she says, trying to calm William down.

He tries to pull himself upright and there is a naked fear on his face. "She is stronger and slyer than seven devils! Even now … I have pleaded, begged …I cannot die before I tell him the truth, but she doesn't understand. She doesn't fear death. She will kill – even now! He says, his breathing shallow and fast.

"Come, lay back down, Uncle William. If you tell me what is bothering you, I will try to help," says Alice calmly, but her heart is almost jumping from her chest. Uncle William doesn't have to name anyone: she knows he is referring to Aunt Emily and Oliver. But will he be willing to trust her with his secret?

Otto leans back tired and closes his eyes. "Oliver knows now. He knows about the hiding place."

"Where is this hiding place, Uncle William?"

He opens his eyes and smiles contently. "That is our secret. No one is allowed to know. Especially not girls."

What can she say now, wonders Alice worried? That Oliver also doesn't know? That he is confusing Oliver with his brother, Henry? But then she will have to admit to knowing Oliver, and that is a fact that can't get out under any circumstances. Then just to be patient and wait until she has gained Uncle William's trust – or until she gets the chance to look for the secret hiding place.

Alice follows Beatrice to Emily's private lounge and stares in amazement at the woman sitting on the gold-plated chair with the dark red upholstery. Emily's hair is done up on her head in elaborate twists and curls, and her face has been made up with professional care. She is dressed in a rose pink nightgown and slippers testimony to riches and a wealthy taste.

In her youth Emily must have been an extraordinary beauty, realises Alice and remains standing next to Beatrice.

"Let me introduce you, Alice," says Beatrice formal. "Lady Emily Howard – nurse Alice Browning."

Emily nods her head haughtily and there is a faint smile on her lips.

"A pleasure to meet you, Lady Howard," forces Alice herself, fighting against the desire to burst out laughing. She feels like an actress in a comedy because only a few hours ago this elegant Lady Howard was a raging lunatic in a loose hanging, white nightdress. Stanton Manor is everything she hoped it would be: a house full of antique furniture, valuable silver- and porcelain ware, original paintings and statues, and the mystery so characteristic of these old manors with all its stairs and long passages. But Stanton Manor is at the same time a very miserable home giving shelter to a dying man with a guilty conscience and an insane woman who threatens to take her own son's life, she thinks bitterly.

Emily waves with a scrawny hand to the chair opposite her. "Sit, nurse Browning. Beatrice will pour us some tea."

"Thank you, Lady Howard," says Alice submissively and sits down on the chair while Beatrice walks over to the coffee table to pour their tea.

"I understand from Beatrice that you are not one of our residents from Arundel?" says Emily, her voice controlled and cultivated.

"That is correct, Lady Howard. I completed my studies in London," answers Alice mechanically.

"Arundel has its origin and continued existence thanks to the Howards," says Emily as if she didn't hear Alice. "The town and its people belong to us because they are all in our service. One can say we are the royalty, which is how the people see us. I hope you understand it is a special privilege to be chosen to live here in Stanton Manor and almost be treated as an equal."

"Alice realises it," says Beatrice quickly when she sees the rebellious expression on Alice's face, and she holds a cup of tea out to her. "Drink, dearie. The tea is warm," she continues cordially, but her eyes plead silently for her understanding.

"Thank you, Miss Crompton," says Alice and continues in a neutral voice: "Stanton Manor is a magnificent old home. I haven't yet had the opportunity to look around, but I have already noticed several treasures."

"There is nothing in Stanton Manor that is not worth a small fortune. You can look around in your free time but don't touch anything. The ordinary worker's class is usually so clumsy and irresponsible in handling valuable ornaments," says Emily with a smile. "The tea is delicious, Beatrice. Let nurse Browning try a slice of your famous apple tart."

"Nothing for me, thank you, Miss Crompton," Alice declines quickly.

She will only choke if she eats anything now, she thinks resentful because Emily's little tea party is nothing but an excuse to humiliate and insult her in a civilised manner.

"Are you hoping to seduce my son with your slender figure, nursy?" Emily's lips jump away from her teeth, her smile sneering. "Allow me to warn you right here: Richard will play with you like a cat plays with a mouse; my son is very well aware of the responsibility resting on his shoulders. He is the sole heir to Stanton Estate, and he will marry the girl of my choice … A girl from our own class."

"I didn't come here to look for a husband, Lady Howard, and for that reason I would very much appreciate it if you can make it very clear to Richard that I am not a mouse and he is not a cat," answers Alice cold.

Emily's face twists in rage and she throws the tea with one jerk of her arm out of her cup in Alice's direction. "How dare you give me instructions, you conceited church mouse? You will not for one moment longer ..."

"Emily!" commands Beatrice as she walks fast towards Emily. "I have warned you: my suitcase is already packed."

"But you heard what she said to me, Beatrice," pleads Emily with the voice of a scared child. "People forget who I am ... Don't you remember? I am Emily Montgomery, the princess of Chichester, who married the sole heir of Stanton Estate."

"Yes, yes, you are, but this visit is now done. You are too sensitive, Emily, which is why these long conversations tire you." Beatrice looks over her shoulder at Alice who has already stood up from her chair. "You can now go, Alice. Lady Howard needs to rest."

Alice nods and relieved she flees from the room. She stops in the passage. Her eyes are on the magnificent crystal chandelier which lights up the stairs and the voyeur, but she hardly notices it. She doesn't want to be here, she thinks rebelliously. She was a fool to offer to help Oliver. Even if she should discover the secret hiding place with all the evidence of Oliver's lineage, it won't change anything for her. Oliver doesn't love her; Oliver would never love her. If she were with Aunt Helen and Aunt Eleanor in Tortington she could at least have talked to Oliver, they could've gotten to know each other better, maybe even have become friends... a very small consolation price, but more than enough to sooth the longings of her heart.

Norman Graham likes her, she tries to console herself, and walks down the passage to have a quick peek on Uncle William.

Beatrice places a chocolate drink in front of Alice on the kitchen table and slowly lowers herself into the chair at the head of the table. "Fat is a strange thing, Alice," she says in confidence. "It feels to me as if my fat first takes a seat and then I follow."

Alice bursts into spontaneous laughter, puts her hand over her mouth and laughs with her shoulders shaking.

"That's better," say Beatrice approvingly. "I had a suspicion you are a cheerful child, but you haven't exactly had any reason to laugh since Doctor Graham brought you here."

Alice's expression sombres. "Stanton Manor looks like a fairy tale castle from the outside, but on the inside..." She stares at Beatrice. "Why don't you find work somewhere else, Miss Crompton? I would go stir-crazy if I were to take care of Aunt Emily."

Beatrice sighs deeply and there is a distant look in her eyes. "You don't understand, child. It is a long story – a promise – which has brought me all the way to this point."

"May I hear the story, Miss Crompton?"

"It's not really interesting, dear. I was the only daughter of a struggling farmer. Our little patch of earth was infertile and also without much water, whereas the rich Montgomery's were blessed with a beautiful farm, a river, and even a fountain. They knew only abundance. But old Charles Montgomery did not have everything. I was just poor Beatrice Crompton, but I was intelligent, if I may say so myself, and after school I became a nurse."

"Are you also a nurse, Miss Crompton?" asks Alice surprised.

"Not as educated as the nurses of today, but I finished my studies when I was twenty. And it was then when old Charles Montgomery came to my father with a suggestion: I would undertake to look after Emily, and as long as I did Charles Montgomery would ensure my parents won't lose their farm."

Alice stares at her in shock. "But that is a very unfair suggestion, Miss Crompton! That meant you would never be able to get married or to have your own family. Why did you ever agree to do it, to almost become Emily's slave?" she asks upset.

"If you love your parents and have five younger brothers still having to finish school ..." Beatrice smiles resigned. "One learns in a large family – especially in a poor family – to be unselfish. Charles Montgomery's offer was to us an answer to all our prayers, it was a godsend, we had hope again. Believe me, Alice, I couldn't accept his offer fast enough."

"And you have never regretted you decision?" asks Alice sceptical.

"How shall I put it , dear?" Beatrice pulls up her round shoulders. "Maybe, in the dark, late night hours, do I sometimes imagine what my husband and unborn children might've looked like... but then the sun rises, and perhaps I receive a letter from one of my brothers and then I know it was all worth it. My brothers all finished school. Two of them became teachers, two became very professionally qualified tradesmen, and the last one is a bank manager today. My father has long since passed away, but my mother is a woman of eighty-three and she takes turns to visit her children and grandchildren... And you ask if I have regrets? No."

"But still... Do you ever visit your family?"

"Until a few years ago I could, but not anymore... not since Emily's health got so much worse. Ever since Emily was a girl of sixteen... She was always an incredibly stressed girl, and a temper... but I have always been able to calm her down. To tell you the truth, I have gotten to love her as a younger sister, maybe because I never had a sister. And then there was Emily's older sister, Annabelle, or Bella as everyone called her. She was six years older than Emily, my age. Beautiful, so beautiful. The Montgomery sisters were blessed beyond what is fair when it came to their beauty with their dark hair and dark eyes. Annabelle was a curious girl, fiercely independent, always reading, always dreaming of traveling to faraway lands and going on adventures and the stories she would write about her travels - to escape her golden cage as she referred to her wealthy upbringing. She was engaged to Henry. Emily was extremely envious of her sister, being the oldest and so beautiful, and engaged to the sole heir of Stanton Estate. Emily would have extreme outbursts. To tell you the truth, she even scared me sometimes."

"But if Aunt Emily could have received psychological treatment –
"

Beatrice's eyes widen in shock. "Do you think the proud Charles and Katherine Montgomery would ever have admitted to the outside world that one of their beautiful girls was mentally sick?

Oh no, dear, they would rather have died. That is why I always had to be near, even when Henry Howard came to visit Annabelle – and Grayson Lumley. Annabelle was so happy that not one, but two men, called on her. Henry was the heir to Stanton Estate, but Annabelle was in love with Grayson. They were cut from the same cloth, looking for adventure and wanting to see the world. That is why she met him in secret – a secret I had to be part of even if it was against everything I believed in."

"Why could she not have been honest with Henry? Why did she have to keep her relationship with Robert a secret?" asks Alice with incomprehension.

"Money," answers Beatrice grim. "The Montgomery's had more than enough money, but they expected Annabelle to marry a wealthy man, a man of their class, to settle and to have children. Henry was the oldest son, old Sir Edward's heir, and therefore they insisted she married him. Grayson Lumley was the nephew of Annabelle and Emily's governess. He was raised by his aunt, Anne Barclay, who lived in a cottage on the Montgomery farm. He and Annabelle practically grew up together, but in two totally different worlds. Grayson was one of the Montgomery servants in the eyes of Charles and Katherine Montgomery, and the two were never allowed to socialise or speak to each other. Until that December… Annabelle was eighteen and Grayson was a student. He came home for the December winter holiday, and that is when everything changed. I do believe with all my heart Annabelle loved Henry, as one would an older brother. And she was content to marry him as was expected of her. But she wanted to travel before settling and starting a family. Henry, on the other hand, had to fulfil his obligations towards his family as the oldest and it was expected of him to complete his studies and to take over the family business from his father. Emily also knew about the secret relationship between her sister and Grayson and being so envious of her sister she told Henry about it. He didn't believe her of course, but Emily told him about a secret meeting they were planning, it was just as spring started, and Henry caught Annabelle and Grayson together in the Houghton

Forest where they were having a picnic ..."

"I am glad for Henry's sake, if a girl can't even be faithful before her marriage, she will definitely not be faithful thereafter."

"That is true, dear, but in those years... the scandal of it all was just too much for the proud Montgomery's and after the news of Henry's death they allowed Annabelle to go on her adventures. And then things turned into William's favour: Henry died during the war in Ireland two years after he left Stanton Manor, and William became the sole heir of Stanton Estate. Three months after Henry's funeral, William and Emily got married and they came to live here with late Sir Edward and Lady Caroline Howard."

"Were they happy, Miss Crompton?"

A smile conjures with soft fingers the happiness of those years back into Beatrice's eyes. "So happy," she answers, her words as soft as the amen at the end of a prayer. "They were like children living in their own enchanted world – until that day when William arrived with little Oliver in his arms I remember thinking in those days: how can a small baby of only a year old bring so much unhappiness into a home? But then the resentment, and the suspicions, and the arguments started; then Emily's hate towards little Oliver was born. And throughout the years it just grew stronger until he eventually left for university. During holidays he either worked or he visited his grandmother Caroline and Eleanor, but he never set foot in Stanton Manor again, except just to greet his Uncle William."

"Does Aunt Emily know who Oliver's real parents are, Miss Crompton?"

"She says so because she has long since also stopped with her accusations that Oliver is William's illegitimate son." Beatrice frowns, shaking her head. "Emily and I have never kept any secrets from each other but after all these years she still adamantly refuses to discuss his parents with me."

"Do you think she knows where Uncle William hid the documents which will solve the secret about Oliver's lineage?" asks Alice hopeful.

"I would not know, child, because as I said: Emily doesn't talk about it."

Alice sighs tensely. "Then there is only one way: I will have to search for those documents and pray nobody catches me."

"I will help with the search, dear, but please, be very careful: if Emily catches you the consequences could be fatal," warns Beatrice with a seriousness that makes the blood in Alice's veins turn cold.

Alice stands on a chair in front of a family portrait in the long gallery, lifts the portrait away from the wall and shines the light from her torch against the back of the portrait.

Nothing, she thinks disappointed. Or is it possible that Uncle William hid the documents between the carton and the back of the portrait? If that is the case, then she would have to take every portrait down and remove the backing – but how can she do that without waking everyone in the house? And if she drops one of these heavy portraits …

No, wait, aunt Eleanor said Uncle William spoke as a child about his and Henry's secret hiding place. A child would also not have been able to lift these heavy portraits. She will simply have to keep looking and hope the documents were stuck to the back of one of these portraits or paintings, she thinks to herself.

She climbs down from the chair – and almost faints from fear and shock when two strong arms grab her from behind and a hand clasps over her mouth and nose.

"If you scream you are dead," whispers an unrecognisable voice in her ear and the torch is grabbed from her and switched off.

She nods in agreement. The pounding of her heart is beating like drums in her ears.

The hand is slowly taken away from her mouth and the voice whispers again: "Come with me," and she feels a hand grab hold of hers.

Alice blinks her eyes, but the darkness is like a thick velvet cloak wrapped around her. She knows it is a man holding her hand because the hand is large and strong. He is a s light-footed as a cat, sure of every step he takes.

"Hold on to the stairs' railing. We have to go down the stairs – quick!" comes the whispered command.

She obeys like someone who is already dead. Is it Richard, she wonders panic-stricken? He knows Stanton Manor like the back of his hand. He doesn't need any light to know where he is going. But if it is him – where is he taking her? She is totally at his mercy because Miss Crompton believes she is fast asleep in her room. If she screams now …

"We are at the bottom," whispers the man again and then he freezes as a heavy key turns in the door's keyhole. "Quick!" he hisses, drags her behind him around the stairs, pulls a door open and pushes her inside. The door clicks close softly behind him.

She remains absolutely motionless. There is a smell of clothes and rubber in her nose, and she realises that she and her abductor are hiding in the stairs' closet. Dimly she hears a heavy door closing, and then the sound of footsteps on the stairs reaches her ears.

"What now?" she asks bewildered.

"Hush!" he warns. He opens the door soundlessly and listens intently.

She hears a door closing on the first floor and tries to shirk away when her abductor grabs her arm again and pulls her closer.

"To the side entrance," he says almost inaudible, and she follows him like an unwilling puppet.

He opens the side door softly, walks out with her and turns around again to close the door. She hesitates only for a second, bents down and bites the hand of the abductor holding onto hers.

"Little pest!" he groans under his breath.

She catches her breath and freezes on the spot. "Oliver?" she asks confused.

He closes the door and rubs his left hand. "Do you have fangs, girl? My hand is bleeding!" he growls, but his voice is still a murmur.

"I wish I bit it off!" she hisses. "You could have given me a heart attack from shock when you grabbed me from behind in the dark!"

"Next time I will first knock you out and then grab you," he threatens. He looks at the dark house and whispers as an order: "Come with me."

They stay in the shadows of the shrubs until they reach an opening in the high fence. Oliver takes her by the arm and pushes her down on a white painted garden chair. "Sit. We must talk," he says gruffly.

"At one o'clock in the morning?" she asks sarcastically, but her heart sings in her ears. Oliver came to her. What does it matter what his reason is? He is here and even if he argues with her for the rest of the night, she will happily endure his insults.

"If I didn't come, Richard would have caught you in the gallery," he says grimly.

"But Richard went to bed early. We all had dinner together and he said to Aunt Emily he was turning in early."

He bents closer to her and in the light of the stars his eyes are the colour of moonlight on a dark lake" silver-grey.

"Then remember in the future never to believe brother Richard. Aunt Eleanor told me coincidentally that Aunt Emily is against Richard's relationship with a certain widow, which is why he is lying about his visits to her. Miss Crompton could also have told you. Did you ask her where Richard was before you started with your nightly detective escapades?"

"No... no, I didn't, but ..." She plucks her head up in anger. "Stop glaring at me, Oliver. I would definitely have heard the front door opening."

"Did you hear when I came in through the side door?" he asks sternly.

"Well, no, but the side door wasn't locked."

"It was, and the lock went off like a gun shot when I unlocked it. You forget: old houses creak at night, which is why you don't hear all the noise after a while; or you just believe it is just a beam, or just the floor creaking."

"Oh ..." she bites her lip guiltily. "In future I will be more careful."

"There isn't going to be a future of detective work for you anymore, little Alice. I refuse to die young because of the stress I have to endure. If I had arrived five minutes later, Richard would've caught you in the act."

"And? He wouldn't have eaten me alive," she says angrily.

"What would your explanation have been?"

"The same explanation I would also have given anyone else: that I was looking for a good hiding place for my diamond necklace."

"Your what?" he asks flabbergasted.

"The necklace I am wearing around my neck: it belonged to my late mother, and I know it is worth a small fortune. Aunt Emily has such a mistrust in her household staff – and that includes me – that she would've believed me if I had said I didn't trust the staff," she explains amusingly.

"That is, if she didn't convince herself that you probably stole the necklace from her," he says bitterly and smiles reluctantly. "I do admire your creativeness, little fire-cracker, but after tonight … I would rather sneak into Stanton Manor myself and search for the documents, at least I know the house."

"Can I then go back to Tortington?" she asks eagerly.

"If you want to, yes, but I was hoping you could gain Uncle Williams trust. Who knows, he might just talk to you about the documents and the secret hiding place one day. Or maybe when he is delirious …" He falls silent and stares at her in silence. "We are friends, Alice, but friendship has no conditions. You can come back to Tortington tomorrow if you can't stay here any longer."

"The poet, Byron, said: Friendship is love without wings," she says impulsively.

"Excuse me?"

"I was thinking aloud. I am not planning to already leave tomorrow…" she stops abruptly when she hears someone loudly calling out to her.

"Alice! Nurse Browning, where are you hiding?"

"Damn! It's Richard. Quick, Alice, he can't see us together. Wait for him there to the left of the hole in the fence," whispers Oliver and forcefully pulls her up.

"Ouch! Wretched bully!" she hisses.

"My hand is still bleeding," he taunts as she quickly jogs to the hole in the fence.

Richard sees her almost immediately and walks with long strides towards her. "Alice!" He grabs her in his arms and kisses her in her neck. "When I couldn't find you in your room, I knew you would be waiting here outside for me. Believe me, I will not disappoint you."

Chapter 5

Where is Oliver? Why doesn't he help her? These thoughts run through Alice's mind as she desperately fights to get out of Richard's suffocating embrace. "Let me go, Richard! I didn't have an appointment with you! Let me go, you wretched octopus!" her voice is shrill and smothered.

Richard laughs in a drunken state. "I like a bit of a fight, nursy, it makes the victory so much sweeter. Come, let me show you how a girl should be kissed."

"No! I will ..." she protests and jerks her head wildly back and forth. She is just half aware of a swift movement behind Richard, and then a dull thud, Richard groans and collapses like a rag doll at her feet.

Her mouth gapes open as she tries to catch her breath and her eyes are wide with fear as she stares at Oliver standing with the thick piece of branch over Richard.

"Are you crazy, Oliver? What if he is dead..." she stammers in panic?

"I am a doctor, girl. I know where to hit someone to not end up with a dead person on my conscience" he answers bluntly. He looks at her and asks grim: Are you very sure you didn't have an appointment with the romantic Richard?"

"Did you forget you dragged me out into the garden, Doctor Howard?" she retaliates irritated.

"I haven't, but why did he come out looking for you here?" he asks suspiciously.

"Probably because I said at dinner the garden looks magical in the moonlight. Aunt Emily then told us she and Uncle William regularly came for midnight walks in their younger days. Richard was reeking of alcohol. In his drunk state he probably remembered my reference to the garden and came looking for me here."

"Well… it is a probability." He looks at her sharply. "As long as you also remember Richard has a bad boy reputation…and that he is also spending his time with Charlotte Jones … e … Hastings."

"The girl you loved?" she asks, without thinking.

Even in the moonlight she can see the expression on his face harden. "Aunt Eleanor enjoys her gossips too much. But we have another problem: Richard. When he comes to, he will wonder who hit him over the head."

"One of the gardeners?" she suggests hopeful.

"Your intelligence is letting you down, little Alice. Not one of the Howard's workers will ever dare to attack the sole heir of Stanton Estate."

"Maybe I should pretend I was also hit over the head," Alice thinks aloud and jumps of fright when she hears a panting mumbling somewhere in the dark garden.

"At my old age… in my nightdress…and the soles of my slippers are so thin…Where is that rascal of a young man skulking around? If I …" Beatrice appears around a dark jasmine bush, shakes to a standstill and curses under her panting breath: "Bloody devil!"

"No blood, Miss Crompton," says Oliver saintly, with a subdued laugh in his voice, "the devil has only been knocked lights out." Beatrice plants her hands on her broad hips and glares at Alice. "No, no, dear, how is it now with you? Was I so wrong in my judgment? I thought you were a decent, innocent child, and what do I find here? Sneaking around in the dark with Oliver and hit another young man lights out." She gives an approving chuckle. "I hope you put some muscle behind that hit, Alice-child. He has been looking for a good hiding a long time coming."

"I didn't touch him, Miss Crompton. But how did you know I was here in the garden?" asks Alice frowning.

I didn't, but I heard this rascal come in. I was laying in my bed listening to him walking to your room and then quickly got into my nightgown and slippers. I was just about to come out of my room when I saw the louse skulking past my room to the stairs. I quickly went to your bedroom, but your bed was empty, so I went after Richard... and here he lays: lights out or dead. What now, Oliver?" asks Beatrice dumbstruck.

"First the truth, Miss Crompton. Alice didn't have an appointment with me. Aunt Eleanor told me about Richard's secret visit to Charlotte Hastings and ..."

"They deserve each other," interrupts Beatrice. "They both got dry peaches instead of souls. There is nothing worse than a shrunken soul with its thoughts only on money and sin, do you hear me, Oliver?" Or are you now also going to pursue that money-hungry gold-digger all over again?"

"I was busy to explain, Miss Crompton," he answers blunt. "I was worried that Alice will start looking for the secret hiding place while Richard was out on his secret visit. I came here, but the house was so dark, and I went back to Tortington. Aunt Eleanor woke up when she heard me coming in at the back door and then I told her about my concern that Richard might catch Alice. She gave me a key for the side door, and I was just in time to warn Alice."

"Warn?" asks Alice indignantly. "This man grabbed me from behind in the dark and then dragged me down the stairs. I almost had a heart attack from shock!"

"I didn't want to wake everyone in the house," says Oliver apologetic. "Alice realises now that it is too dangerous to search for Uncle William's secret hiding place. I have a key for the side door: I will sneak into Stanton Manor at night and look for the documents myself."

"That is all simply good and dandy, child," says Beatrice and she plaits her fingers together over her stomach while she sympathetically considers the motionless Richard, "but what do we say to this rascal when he joins us again in the land of the living?"

Oliver hesitates for a second and then holds the branch out to Beatrice. "You hit him over his head, Miss Crompton."

Beatrice quickly steps backwards. "Me? But why would I ever do such a thing, child?"

"Oliver and I came out into the garden and were sitting on the bench behind the fence when Richard came calling out to me," explains Alice. "We couldn't let Richard see us together, that is why I slipped back through the hole in the fence. Richard saw me and he grabbed me … and he … and he just started kissing me. He can be grateful Oliver only hit he over the head, I was going to bite off his ear."

"That's the truth, Miss Crompton: Alice bites," says Oliver and looks at the bitemarks on his hand in the moonlight and glares at Alice.

"Good, that is what I like to hear! Bite every single man to pieces if they try to kiss you against your will, dear," says Beatrice impressed.

"I didn't try to kiss her, Miss Crompton," says Oliver upset.

"Yes, yes, child, I believe you. Give me that branch. I should probably sit here with this drunk skunk until he wakes up ," says Beatrice with an unwilling acceptance.

"A few hard slaps will wake him up fast, Miss Crompton." Oliver hesitates a moment and glances over to Alice. "And you, girl, make sure to lock your bedroom door at night. I will not always be here to protect you from Richard. Good night, Miss Crompton … Alice."

"I don't need a babysitter, Doctor Howard. I can bite!" she mockingly calls out to him.

"Hush, child!" warns Beatrice, and groans as she gets down and sits next to the motionless Richard. "Richard?" She first shakes him gently and then grabs him harder by his shoulder. "Richard, open your eyes. Richard!"

Richard groans in his sleep, mumbles something incomprehensible, turns on his back and starts to snore lightly.

"But ..." Beatrice stares at him. "I thought the devil was unconscious but, in the meantime, he is sleeping off his drunken stupor!" she blurts out angry. "How hard did Oliver hit min, Alice?"

"I don't know, Miss Crompton, but Richard was definitely drunk. If he weren't drunk, he would probably have gotten to by now."

"In that case..." Beatrice looks up at the stars above them. "It won't rain before sunrise. Come, come, help me get up, dear. You and I need some sleep."

"And Richard then?" asks Alice worried.

"Are you up to carrying him to the house, child?"

"No...no, he is too heavy."

"Exactly. Let him sleep right here. Nothing will happen to him," says Beatrice indifferent and pulls on Alice's hand to get on her feet. "My goodness, the hardships I have to endure thanks to this creature. But let's hurry, dear. Emily has this nasty habit of waking up in the middle of the night to order bacon and eggs."

"I must also have a quick peek at Uncle William and see if he is still all right," says Alice concerned and stretches her steps. "But what do I say to Richard if he should ask me about tonight?"

"You just send him to me, Alice. I have also enjoyed putting the lad in his place," says Beatrice with a slight smile.

An ally such as Miss Crompton can actually make her stay in Stanton Manor bearable, thinks Alice grateful. Oliver will regularly come to Stanton Manor at night to search for the documents and maybe she will get to see him ... No, she is living in a fool's paradise. Oliver is totally unaware of her existence as a woman, as a girl who could love so unconditionally... The moment he knows who his real parents were, he will go back to

Charlotte Hastings, and she, Alice, and Aunt Helen will return to London, and over time she will learn to forget about her foolish love...

Beatrice watches with a feeling of satisfaction as Richard walks into the kitchen, his hair tousled and his clothes a mess. He stumbles to the nearest kitchen chair and sits down with a deep groan. "Black coffee with a shot of whiskey, please, Miss Crompton," he requests. His voice a hoarse rasp.

Beatrice plants her right hand on her hip and starts in a rage: "Has my kitchen suddenly become your bar, young Richard? And you, with all your pride and haughty arrogance, you condescend yourself now to sit at my kitchen table, instead of sitting at the dining room table and ringing that blasted bell ad nauseum?"

Richard holds his head in both his hands, unable to look up. "Please, Miss Crompton, please talk softer. My head is going to split open. Please, Miss Crompton, just some coffee – with or without the whiskey."

"I see. You can party all night until the sun comes up and then you expect me to jump when you say jump. Get your own coffee. I am busy preparing your mother's breakfast," answers Beatrice intentionally callous.

"I wasn't partying, Miss Crompton. Someone attacked me in my own garden." Richard looks up, revenge burning in his eyes. "I will make sure she leaves this house today still, Miss Crompton. My father can get another nurse, but we don't need her type around here."

Beatrice places a cup of coffee and two headache tablets in front of Richard. "Drink, you unfortunate thing. Maybe you will make more sense if your head doesn't hurt."

Richard swallows the tablets, drinks the coffee and shudders obviously. "I know what I'm saying, Miss Crompton. Last night that nurse lured me to the garden on purpose and then she and her low-life friend waited for me, and they hit me over the head. They robbed me of every cent I had!"

"Really? Is your wallet missing?" asks Beatrice innocently.

"No, but the money is gone. As soon as my mother hears what Alice…"

"Stop! Stop right there, or I might just hit you over the head with a pan," threatens Beatrice and plants herself squarely in front of the confused Richard.

"What is the matter, Miss Crompton?" he asks surprised. "Do you think I am lying?"

"I don't need to think, child, because I know you are lying. Did you forget I helped to raise you and Oliver? Did you forget how often I had to protect Oliver because you always twisted the truth and falsely accused him when you did something wrong?' she asks angry.

"Goodness, Miss Crompton, I was a child then. Oliver has got nothing to do with this incident. As I said: Alice made an appointment with me to meet her and when I went to the garden…"

"Yes, yes, I already heard this lie," she abruptly interrupts him. "Let me save you from yourself, child. I know you snuck out of the house last night just after nine to pay your happy widow a visit."

"Miss Crompton!" Richard's eyes widen in fear. "If you tell my mother…"

"Yes, Richard? Then what?"

He bites down hard on his teeth; she can see the muscles in his jaw bulge. She reads the bitterness in his eyes as he starts to talk again: "I am twenty-eight years old, and I have never said this aloud: my mother is a crazy woman. She…"

"Don't, Richard," warns Beatrice, suddenly feeling sorry for him. He is a very handsome, dark like Emily, but with the strong features of the Howards. And when he forgets that he is the sole heir to Stanton Estate he is just an unhappy child who grew up in the shadow of an overbearing, sick woman, and an interested father, she thinks sympathetically.

"Is it going to make my mother normal if I keep denying it, Miss Crompton?"

"Your mother struggles with her nerves, child. She is a very tense person, even as a child, and sometimes she behaves uncontrollably, but she isn't crazy. Think for yourself, Richard: she has spoiled you since you were a baby, nothing was ever good enough for her only son. She loves you, child."

"Love?" His lips pull into a sneering smile. "Do you call it love when a mother blackmails her own child?"

"I don't know what you are talking about?" says Beatrice confused.

"No, Miss Crompton. You won't. Because my mother is sly enough to never talk to me about it when you can hear her. When I was small, I could do nothing wrong in her eyes, but since I have become a man ... Every time I go out with a girl who she doesn't personally approve of, she threatens to tell the truth about Oliver; to force my father to make Oliver his heir," he tells her with a bitterness bordering on hate.

"The truth about Oliver? What are you talking about, Richard?"

"Don't be sanctimonious, Miss Crompton. Everyone suspects it: that Oliver is my father's illegitimate child. But illegitimate or not, he is a Howard, and my parents did adopt him. And he is older than I am. He has much more right to Stanton Estate than I have," he answers, his voice hoarse with emotion.

"Did your mother tell you that Oliver was your father's illegitimate son?" asks Beatrice amazed.

"Yes – a thousand times, yes! That is why I must obey her in everything. Because if I don't my mother will convince my father to disinherit me and that ... that foundling child will walk away with my inheritance. Do you know how it feels to live in constant fear? Sometimes I wish my father could just die already, before he has a chance to change his will. Other times I wish something would happen to my mother, and sometimes I wish I just had the guts to walk out of this house and never come back. I hate Stanton Manor and the cursed transport company. That is why I like to visit Charlotte. With Charlotte I at least feel like a human being ...like a free man."

"When you were still a little boy, you always said you wanted to become a farmer," it comes deep in thought from Beatrice.

"I still want to become a farmer, but I don't even dare speak of my biggest dream in my mother's presence. Oh, no, because I am the sole heir of Stanton Estate, the sole heir to all their treasures. And her money. Her family-farm. Do you know what I will do, Miss Crompton? I will get rid of this wretched place and move to the farm."

"You take after your grandfather, Charles Montgomery," says Beatrice in awe but then continues in a strict voice: 'but you mustn't forget that you are also a Howard, dear. Who knows, maybe one day you will have a son who might be interested in this old house and the transport business."

"It is a house of hate," he says rebellious and suddenly looks uncomfortable. "Don't repeat what I have told you, Miss Crompton. And if there is a cup of coffee left for me…"

"I don't speak out of turn, Richard. But about last night…"

"That is a matter between my mother and me, and that cunning nurse Browning," he says stubbornly.

Beatrice presses with her hands on the table and looks intently at him. "No, Richard, it is a matter between you and me," she says intensely.

He frowns in incomprehension. "Are you going to protect the girl, Miss Crompton?"

"No, child, I am going to protect you. I was with Alice in the garden last night when you, in your drunken state, grabbed her into your arms and kissed her against her will."

Richard blushes blood-red and looks down at his hands. "I see. You hit me over the head and just left me laying there in the garden."

"What did you expect? That I, a woman of sixty, and the tiny Alice should've carried you back to the house and tucked you in?" she asks disapprovingly.

"Well…" He smiles embarrassed. "I should probably be thankful you didn't kill me." He looks at her, worried. "You won't say anything to my mother, Miss Crompton?"

"I won't. But I can't speak for Alice. I mean, you do owe her an apology," she answers strictly.

He presses his lips together and pulls up his shoulders. "Why not? She is an incredibly beautiful girl and if I can convince her I am not a jerk, we might become friends... good friends."

"You leave Alice in peace, Richard. If you bother her, I will tell your mother about your secret visits with Charlotte," warns Beatrice.

"Blackmailer!" he says, pretending to be upset. "Even if you don't believe me, Miss Crompton, I can behave like a true gentleman. How about that second cup of coffee now?"

"You are old and ugly enough to get your own coffee. Your mother will just become upset unnecessarily if I am late with her breakfast," answers Beatrice, picks up the tray and waggles out of the kitchen.

Matron Frances smiles her brightest smile when she looks up and sees Oliver standing in her office door.

"Doctor Howard..."

He steps inside.

"And to what do I owe the honour this morning? Please, sit. Have a cup of tea with me."

"I'm early, my apologies to just barge in like this." He thanks her for the cup of tea. "I didn't expect to find you here so early."

She blushes lightly. The man's purple-blue eyes fascinate her when he looks at her like this.

"I usually come to the office very early," she says with a smile around her full lips. "It does happen from time to time that I don't have enough time to finish the day's work, and then I have to either take my work home or I have to come in early to finish everything before the new day starts."

"Yes, I can imagine that the clinic can become quite busy, Matron."

"Busy is a very accurate description, doctor Howard," she says laughing. "Especially when the ambulance arrives with an emergency. But luckily, that doesn't happen every day."

"Yes, luckily not," he says, lost in thought, and puts down his empty cup. "Anyway, the reason I'm here, " he says as he suddenly gets up and thanks her for the tea. "There is a matter I want to discuss with you in regard to my uncle's care. I first need to run it past doctor Graham, of course."

The sparkle in her brown eyes is very evident as she looks at him and answers, "Of course, doctor Howard, I'm at your disposal whenever you want to talk to me. About anything at all. I could also meet you somewhere in town if you would like it to be a more personal meeting."

"Thank you, Matron. Your office will be more than adequate. I shall be in touch." He thanks her, then excuses himself and walks out of her office.

She smiles broadly. The man is already noticing her, she thinks dreamily. And he wants to discuss family matters with her, maybe he wants to introduce her to his family. This is going even better that she could've have imagined. She just knows that she has already managed to capture his heart.

Completely unaware of her thoughts, Oliver walks down the hospital passage in long strides to where he finds doctor Norman Graham in his office.

"Ah, just the man I was looking for. I tried to contact you at the hotel a little earlier, Oliver. But apparently you were already on your way here." Says Norman, getting up from his chair. The two men shake hands. "Come, please, sit. We have a few matters to discuss."

"Yes, that is why I'm here. We didn't get time to talk much the other day." He starts, while Norman Graham listens to him intently. "Firstly, I want to thank you for your help to get Alice in at Stanton Manor to look after my uncle. My Aunt trusts you, and my uncle's health depends on you."

"Oh, please, think nothing of it. It's all part of a day's work. How is Alice adapting to life at Stanton Manor?" Norman asks.

"That is precisely the second matter I've come to discuss with you."

Doctor Norman notices the seriousness on Oliver's face. And he knows in these early morning hours that Oliver Howard isn't a man to be taken lightly. This man sitting in front of him, is a

Howard, and he knows what he wants.

"Please, how can I be of assistance?" asks Norman

"Alice is doing a wonderful job taking care of my uncle. Maybe too much so. She is on call twenty-four hours a day, every day. It is my professional opinion, for the health and well-being of both my uncle and Alice, that it would be appropriate to arrange a night-shift nurse for my uncle to relieve Alice. Alice could get a decent night's rest, and should any emergency occur, she is available right down the passage." Oliver explains.

"That sounds like a very wise idea, matter of fact," Norman agrees, rubbing his chin. "Who do you have in mind?"

"I don't. I've just spoken to Matron Frances, and with your approval I will ask her to nominate the most appropriate candidate."

"You have my complete approval. Please, make the arrangements with Matron Frances as you see fit."

"Thank you, Norman." The two men chat a little while longer, then Oliver gets up, they shake hands, and Oliver leaves the clinic.

Alice looks up from the book she is reading and smiles guiltily as she looks straight into William's eyes as he is watching her. "Uncle William, why didn't you tell me you were awake? Do you need anything?" sha asks and places the book down on the table next to her chair.

His lips turn into a smile. "The youth is so beautiful ... and innocent... like a beautiful sunrise which passes too quickly," he answers.

Memories of hie own youth is like a soft glow which covers the dark, splintered years of his adulthood. The things he has done...

"Was your youth as beautiful, Uncle William?" sha asks, relieved to find no signs of pain on his face.

"As beautiful as only a young person's dreams can be. Emily and I ..." He looks at her and his eyes beg for understanding. "She wasn't always like this. We were happy, she and I. Maybe I should never have brought him here, that is what changed her."

"You are referring to Oliver?" she asks hesitantly.

"Yes…yes. I believed that she had loved me enough to understand, but she couldn't or wouldn't. When Richard was born a year later, she wanted me to place Oliver in an orphanage. All those arguments … all these years of resentment and hate… but I did the right thing.

"Oliver doesn't know who his parents are, Uncle William," says Alice in a whisper, her eyes on the bedroom door.

William smiles secretively. "He wil know soon enough. He knows where the hiding place is."

"No, Uncle William, he doesn't. If you don't tell him where to…"

"He knows," interrupts William her with finality and closes his eyes.

Alice stares powerless at him, wishes she could shake the truth from he, but realises he is already in the world between life and death. Is he going to take his secret with him to his grave? No, she will not allow that to happen. Oliver will never marry if he doesn't know who his parents were. But if he finds out – will he go back to Charlotte Hastings? Is her love for him selfless enough to let him be happy with Charlotte, she asks herself and sighs dismayed? But as long as Oliver's past is cloaked in mystery, they will remain friends. Does she want to forever lose the man she has fallen in love with so deeply?

A knock on the door lets her return to the present with a feeling of gratitude. She quickly gets up, walks to the door, and opens it.

"You!" she says stunned and stares at Richard who stands there with a bouquet of red carnations, smiling sheepishly at her.

"Yes, it's me, but this time I'm sober, nurse Browning." He holds the bouquet out to her. "I would not blame you if you threw my flowers in the dustbin, but it is my way to apologise for my appalling behaviour last night in the garden."

"Then you at least remember what happened," she says stiff.

"Well… not everything, but Miss Crompton made it very clear to me how badly I behaved. I promised her I will not bother you. E… what about the bouquet?" he asks uncomfortably.

"I will tell your father you bought him the flowers for his room," she answers coolly and takes the flowers from him.

"So, I am forgiven?" he asks hopeful.

"I am here to take care of your father, Mr. Howard. That is …"

"Richard. Call me Richard. I promised I will behave myself, didn't I," he interrupts her.

"So, your mother will have a reason to throw her tea at me? No, thank you. I prefer to remember that you are Mr. Howard, one of the royals of Stanton Estate," she answers cold.

A bright red blush spreads over his cheeks and neck, but he looks her straight in her eyes. "Are you judging me to be in the same category as a mentally unstable woman, nurse Browning?"

She sharply pulls in her breath and for the first time looks at him with compassion. Who is the real Richard? The young man full of bravado who, just yesterday, asked his mother whether she hired her for his amusement, or this man looking at her with his pain so obvious in his eyes?

"First impressions are difficult to forget," she answers.

"Still, one's first impressions can be wrong. I will be honest: I can't act like a friend towards you when my mother is in the vicinity. But Stanton Manor is a lonely place full of dying and sick people. I would welcome a friend."

"Only friendship?" she asks suspiciously.

"Only friendship," he assures her.

She smiles. "Fine. As long as you remember Miss Crompton has a very strong right arm and she doesn't miss."

He feels his head and smiles. "It is almost impossible to forget. If we are going to be friends: may I call you Alice?"

"Obviously, but not – "

"- not in my mother's presence," he finishes her sentence for her, and they laugh muffled. "I actually wanted to ask you: can you ride horseback?"

"Like a champion. I grew up in the countryside and my father has a farm where he keeps horses for my brothers and I."

"Then, Miss Alice, I now cordially invite you to go horseback riding with me. We have several horses, but I usually ride alone." He looks down the passage towards Emily's bedroom door. Since my father got sick my mother's behaviour has become more unpredictable – so, I don't bring friends over anymore."

"I understand and I appreciate the invitation. I would love to join you when my obligations to your father allows me to."

"Fantastic! Let me know when you are free," he says pleased, nods his head, and walks away to the stairs.

It is wonderful what a knock over the head can do, thinks Alice amused, closes the door, and takes the bouquet to the dressing table. No, now she is being unfair, she admonishes herself. She was too quick to judge because she knew beforehand Oliver and Richard are arch enemies. But Richard has his own hurt: he lives in extravagant wealth, but Stanton Manor isn't a home to him, but rather a prison.

Eleanor looks up in surprise as the backdoor opens without a knock and Beatrice enters with waggling grace.

"Oh, my heart! I am exhausted!" she heaves and flops down on the nearest chair. She takes a lace handkerchief out of her pocket and clads at her sweaty face. She leans back in the chair and tries to fan herself with the handkerchief.

"For goodness's sake!" says Eleanor impatiently and props a big male handkerchief in Beatrice's chubby hands. "Fan with this, Beatrice. You won't be able to cool down a gnat with that little piece of damp lace."

"You can be so unladylike, Eleanor," says Beatrice offended.

"But at least practical," says Eleanor and place a large glass of cold-drink in front of Beatrice. "Drink, Beatrice, and then tell me what on earth possessed you to walk all the way here. Is your car broken?"

Beatrice gulps the cold-drink, puts the glass down and pants: "More."

"You will get stomach cramps if you swallow cold things so fast," warns Eleanor.

"Yes, yes, Eleanor, you might be eighteen years older than me, but you aren't the all-knowing. I know my own stomach," says Beatrice angrily, reconsiders and then says mysteriously: "You will never guess what the young Richard told me about four days ago."

"No, I won't. But Richard's comings and goings don't interest me in the least. How is Alice? Helen and I are nervous wrecks because we haven't heard anything from her since she left," asks Eleanor while she refills Beatrice's glass.

"Absolutely wonderful, Alice knows exactly how to manage Emily by now, and she is taking such good care of William. She and Richard also get along very well, and they go horseback riding most afternoons," she informs Eleanor pleased.

"Does Alice trust that ladies-man?" asks Eleanor surprised.

"Yes, alright Eleanor, everyone doesn't only have bad in them. Not that I blame you because until Richard opened his heart the other day and started talking, I also misjudged him."

"So, now you believe he is all innocent?" asks Eleanor skeptical.

"That is not what I said but Emily is blackmailing the child. She told him Oliver is William's illegitimate son and if Richard doesn't obey her every whim, she will make sure he is disowned. You took care of Richard's grandmother Caroline, Eleanor. You tell me what the truth is."

Chapter 6

"That is the truth I've been looking for my entire life, Aunt Eleanor," says Oliver, and follows Helen into the kitchen.

"Eavesdropper!" scolds Beatrice him. "I punished my own flesh to come here to have a private conversation with Eleanor and look what happens! A house full of guests take over!"

Oliver smiles tauntingly. "I saw a cloud of dust coming this way and I knew you were on your way, Miss Crompton. Is your car broken again?"

"Hush, Oliver!" commands Eleanor. She smiles at Helen and turns to Beatrice. "This is Helen Upton, Alice's aunt, Beatrice. Helen, meet Beatrice Crompton, Emily's Lady-in-waiting."

"My dear, I am so glad to meet you," says Beatrice heartily. "Alice is such a lovely child, so helpful and all. She has told me so much about you."

"Nice to meet you too, Beatrice," greets Helen. "If this is a private conversation, I will excuse myself."

"Sit, Aunt Helen," instructs Oliver. "You are well informed of my search about my real parents." He turns to Beatrice. "Did I understand correctly, Miss Crompton? Did Aunt Emily tell Richard that I'm Uncle Williams illegitimate son?"

"That is what I said, yes, and that is why I chastised my poor little body to walk all the way here. You know Emily: she has the hearing of a bat. If I should get in my car, she will have a fit again, and accuse me of conspiring with Doctor Graham to have her committed to a mental institution. That is why I had to walk," she tells them and rubs her aching legs.

"You are a star, Miss Crompton," smiles Oliver, but he looks at Eleanor with anticipation. "Grandmother Caroline was the only Howard who ever made me feel welcome at Stanton Manor, Aunt Eleanor. She insisted that I call her grandmother, while a called my adoptive parents Uncle and Aunt. Did she perhaps know something about my birth which Uncle William has kept hidden from me all these years?"

Eleanor stares at him in silence, sympathy and sadness taking turns on her face. "I wish I knew the truth, then I could've given you the answers you so desperately want, Oliver, but I can only tell you what had happened a short while before late Charlotte passed away."

"And that was?" he asks tense.

"Caroline realised her time was running short. She summoned William to come here, and she asked him if you were his illegitimate son. William strongly denied it."

"Because he wanted to protect Richard's inheritance?" asks Beatrice suspiciously.

"No, Beatrice. I kept an eye on William because I was in the room with them. William was extremely nervous and obviously upset, but I cannot believe that he would have lied to his own mother on her deathbed." Answers Eleanor assertively.

"Then Uncle William is still the only person who knows the truth about my parents," says Oliver with despair.

"Emily will also know, but she would rather burn at the stake before telling anyone the truth about it," says Beatrice upset.

"But why all this secretiveness about your lineage, Oliver?" asks Helen who was listening objectively at their conversation. "If you really are the son of two of William's old university friends, then why are they making it such a big secret?"

Oliver looks at her sharply. "What you are saying makes sense, aunt Helen. I am not planning, after thirty years, to go knocking on the door of the parents who gave me away as a baby. I just want to know who my parents are. And I have said exactly that to Uncle William so many times."

"But if William promised these people to keep their identities a secret..." Helen sighs and shakes her head. "It is probably a case of honor to William do not break his promise."

"Then why did he tell me that I would find the documents about my birth in this secret hiding place?" asks Oliver quickly.

"Trickery," says Beatrice irritated. "William probably realises this that you don't know where the secret hiding place is."

She looks at Eleanor. "How about something to eat Eleanor? The cold drink does nothing for the empty spot in my stomach."

Eleanor walks into the pantry, takes the lit of a cake tin and places the tin down in front of Beatrice. "Help yourself, Beatrice. I can't think about my stomach when there is more important business we have to deal with."

"I think better when I chew," says Beatrice, and props a jam tart in her mouth, closes her eyes, a blissful expression on her face.

"Beatrice," starts Helen in a serious tone, "you said Emily is blackmailing Richard that he would lose his inheritance to Oliver if he doesn't do as she says. Does she say these things in your presence?"

Beatrice is hand with a second jam tart Freezes between the cake tin and her mouth. "I am eating now, Helen," she says surprised.

"Answer Helen's question, Beatrice, or I'll put the cake tin away," threatens Eleanor.

"Spiteful old woman!" says Beatrice upset, but she answers: "Yes, Helen, when Emily gets angry, she doesn't care who listens."

"Have you never asked her whether Oliver is in fact really William's illegitimate son?" asks Helen again.

"My dear, have you lost your mind?" Says Beatrice dismayed. "I am Emily's Lady in waiting, but when she speaks to a third person, I become a fly on the wall. I hear, but I don't hear. That is what her late parents expected of me, and that is what I do to this day. I pretend that I am never eavesdropping on her conversations, understand?"

"But if you were to ask her about it, miss Crompton?" asks Oliver hopeful.

"Then the poor thing ends up in a mental institute. No, Oliver, I realize Emily is not an easy person to live with but if one knows how to handle her... For so many years I have considered her a sister... a sick sister who needs my help. That is why I make sure she doesn't get upset unnecessarily, because then ..."

"Then she goes crazy, right, Beatrice?" asks Eleanor tightly.

"It's his fault!" says Beatrice in Emily's defense. "I don't deny it: Emily was a spoiled, only child; a wealthy man's only child, and she could never stand any opposition. But she was so happy when she and William got married. Don't you remember, Eleanor? Don't you remember how happy she and William were just after they got married?

"Yes, Yes, I remember."

"She was like any normal, young bride ... until that terrible day when William arrived with Oliver. William demanded that they adopt the baby and then... Their arguments were behind closed doors because William wanted to make sure that I couldn't hear what he was saying to Emily. I could only make sure that she drank her calming medication regularly and to console her when she was crying her heart out," recalls Beatrice, the cake tin in front of her forgotten.

"But still, Emily did calm down after a while, especially when she became pregnant," says Eleanor. "She was so proud when Richard was born, even more so than William. She was calmer then, wasn't she, Beatrice?"

"Yes, because she was the mother of the heir to Stanton Estate. That is why she raised Richard as if he were a little prince; why she never denied him anything. I believe she poured out all her love on Richard because she lost all interest in William."

"But not in me," says Oliver bitter. "She never let one opportunity pass her by to remind me I was only a foundling. Luckily, Uncle William did show some interest in me sometimes - and of course you, aunt Eleanor. You and grandmother Caroline made sure I received the love which Aunt Emily could never give me."

"And what about me?" asks Beatrice hurt. "Didn't I give you hugs when Emily wasn't in the vicinity, Oliver?'

"You did, miss Crompton, but it was very seldom if ever because Richard learned from very young to tell aunt Emily everything. I realised from a very young age that you were as powerless as I was. We were both aunt Emily's and Richards loyal slaves."

"Emily's happiness has always been my priority," says Beatrice apologetic and frowns bothered. "That is why I resent William for his spitefulness."

"But is the poor man not dying?" asks Helen stunned.

"Oh, he is, but he pretends to be delirious and then he says to Emily over and over again that the truth must come out. The poor woman is in a state! That's why I don't visit so often anymore, Eleanor, because I can see William's rantings has her all worked up."

"What truth is William referring to Beatrice?" asks Eleanor sharply.

"How should I know that? He doesn't say, and Emily says even less. She only starts yelling and threatening and... and sometimes she just starts laughing as if she has totally lost her mind. But it is all his fault. He terrorizes her, almost as if he enjoys seeing her in such a state."

"Is it maybe the truth about me miss Crompton?" asks Oliver trying to compose himself.

"But, child, I just said I don't know. And now I am going to eat because I'm also only a human of flesh and blood with a hungry stomach," she says, and grabs the cake tin with her left arm tight to her chest and with her right-hand stuffs one jam tart after the other into her mouth.

Eleanor stays at her disapprovingly. "I've always wondered why you have such a huge jaw, Beatrice, but now I know: chewing is your only form of exercise."

Oliver grins, takes Eleanor by the arm, and walks with her down the passage to the front patio. For a moment they listen to the shrill cries of the albatross flying over their heads and feel the South easterly wind blow through their hair.

"Alice and Richard go horseback riding," he says evenly. "Aunt Eleanor, did you hear win miss Crompton told aunt Helen about it?"

"I heard, yes. does that upset you?"

He hesitates, his eyes on Eleanor's face. "I know aunt Emily," he eventually says. "Even when we were children, she was jealous of Richard's friends - his male friends. He was fifteen when I went to university, but he already knew then that aunt Emily would get one of her infamous fits the moment he spoke about a girl. Richard is to aunt Emily not just her son; she believes he is her personal property which she cannot and will not share with anyone."

She stares at him distressed. "You believe Alice and Richard goes horseback riding without Emily knowing about it?"

"I know they keep it a secret because if aunt Emily should hear about it..." he frowns worried. "Alice agreed on my behalf to become Uncle William's private nurse, but her friendship with Richard puts her life in danger. She must return to Tortington, aunt Eleanor."

"Surely it can't be that bad, Oliver? I remember from my younger years that Emily has always been a highly strung child, but she has never been a danger to anyone. You did hear after all what Beatrice told us: there was always a good reason for Emily's outbursts," says Eleanor calmingly.

"Miss Crompton is being protective over aunt Emily, and that makes me wonder if she would actually tell us the entire truth. Have you forgotten aunt Eleanor: aunt Emily wanted to attack me with a pair of scissors, and that was only for visiting Uncle William?"

"I did forget," admits Eleanor, concern in her eyes. "I must have a serious talk with Alice, but how to arrange something…"

"Leave that to me aunt Eleanor," he interrupts her reassuringly. "I actually had a second visit planned to Uncle William because my nightly visits to Stanton Manor have so far been fruitless."

Oliver parks behind Stanton Manor's horse stables, he gets out of his car and watches displeased as Richard and Alice come riding towards him.

"Wait there!" Richard demands him and rides closer with Alice.

Oliver waits for him in silence his face an expressionless mask. He had hoped to sneak into Stanton Manor unnoticed to talk to Uncle William, but Richard's unexpected appearance makes his visit impossible now, he thinks frustrated.

"That is what I like, brother Oliver: at last you realize you don't have the right to enter Stanton Manor through the front door. If you have come to visit miss Crompton, I will tell her you are waiting for her in the kitchen," says Richard sneeringly, still mounted on his horse.

Alice looks at Oliver upset, but Oliver avoids her eyes and asks gruffly:

"Aren't you a little too old by now to still act like a spoiled brat, Richard? Or are you trying to impress your girlfriend?"

"I will surely…" Richard starts threatening Oliver and lifts his whip.

"Don't, Richard!" Alice calls out upset and grabs his arm. "For goodness's sake, why don't you just ignore the man? Or if he is trespassing on your property: phone the police."

Oliver laughs angry. "Let him go ahead, miss. I cannot wait to pull him off his horse and give him a proper hiding."

"Try that and you will be behind bars, you cursed foundling child!" snarls Richard and gets off his horse. "Why are you here? My father is sick. He is not allowed any visitors."

"I have already visited Uncle William, but this time I am here on request of nurse Browning's aunt, aunt Helen Upton." Oliver looks at Alice who is watching him tensely. "Your aunt is visiting in Tortington, the white house at the top of the hill. She is planning to vacation here for a few weeks, and she has asked that you come greet her."

Alice smiles in a forced surprise. "Is aunt Helen visiting here? That is wonderful news! Thank you for coming all this way to tell me, doctor Howard," she answers and dismounts her horse.

Richard glares at her suspiciously. "How do you know him?" he asks brusquely.

Alice sharply pulls in her breath, looking for an acceptable explanation, and Oliver answers evenly: "I met nurse Browning in my old friend, doctor Norman Graham's, rooms when I asked him about a private nurse for your father." He turns to Alice. "When would it be convenient for you to visit your aunt, miss Browning?"

"Tonight, around half past eight, after I have given Uncle William his last injection for the day. And now, you both must please excuse me, I have left Uncle William alone long enough. Thank you for your trouble, doctor Howard. Goodbye," she greets and walks across the cobblestones in the back yard to the nearest side door.

"Tomorrow afternoon, same time, Alice!" calls Richard after her, but she doesn't look back. He turns back to Oliver with a sneering smile. "She is eating out of my hand, the pretty little thing. I should probably thank you for arranging such a pretty nurse for my father."

"Isn't Charlotte your bride to be then?" asks Oliver mockingly.

"What do you know about me and Charlotte?" asks Richard sharply.

"What all the town's people tell me: you two haven't stopped celebrating since her beloved husband's funeral."

Richard throws his head back and laughs out loud. "Fantastic! As long as everyone knows Charlotte is mine, I have no reason to be worried." His lips twist into a humorless smile. "And that includes you, brother Oliver. You have succeeded in stealing Tortington from me and you can brag with your prestigious education, but you remain the foundling child of Stanton Estate. I believe Charlotte would want to be able to tell her children one day who their grandfather and grandmother was."

Oliver balls his fists next to his sides, his eyes like dark, glistening marble in his unnaturally pale face. "I could care less about what you and Charlotte are up to but if you harm nurse Browning in any way..."

"A-ha, is that how the wind blows?" Richard claps his tong sympathetically. "You are a born loser, Oliver. Have you not learned by now? Us, the rich, always get what we want? A beautiful bride like Charlotte and a pretty, little thing like nurse Browning to make sure I don't get bored... and both under the same roof. Do you envy me?"

"No, I feel sorry for you because you will need a plastic surgeon if you touch Alice," answers Oliver forcefully and quickly walks back to his car.

"I always enjoy some competition, old friend, because I always win!" Richard shouts at him and starts laughing uncontrollable. Oliver slams the car door close behind him and switches on the engine with a shaking hand. He will kill him if he doesn't leave now, he thinks. A fog of white-hot rage swimming before his eyes. Richard's insults are to him like the forever blowing southeastern wind: he doesn't even notice it. But Alice...small Alice with the long, blonde hair and her extraordinary eyes ... No, she isn't small; she is an adult, a registered nurse who should realise Richard is playing her for a fool. As long as she isn't stupid enough to believe Richard actually loves her, he worries as he drives unnecessarily fast back to Tortington, as if he hopes to race away from his troubled thoughts.

Beatrice hands a basket over to Alice and opens the back door. "Tell Eleanor, the jam tarts I ate this morning at her house weren't too bad, but now she can taste what a jam tart should taste like. And don't you worry about William, Alice. Emily is less of a bother since Richard has been here to chat with her in the evenings. I will keep an eye on William."

"Thank you, miss Crompton. I won't be too long. Goodbye," greets Alice and closes the kitchen door behind her.

She stands still for a moment so her eyes can adjust to the dark and jumps of fright when a big hand closes around her arm.

"My car is parked behind the stables. Come!" says Oliver formally, takes the basket from her and pulls her with him.

"Beast!" she groans, still breathless from her fright. "Why do you sneak up on me in the dark every time, Oliver? What are you doing here in any case? I was planning to drive to Tortington in my own car."

"Stop pulling away, girl, or I shall pick you up and carry you to my car," he says impatiently. "And if you dare to bite my hand again, I'll pull your teeth one by one."

"Bully! Just because you are physically stronger than I am, you believe you have the right to order me around. But that is so typical of you chauvinistic...e..."

"Pigs?" he suggests helpfully.

"I can think of worse names," she answers snide. "Why did you come to fetch me? I have my own car."

"Consider me Richard's twin brother: I find you absolutely irresistible," he teases.

"Please! Don't make me laugh, doctor Howard! Richard is gallant and thoughtful. He doesn't push and pull me around by my arm as if I am a rag doll," she says livid.

"Really? You prefer to be embraced and kissed by a drunk man!" He laughs sarcastically. "I will remember that next time I am waiting for you in the dark nurse Browning."

"Richard has already apologized to me for his appalling behavior. We are now friends."

"Friends?" he asks skeptically and stays standing next to his car. "You, little Alice, are head over heels in love with the rich, handsome Richard Howard. Shall we hope that your being in love is only a temporary convulsion and that you would outgrow it very soon?"

She stares at him with all the fury and humiliation in her but knows that she must stay silent, or she would burst out crying. How can any man with his education have such an extreme lack of intellect? She feels as if there are bright, red letters on her forehead proclaiming to the entire world that she has fallen in love with this large, dumb man standing in front of her; but he accuses her of being in love with Richard. On the other hand: as long as he believes that she is in love with Richard, her love for him will remain her secret. She prefers to see disdain rather than sympathy in his eyes.

"My feelings for Richard are none of your business, Oliver. I know what I am doing," she says coldly.

"It is precisely because you don't know what you are doing why I am warning you, little Alice. Richard is interested in Charlotte Hastings. They are planning to get married," he says urgently.

"They aren't married yet, or even engaged," she says stubbornly, her face turned away from him.

He puts his hands on her shoulders and his unexpected touch sends her blood rushing through her veins.

"Please, Alice, listen to me. Richard loves Charlotte. He admitted to me that he is planning to marry her. He… he is just using you."

She jerks her head up, her eyes flashing in his. "You are a mean bully. How dare you insinuate that I would ever allow any man to use me? I will never put myself in that position ever again! Do I look like the sort of girl who… who…e… who wants to be used?" she asks furious, suddenly she is back in London in that street café with Robert.

"Love can do strange things to a girl," he answers seriously. "I'm a doctor. I know."

"And I am a girl, I also know, doctor Howard. Remember that in the future, and don't try to play the role of my father," she says through tight lips.

Her blonde hair is silver-white in the moonlight, her features fine and fragile, he thinks and wishes he could read the expression in her eyes. Does she know how beautiful she is? If he took her in his arms right now and kissed her, would he be able to make her forget about Richard, he wonders? And is alarmed by his own thoughts. What possesses him to think about something like this? A light flirtation would suit him, but Alice… she is not one of his experienced girlfriends who have long since lost their faith in the undying love. Alice is a girl with the innocent faith of a child in a fairy tale where the hero and his princess live happily ever after.

"A snowflake," he murmurs.

"Excuse me?" she asks dumbfounded.

He flashes a smile. "You remind me of a snowflake. Pretty to look at, but when you try to hold it, it melts in your hand."

"You've been holding my shoulders for hours now and I have not melted yet," she says upset.

"Don't always over exaggerate, little firecracker," he says and takes his hands off her shoulders. He looks at her cynically. "You still believe in the undying love, right, little Alice?"

"Obviously. But I know a marriage isn't just moonlight and roses... or a fairytale from a children's storybook," she answers, almost as if she can read his mind.

"Undying love is a fairy tale. I am convinced that my parents believed at a time that their love for each other was undying - until I showed up... Uncle William and Aunt Emily also thought they had an undying love, but their love turned into hate." His mouth pulls into a bitter grin. "What have you got to say now, clever Alice?"

Alice hesitates. "My father never remarried after my mother passed away. He once told me that no other woman could ever take her place in his life. And Aunt Helen never got married because she could never forget the one man she had loved."

"Exceptions. As long as you remember Richard is not like your father. Let's go," he says and quickly opens the car door before she can continue her reasoning.

They drive in silence through the moonlit night to the white house on top of the hill. The silence between them echoes the emptiness in her heart. Why did she fall in love with this man sitting next to her, she asks herself hopeless? He never gave her any reason to think they could be more, but she also didn't ask to fall in love with him. A futile love built on the foundation of tears, that's all that will remain for her if she doesn't find a way to smother these feelings she has for this man next to her.

Helen walks into the lounge with a tray with tea in her hands and places it down on the coffee table nearby. "What happened to Oliver? Didn't he say he would have tea with us?" she asks Alice who sits on the couch and stares out in front of her tensely. "He realized we wanted to talk alone, Aunt Helen," answers Alice without looking at her.

"Did the two of you have an argument?" asks Helen quickly.

Alice frowns impatiently. "He is a nosy old man, Aunt Helen. He has decided that I am in love worth Richard Howard, and he gave me a drawn-out moral speech. Goodness, I'm not sixteen years old! I am very well aware of Richard's relationship with Charlotte Hastings. I just go horseback riding with him every so often because I happen to like horseback riding."

"With or without Emily's knowledge?" asks Helen sternly.

"Without her knowledge. Aunt Emily made it extremely clear I am merely a servant. But seeing that I do have a degree I am allowed to eat with them at the dinner table," she answers with a skewed smile.

Helen gives Alice her cup of tea and sits down next to her on the couch. "Emily's haughtiness amuses you, but you don't realize you are putting your life in danger if you go horseback riding with Richard, dear."

"Nonsense!" Alice stares at her in surprise. "I realize aunt Emily doesn't believe I am rich enough to socialize with Richard, but what can she actually do if she finds out that we go horseback riding together?"

"I am just repeating what Oliver said to me, Alice: Emily believes that Richard is her personal property. She will never share him with any other woman. You are aware of his relationship with Charlotte, but has Charlotte ever been to visit at Stanton Manor?"

"No... but that is because aunt Emily can behave so unpredictably. I believe she is an embarrassment to Richard, which is why he doesn't bring his friends to his house."

"It is much more serious than that, my child. I don't doubt that

Emily will physically harm you if she realizes this that you and Richard are friends. That is why…"

"Don't exaggerate, Aunt Helen," interrupts Alice her upset. "Aunt Emily is very calm these days. Oliver only told you a bunch of scary stories because he believes I am in love with Richard."

"The truth isn't just a story, Alice. Emily threatened to attack Oliver with a pair of scissors when she found him in William's room. Beatrice will corroborate what I am telling you."

Alice stares at her unhappily. "Do you want me to come back to Tortington, aunt Ellen?"

"Yes, dear. We did plan to have a vacation together, after all. Oliver is worried about your safety and seeing as you went to Stanton Manor on his behalf, he feels responsible for you," says Helen calmly.

"And Uncle William, then?"

"Oliver already spoke to doctor Graham to arrange for an extra night-nurse, I'm sure he can also arrange another fulltime nurse in your place. Please Alice, I want you here safe with me."

"I can't come back now, Aunt Helen. I am winning Uncle William's trust. It is quite possible that he will actually tell me where the secret hiding place is. I must stay there until I know that," says Alice with an urgent seriousness.

Helen stays at her in silence and then sighs dismayed. I can't force you, dear, but with Emily is going to approve of it or not: from now I am coming to visit you regularly at Stanton Manor."

Alice walks up the wide stairs light-footed. She sees William's bedroom light is on as she reaches the landing, and she stretches her steps. Why is he awake, she wonders concerned? She was away for two hours but after his injection he should not have any pain.

"… lovely bride… my beautiful Emily… do you hear the church bells? It is our wedding day, Emily," Alice hears William deliriously talking and shocks to a standstill. Miss Crompton had warned her: William only preteens to be rambling about his wedding day wing Emily is arguing with him. What is Emily doing in his room at this time of the night?

She moves closer silently and peeks around the door frame. Emily stands in a threatening posture bent over William and whispers furiously: "The letters and the documents - where did you hide them, William? Talk, you helpless idiot, or I will smother you with your own pillow!"

Chapter 7

A hopeless fear nails Alice's feet to the floor. William is a helpless, dying old man and her patient and therefor her obligation to protect him. But Emily is an unstable woman who will be driven to murder through her own fury and frustration.

"My beautiful bride ... my beloved Emily..." she hears William speaking deliriously. "Do you hear the wedding march, Emily? It's our wedding march... I am the luckiest man on earth, my darling..."

"Idiot!" curses Emily in a muffled voice, grabs William by his shoulders and jerks him around like a lifeless rag doll. "Listen to me, William. I have to destroy the letters and the documents. Where did you hide them? William... William, do you hear me?"

Emily isn't immediately going to act on her threat to smother William with his own pillow realises Alice, turns around and runs down the passage to Beatrice's room.

Alice opens Beatrice's bedroom door without knocking and

switches on the main light.

"Goodness!" protests Beatrice muffled from under her duvet and sits up with a groan. She blinks her eyes quickly to adjust to the light, but Alice has already reached her bedside.

"Come quickly, miss Crompton. Aunt Emily is with Uncle William in his room, and she is threatening to smother him with his pillow. Come, please, miss Crompton!" she pleads desperately and pulls Beatrice by her arm.

Beatrice's eyes fly wide open, and she is wide awake at once. "Smother, you say, child" Quick, give me my gown. And I must get my slippers – where are they hiding now?" she asks and bents down laboriously.

Alice kneels in front of Beatrice and puts her slippers on her feet. "What are you doing, Alice? I can put …" she protests.

"For goodness's sake, miss Crompton, you are wasting time. Just come!" begs Alice, her voice hoarse with held back tears. Why is she so powerless? If William dies tonight, it will be her responsibility, she thinks guiltily.

"Decent," says Beatrice and puckers her lips primly. "I am an unmarried woman, a spinster, Alice, I have to be decent when I appear in a man's presence."

"What would being decent help you tonight, miss Crompton, if Uncle William is already dead?" asks Alice bitter.

"Emily won't murder anyone," says Beatrice with a determined conviction. "But let's go, dear, before you burst into tears."

If anything happens to Uncle William…"

"Hush!" warns Beatrice and sneaks down the passage to William's room.

"… the most expensive engagement ring, my darling. But it is still not good enough, Emily. Nothing is good enough for my beautiful bride," mutters William as Beatrice and Alice reach his bedroom door.

"You have a choice, William," hisses Emily who has her back turned to the bedroom door as she bends over his bed. "You are going to tell me where you are hiding those letters and documents, or you will die. I will not allow a foundling child to walk away with my son's inheritance. Speak, William, or you will die tonight!"

"Oh, is this what is going on in this house at this time of the night!" taunts Beatrice, her arms crossed over her chest.

Emily jumps around and yells shrill: "Beatrice!"

Beatrice ignores her and speaks to Alice: "You heard with your own ears Lady Howard threatening to murder her helpless husband, nurse Browning. You will be able to testify under oath in a court that Lady Howard is not acting in a normal state."

Alice fights against the desire to burst out in a hysterical laughter when Beatrice cunningly winks at her but succeeds to reply with a convincing sternness: "Yes, miss Crompton. I heard every word, and I would be willing to testify in a court."

"In that case, dear: let us go pack our bags. I don't feel safe for my own life in a house with a murderer."

"Beatrice, please!" Emily storms closer and grabs Beatrice's arm. "Beatrice, listen to me. You can't leave me now! You know I need you. Forty years, Beatrice... You have been taking care of me for forty years. I can't be without you," she begs with the helplessness of a child.

Beatrice's expression remains merciless. "I never took care of you, Emily. I was your Lady in waiting ... when you still behaved like a normal woman. But if you are planning a murder... I am not going to hang with you for a murder you committed."

"I was just talking, Beatrice. You know I would never murder anyone. I just wanted William to listen to me," she explains guiltily.

"That's what you say now, but I'm not a child anymore. You need someone to keep an eye on you twenty-four hours a day. I don't have the strength anymore do give you the attention which you need, and that is why I will be leaving tonight still, Emily," says Beatrice decidedly.

"You don't dare! You made my parents a solemn promise to be my Lady in waiting for the rest of your life. Did my father not ensure that your father did not lose his farm? The magnanimous Charles Montgomery showered you Crompton's with his generosity, and that is why your brothers have their educations today. How can you be so ungrateful, Beatrice?" asks Emily vehemently.

"Hard work, blood and sweat, and all our own personal sacrifices ensured that my father never lost his farm. The only thing he ever received from your father was my monthly salary. My father passed away many years ago and my brothers are all independent and have their own families. They have for many years now not needed my meager salary anymore," answers Beatrice with obvious pride.

"But you still need your meager salary. What will become of you? You have your own room, and your meals are free. You live in luxury. If you leave me, I will make sure no-one else ever hires you again," says Emily tauntingly.

Beatrice's stomach and shoulders shake with her laughter. "But how does your poor mind work, Emily? You said it yourself: I've been in your service for forty years. I had nothing to spend my money on. As you rightly said: my meals have been free. I don't have a husband or children, nor property. I never travelled; I never saw this wonderful world. I don't even get to visit my brothers or my aged mother anymore, Why, Emily? Because I have you. Always you. Always here. I didn't waste my money. Ever since my father hadn't needed my salary anymore, I saved it. I have more than enough – and I have five brothers who will welcome me with open arms because I sacrificed so much for them."

Alice's watches in amazement how Emily's face suddenly crumbles and tears well up in her eyes and flow down her cheeks. "You cannot go away, Beatrice. Don't you understand? You are the only person in my life I can trust unconditionally," she sobs.

"Because I never betrayed you," says Beatrice in a firm voice. I know you like the back of my own hand, Emily. Your uncontrollable outbursts and hysteria are only clever acting to make everyone around you dance to your tune. You are a woman of fifty-six, but you carry on like a spoiled little brat whenever you don't get your will. It doesn't bother you that people think I am taking care of an insane woman, as long as you can wield your scepter on Stanton Estate. Am I speaking the truth?"

"My parents never opposed me. I always got what I wanted. I've always been hypersensitive and stressed. The doctor told them it would be better to just give me whatever I wanted," answers Emily contrite.

"The doctor was a quack with the intelligence of a bullfrog. Unfortunately, your parents believed him because they could afford to spoil you. If you had been my parents' daughter, you would've attended a public school and would've sweated out your fragile nerves behind the plough in the field. But, no, the spoiled Emily had to have a governess and a Lady in waiting, and that is why you made such a huge failure of your life and your marriage," says Beatrice damning.

"I did not! Take that back!" protests Emily. " You know how happy I was shortly after our wedding, Beatrice. But he brought that foundling child here: he is the cause of all my sorrow and misery."

"No, Emily. You were too selfish to share William with anyone. You were jealous of all the attention William was giving to the little Oliver because you always had to be the centre of his existence. You even expect Richard to give up his youth on your behalf, but he isn't your paid Lady in waiting. Richard has the right to his own life and happiness. If I should change my mind and decide to stay, you will do as I say, or I will pack my few things right now," threatens Beatrice.

Emily glares at Beatrice with resentment and then looks down. "You upset me, Beatrice. I don't want to argue with you. Let's go to my room," she says timidly.

"Are you going to listen to me, Emily?" asks Beatrice and stays standing in the door.

"You know I need you," Emily answers resentful.

"Oh, I know, therefore you shall do as I say. Come!" commands Beatrice and walk a timid Emily back to her bedroom.

"Oh, my..." Alice sighs in audible relief and walks over to William's bed. She sees his eyes are closed and quickly puts her hand on his wrist.

He opens his eyes and smiles weakly. "I just look like the dead, child, but I'm perfectly alright," he reassures her.

"I am so bitterly sorry I wasn't here to prevent Lady Howard from upsetting you, Uncle William," she says rueful.

His smile widens. Did you not listen to Beatrice? I have been married to Emily for thirty years. She is as normal as I am, but she uses her fake nervous disposition to threaten us all and have us all obey her like puppets on a string."

"But she wanted to attack Oliver with a pair of scissors!"

The smile doesn't leave his eyes. "Because she believes her frail nerves gives her the right to act irresponsibly." He's expression sombres. "That is why I'm sometimes afraid of her, Alice. she is so used to getting her way. Nobody can predict what she will do if one opposes her."

"And still you brought Oliver here when he was only a baby? Were you not afraid then that she might have done something irresponsibly?" she asks confused.

"No, because she knew I was only fulfilling my duty. I gave her wish, I agreed to remain silent about Oliver's lineage… and today I bitterly regret it." He looks at her for a moment in silence. "You know my time is very short, Alice."

Alice swallows hard, she searches for the words of comfort, but she knows she is not capable of deceiving him. "I know, Uncle William."

"That is why the truth must come out. Is Oliver happy that he now knows who his parents were?"

"He doesn't know yet, Uncle William," she leans closer to him, her eyes bleeding in his. "You are confusing Oliver with your brother Henry, Uncle William. you and Henry had a secret hiding place, but Oliver doesn't know where that is."

"Oliver knows. I told him years ago. If he thinks carefully, he will remember," answers William with an unwavering certainty.

"Did you not perhaps tell Richard, Uncle William?"

She knows the pain on his face is not caused by physical pain.

"Richard was never my son. Emily made sure of that. She said I could have the foundling child, but Richard was hers. I would never have told Richard about the hiding place."

"But if you should tell me about it…" she starts, but William closes his eyes to end the conversation.

Alice sighs dejected and moves to the window. Is it true that Uncle William told Oliver about the hiding place, she wonders? No, it cannot be, because he would have remembered about it. Oliver will never love her, but maybe he will remember her with gratefulness if she manages to discover the hiding place. To-night, she is too tired, but tomorrow night she will start with her search again, she decides and turns around to switch off the bed-side lamp before she walks to her own room.

Emily takes place at the breakfast table and looks offended at the empty chair to the right of Beatrice. "Where is nurse Browning, Beatrice? Did you not explain to her that I expect everyone to be punctual for meals?"

"Alice is aware of that, but doctor Graham is busy to examine William. He needs Alice to assist him with the examination," says Beatrice calmly.

"That explains it then," says Emily reasonable and folds open her serviette on her lap. She looks at Richard. "You may say grace, Richard."

He obeys, opens his eyes, and asks astonished: "What has happened to put you in such a good mood, mother? Did you sleep well?"

Emily flashes a glance at Beatrice and answers gregariously: "Beatrice told me that nurse Browning is Helen Upton's niece. One never realises how small the world is… Helen is the daughter of your grandparent's doctor, doctor Thomas Browning. I was surprised to learn Helen was visiting at Tortington. I would very much like to see her again."

"Do you know Alice's aunt, mother?" asks Richard impressed.

"You are becoming too familiar, Richard. Don't forget; nurse Browning is in my service," says Emily disapprovingly.

"It is difficult to forget if you keep reminding me, Mother" he reacts annoyed. "Still: I know nurse Browning likes horseback riding. She spends hours in father's room. Do you have anything against it is she should join me to go horseback riding, Mother?" Alice, walking into the dining room with doctor Norman Graham, stops dead in her tracks when she hears Richard's request to Emily.

"No!" shrieks Emily and grabs her knife like a weapon in your hand. "Don't taunt me, Richard! You are the sole heir of Stanton Estate, and you will marry a girl of my choosing. Don't you realize that you embarrass yourself when you go out with one of the servants?"

"Be reasonable, Mother," says Richard stubbornly. "I didn't say I wanted to marry Alice. What harm is there to go horseback riding with her?"

"It will start with horseback riding, but where will it end?" asks Emily in a shrill voice. "The nurse is from the workers class. She would give her front teeth to marry a rich man like you."

"No, I won't, Lady Howard," says Alice with a cold pride and walks to the table, "Because it so happens, I am already engaged."

Emily's mouth twists into a sneering smile. "Is that so? Who is the poor wretch? A farm worker?"

Norman sees how the blood drains from Alice's face and steps closer quickly, he places his arm around her shoulders protectively. "Alice is my fiancé, Lady Howard," he says with a broad smile.

He hears how Alice gasps for breath but only smiles even broader when she stares at him confused.

"Isn't love just wonderful?" asks Beatrice who was too busy nourishing her inner being to take any notice of Emily's and Richard's small talk. Her smile equals the warmth of the summer sun when she turns and looks at Norman and Alice. "A doctor and a nurse - the two are made for each other. Congratulations, doctor Graham. You are getting a wonderful bride."

"Thank you, miss Crompton,' says Norman, and he squeezes the silent Alice's shoulders encouraging.

"The girl isn't wearing an engagement ring," says Emily suspiciously. "Nurses don't earn too much, but as a doctor you should probably be able to afford a decent ring for your girl, doctor Graham?"

"Without a doubt, but since Alice started working here, she hasn't had one day free so we could go and find her a ring." He turns to Beatrice. "I assume Lady Howard does not need my professional services today?"

"She has everything she needs thank you, doctor Graham," says Beatrice, and waves towards the dining room door. "Go, go Alice, walk your fiancé to the front door. The two of you don't get near enough time alone together."

"The breakfast…" Emily starts offended.

"Can wait," interrupt Beatrice her. "Goodbye, doctor Graham."

"Goodbye, miss Crompton. Lady Howard…" greets Norman and quickly walks with Alice out of the dining room.

They walk to his car in silence, look at each other and laugh embarrassed.

"I should probably thank you," says Alice, a blush turning her cheeks red.

"I expected a slap in the face," he confesses and continues concerned: "I said that to protect you, Alice. Everyone in Arundel is aware of Lady Howard's unnatural possessiveness over Richard. Or are you really engaged to someone else?"

"Are you denser than Lady Howard? You can clearly see I am not wearing an engagement ring."

"Oh… yes, of course. Then you won't mind wearing my ring?" he asks hopeful.

"We don't know each other, Norman! An engagement is a serious matter," she protests.

"Your safety is of greater concern. An engagement ring will protect you against Lady Howard's jealousy… and hopefully keep Richard at a distance."

"Now you sound like Oliver. Does Richard really have such a bad reputation?" she asks in disbelief.

He smiles askew. "Oh, he has a reputation, but I hold Lady

Howard responsible for that. He realises his mother will do anything to prevent him from getting married and that is why he flirts with anyone and everyone as he wants." he frowns in contemplation. "But these days the people or talking less about his escapades. I have a suspicion he really loves Charlotte Hastings."

"I know he loves her. Richard and I have secretly gone horseback riding in the afternoons. He has told me, but nothing would make him happier than to marry Charlotte and to permanently move to the farm in Chichester," she tells him.

"And Stanton Estate, then?" Norman asks in surprise.

"As long as Lady Howard rules in this old house, no one else will ever be happy there. I don't blame Richard for hating that old place. Lady Howard keeps him a prisoner there."

"Let's then hope that Richard will soon have the courage to marry Charlotte," says Norman. He opens his car door but lingers. "Shall we continue with our fake engagement until you leave Stanton Manor?"

She hesitates. The vision of a dark man with purple blue eyes flash before her mind's eye. She doesn't want to wear anyone else's but Oliver's engagement ring, but the chances of that ever happening is a round zero. She was a fool for falling in love with him and an even bigger fool for holding onto the hope that he might also love her one day. Who knows, maybe Norman can help her forget about her feelings for Oliver, she thinks; but doesn't believe herself.

"I won't set any demands on you, Alice. I think you are beautiful and desirable, but I also realize that you don't know me. You can't possibly love me. I can only hope that you will learn at least to like me when we get to know each other better, but in the meantime… it is only a fake engagement," he pleads.

She smiles forced. "I will wear your ring with gratefulness, Norman, especially if it protects me against Lady Howard."

"Done. Let me know when you are free to look at rings. And I think it should be a good idea if we host an engagement dinner at my house with some close friends, just to quell any doubts Lady Howard might still harbor. I will arrange that." He says, bends closer and kisses her on her lips. "That is for the curious ones who might be watching us," he says apologetic, gets into his car and drives away.

Now she is an engaged girl, Alice thinks miserable, and walks slowly back to the dining room. What would Oliver's reaction be when he hears about her engagement? Her heart is beating out of her chest, her heart still holding onto him. No... no, she must stop thinking about him constantly. Her engagement ring will be her talisman to protect her against her own foolishness. The last thing Oliver will do is to bother himself with an engaged girl, she thinks with a feeling of loss. She tries to look joyful when she re-enters the dining room.

Oliver sits on a high rock, his eyes squinted against the sun while he stares over the valley and the river Arun in the distance. Must he return to London, he asks himself for the umpteenth time. His visit to Uncle William was fruitless. Maybe there is a secret hiding place in Stanton Manor; maybe there are letters and documents with information about his parents; but where must he start searching? He lived in Stanton Manor for sixteen years and with the curiosity of the child he poked around every nook and cranny, but he never discovered a secret hiding place. How can he expect he's short nightly visits to offer better results?

He is and he remains a man without a lineage, without an own name... and without a future. If he were the adopted child of loving foster-parents, he might have felt differently about the matter. But even if he wanted to, he cannot forget sixteen years of humiliation in Stanton Manor. Foundling child. How old was he when he decided for the first time to one day find his own parents; when he would be able for once and for all to silence aunt Emily's and Richard's mouths for good; the day when he could say to them: "I have my own blood. I know where I come from. I know who I am."

Only a child's dream, he thinks bitter and turns around when he hears the droning of a car's engine. He doesn't recognize the white sports car and quickly gets up, not in the mood for company. The car drives closer and stops a few meters from him. He turns his back on the motorist and starts walking away with long strides.

"Oliver! Oliver, don't you recognize me?" calls a clear female voice and he hears the car door quickly opening and closing.

He turns around slowly and sees Charlotte Hastings in a floral green summers dress walking towards him. She hasn't changed, he realises. She is beautiful... no, she is breathtakingly beautiful the thought hits him unexpectedly and he remains standing. The sun paints her hair copper red and reflects warmth in her chestnut brown eyes. She is tall but the curves of her figure accentuates her femininity and makes her appear shorter. She comes to a standstill in front of him and smiles up in his face.

"Are you not going to greet an old girlfriend, you beautiful man?" she asks. She doesn't wait for his reaction but puts her arms around his neck, stands on your toes and kisses him full on his mouth.

"Hello, Charlotte," he greets, annoyed with himself for the hoarseness in his voice. He clears his throat and says formally: "I have heard about your husband's passing. My condolences."

She lets go of him and lifts her shoulders indifferently. "I don't make a murderer's den of my heart so I will confess to you: I am neither sorry nor happy about my husband's death. I never loved him, but I was good to him, because he treated me like a queen. I believe I also succeeded in making him happy."

"I understand," he says brusquely and avoids her eyes.

She puts her hand on his own. "You loved me, Oliver," she says in a soft voice.

He looks at her sharply. "I never said that."

"No, but a woman knows. What you didn't realize was that I also loved you... but you were a poor student. I have had to do without too much in my youth to end up marrying a poor man."

"So, you admit that you married for money?"

"Why would I deny it? Do you remember where I come from? I was one of the nine Jones's who grew up in a small two-bedroom house on the other side of the railway. The times when my dad was sober, he went out with the fishing boats to earn just enough money to go drinking again. Do you know what it feels like to live off scraps, to depend on charity?" she asks with a bitterness that does not meet her youthful appearance.

"We went to school together. Did I ever treat you any different from the rich children?" He asks, forcing himself to stay calm.

"No, but..." she searches his eyes. " I was young when I realized how men looked at me. I knew I was pretty and desirable and every time I had to wear a stranger's second-hand washed-out dress; I swore to myself that I would one day marry a rich man so other people would wear my old clothes."

"Then I should congratulate you, as I understand it you are a very wealthy widow," he says cynically.

"Can you blame me?" she asks offended. I loved you but I married Thomas Hastings for us. I knew about his weak heart. I never wished him dead, but I could always dream about the day I would be free again to marry you, Oliver."

Oliver looks at her, his face expressionless. They were best friends; he thinks to himself. More than that, they were inseparable. And yet, their relationship didn't grow any further after school despite the dreams they had to leave this place together. They both went in their own separate directions. Charlotte went to Chichester and started working as a receptionist in Thomas Hastings' office. He left to study medicine in London. In the beginning they used to contact each other on a regular basis, until they both eventually realised that they were leading vastly different lives and now also had very different goals. Yes, he grins to himself, precisely because they had quite different goals. She wanted a rich husband, and he wanted to become a cardiologist.

"Free and rich." His laugh is void of any humour and he shakes his head. "I can't help but have an involuntary admiration for you, Charlotte, but I had my own reasons why I never actually asked you to marry me."

"You were a penniless student who were supported by the Howards," she says quickly.

"That is true, but…"

"That is all in the past now, Oliver. You are a successful cardiologist now, and the owner of Tortington. I am probably richer than you are, but even if you hadn't had one cent, I would still be willing to marry you."

The expression on his face hardens. "You didn't give me the opportunity to finish talking, Charlotte. It wasn't my poverty which prevented me from marrying you. I had another reason… but that doesn't matter anymore."

"I am glad because then my sacrifice wasn't in vain. Do you know how lonely a person can be when you have to act the entire time? I longed for you embraces and your caresses, but I had to…"

"That's enough, Charlotte," he interrupts her gruffly. "Your sacrifices were worth it; you gained the wealthy you so desperately wanted. And Richard's love. Who knows, one of these days you might become even richer than you are now when you marry the sole heir of Stanton Estate."

"Goodness gracious, Oliver, don't tell me you are jealous of Richard? He amuses me but you are the man I love, the man I've always loved," she says offended.

He lets his gaze move slowly over her, searching for the love he once had for her, but he doesn't find it, he finds only a feeling of unknown emptiness. What happened to Charlotte, the carefree girl, his best friend, from his youth? Charlotte with the dancing eyes and cheerful laughter, the young girl who, only yesterday was still the long-legged girl in her shorts, building a raft with him on which they were going to escape with together down this very same river Arun flowing below them right now. But he knows the answer: Charlotte doesn't believe in love. Little Alice still believes in the undying love, he remembers and turns his head away. His gaze follows the river and flows over the rolling green hills of this valley. The same green as Alice's eyes. Alice… Alice… pulses her name with every beat of his heart through his entire being. What does Alice have which Charlotte never had, he asks himself puzzled. Innocence? Or maybe just a child's faith in the all-conquering power of true love? For Alice love is the only reason, love is the only truth in everything. Alice would never marry a man for money...

"Did you hear what I said, Oliver?" asks Charlotte, standing tense next to him. "I have loved you all these years."

"I heard you," he says without looking at her, "but I am not a student anymore, Charlotte. You were married and you know the old saying: Time heels everything, even a broken heart."

"Don't you love me anymore?" she asks devastated.

He looks at her with a faint smile around his lips. "Back then I believed I loved you, but I guess adulthood has given me a better perspective. You changed; as did I. Whatever we had, whatever we thought we had, belongs in the past now."

She jerks her head up offended. "I am sorry I wasted my time, haughty doctor Howard. Don't expect an invitation to Stanton Manor once Richard and I are married," she sneers, turns around and walks back to her car.

He doesn't look back when he hears her driving away. The image of a blonde girl with flashing green eyes is his only thought. Alice could never act, could never hide her true feelings. He can love a girl like Alice because she doesn't play around with love.

Eleanor covers her face with her hands when Beatrice steamrolls into her kitchen for the second time in two days taking a seat at the kitchen table, panting for breath.

"Oh, oh, oh! The test of all tests! People say I'm fat, Eleanor, but I tell you this today: it is my cross to bear. I walk and my fat walks with me... I am breaking my back carrying my fat," bemoans Beatrice her fate and fans herself with her dainty lace handkerchief.

"You are carrying yourself and your fat to an early grave, Beatrice Crompton!" scolds Eleanor, already busy pouring her a glass of cold drink. "What are you doing walking around under this warm sun, Beatrice? You could've phoned if your news was so urgent."

Beatrice drinks the glass of cold drink and places the empty glass down in front of Eleanor. "More!" she demands out of breath.

"Cool down first, Beatrice. All right, now tell me what disaster hit the people of Stanton Manor this time?" asks Eleanor curiously.

"Disaster? Who said anything about a disaster?" Beatrice leans back on the creaking kitchen chair and smiles contently. "It is the most wonderful news, Eleanor. You will never guess, the pretty Alice and doctor Norman Graham got engaged. What do you have to say about that?"

"Damn it!" roars Oliver enraged from the passage door, his eyes gleaming coals in his unnaturally pale face, while he storms menacingly towards the startled Beatrice. "Why do you lie to us, miss Crompton?" he asks gruffly and grabs Beatrice roughly by her arm.

Chapter 8

Beatrice slaps Oliver's hand which is still holding her shoulder. "Rude rascal!" She scolds him offended. "Here I am struggling to regain my breath after walking all the way here, and what do you do? Give me the fright of my life! What's bothering you, child? I brought wonderful news; I didn't come here to argue with you."

Oliver glares at her angrily. "Is the lie that Alice and Norman Graham are engaged you are wonderful news, miss Crompton?"

"But will you stop making me out to be a liar? answers Beatrice now also losing her temper. "No, Oliver, how do you know me by now? Am I a gossip, or do I always speak the truth?"

Oliver, now uncertain of himself, looks at Eleanor who is standing in silence at the head of the table watching him with the wisdom of the ages. "Is it the truth, aunt Eleanor?" he asks curtly.

"I cannot, for the life of me, think of one reason why Beatrice would walk all the way here under this beating sun just to come and tell us a lie, child. If Beatrice says that Alice and doctor Graham are engaged, then it is so," she answers calmly.

Beatrice smiles tauntingly. "Tell him, Eleanor. Imagine! The impertinent child shaking me around by the shoulders and telling me I'm a liar. What is wrong with you, Oliver?" she wiggles her little nose sniffing the air. "Did you perhaps have too much to drink?"

"I don't think it is alcohol that has the man behaving like a bear with a sore head, Beatrice," says Eleanor meaningful.

"What is that about alcohol?" asks Helen and enters the kitchen. She sees Beatrice sitting at the kitchen table and smiles welcoming. "Good day Beatrice. how is my niece?"

Beatrice glares distrustful at Oliver. "My lips are sealed, Helen, I'm afraid if I should open my mouth to tell you the wonderful news this unmannered bear of a man might slap me," she answers offended.

Helen becomes aware of the tense atmosphere in the kitchen; as if a cold cloud has drawn into the room and covered them all. She takes turns looking from Oliver to Eleanor, a wordless question in her eyes.

"Beatrice exaggerates as usual, Helen," says Eleanor nonchalantly. "The news that Alice and doctor Norman Graham had gotten engaged upset Oliver just a bit."

"What?" Helen stares at her speechless and then turns to Beatrice dismayed. "Is that the truth, Beatrice? Did Alice get engaged to a complete stranger without my knowledge?"

"You see, who's exaggerating now?" asks Beatrice now also upset. "Doctor Graham is not a complete stranger. He has been our personal physician for almost four years now, and he often does house visits at Stanton Manor. You know yourself, Eleanor: doctor Graham is almost like family."

"Maybe to the Howards and to you, Beatrice, but Alice met him scarcely a week ago," says Helen disapprovingly. "How often has he visited her, Beatrice?"

Beatrice lifts her shoulders indifferently. "Now how would I know, Helen? I keep myself busy with the troublesome Emily. I don't have eyes in the back of my head to see what Alice is doing behind my back."

"Alice doesn't know the man." interjects Oliver bluntly. "Surely you aren't just going to leave the matter at that, aunt Helen?"

"Obviously not, but if the girl is serious… she is of age and I can't prescribe to her what to do," answers Helen worried and looks at Beatrice. "I would like to talk to Alice, Beatrice. Are you driving with me?"

"Not before I've had a second glass of cold drink and something small to eat." Beatrice looks accusingly at Eleanor. "I have long since cooled down, Eleanor. Where is my second glass of cold drink? And what about a little something tasty to eat?"

Eleanor fills the glass in silence and then walks into the pantry. she returns with a basket in her hands and places it down in front of Beatrice. "The jam tarts you sent with Alice, is as chewy as shoe soles and to top that off, it's burnt. You can eat them on your way back to Stanton Manor, Beatrice."

"But would you listen too such a pretentious soul!" says Beatrice furious. "My jam tarts as chewy as shoe soles, Eleanor Wallace, but what about the tarts you bake? You are stingy, my old friend, because you always only put a lick of jam in your tarts." She scratches around in the basket and takes out one tart. "This is what a jam tart should look like, Eleanor: it looks a little pot belly piglet stuffed with jam."

"Helen is in a hurry to leave, Beatrice. Finish your cold drink," says Eleanor calmly.

"Hurry, hurry, hurry… and what for? We all know life is a one way heading to the graveyard," Beatrice says in resentment, drinks the cold drink and pats her mouth with her lace handkerchief. She gets up with a groan. "Now what are we waiting for, Helen? I have my jam tarts."

"I'll be back soon, aunt Eleanor," says Helen and walks out the back door.

"Slow down!" says Beatrice in a pitched voice. "I can't jog with my cross of fat to carry with me." She wobbles to s stop in the back door. "Goodbye, Eleanor. I am a compassionate person and therefore I shall forgive you for your snide comments about my jam tarts. And you, Oliver, don't need to look so miserable. I have already forgiven you, even though you assaulted me without reason. Goodbye, child."

"See you later, Beatrice," greets Eleanor, smiling and shaking her head. She turns to Oliver who sits on a kitchen chair staring out in front of him, silent and obviously disgruntled. "Do you love Alice, Oliver?" she asks straightforward.

Her question hits him like a fist between his eyes and he jerks his head up. He stares at her disconcerted, disbelief clouding his eyes. "What makes you ask that, aunt Eleanor? Alice is a stranger to me, the same way as Norman Graham is a stranger to her."

"I see." Eleanor's eyes fill with laughter, but she asks with composure: "Do you believe love is a science, child? Does everything happen according to a schedule? Today you meet a girl, six months later you fall in love with her, and a year later you get married?"

He stares at her offended. "I have only loved a girl once but when I saw her again this morning..." he frowns in amazement. "I said it to Alice, and I know it is true: love is just a temporary convulsion which one outgrows."

"Are you referring to your feelings for Charlotte Hastings?"

"Yes, aunt Eleanor. There was a time in my life that I believed I could never be happy if I did not marry Charlotte."

"And now you feel differently about her?"

He smiles bitter. "Without a doubt. It is one convulsion I quickly outgrew."

"Being in love is not love, Oliver. If you don't know what the difference is, then you have never loved."

"I cannot afford to love a girl - and you know why, aunt Eleanor," he answers sullen.

"Oh, I know you believe that you do not have the right to love someone because you know nothing about your lineage, but the day when you realize you love someone, truly and deeply love someone... no one asks for that kind of love. It just happens."

He looks at her cynically and lifts his shoulders. "Let's not waste our time debating fatuous matters, aunt Eleanor. I would really appreciate a cup of tea right about now," he changes the subject. Eleanor looks at him with sympathy, she wants to say something, but decides against it. Life itself is the best teacher, she thinks to herself and switches on the kettle.

Doctor Norman Graham sits lost in thought with his chin resting on his hand. Then he smiles as he thinks about Alice. They are engaged. And tonight they will announce it at their engagement dinner at his house. Yes, yes, it is only a fake engagement – for now. He was almost certain Oliver would've jumped at the opportunity to ask her out to dinner, and start seeing her, but for a change Lady Luck is smiling down at him, Norman Graham. Oliver might realise his loss yet. Maybe he should try to find out what Oliver's feelings really are towards Alice tonight at the dinner.

Alice is one of the most beautiful girls he has ever seen. And in the past few weeks they've gotten to know each other a little with their daily communications regarding uncle William's care. She isn't just very beautiful; she is also very intelligent and a very good nurse. She can move to Arundel. They can build a life here. Could fate have brought them together? They do make the perfect couple.

Norman smiles and shakes his head. Concentrate good man, he chides himself. He makes a few notes in a patient's file, and then he suddenly gets up. It is time for him to find a partner to join him in his practice. Being the superintendent of the hospital and seeing patients keeps him extremely busy. He is tired of the personnel's complaints and everything in general that goes wrong from time to time. He needs someone with a firm handle on people and who won't put up with any non-compliance in the clinic.

He walks out of his office. Yes, the moment he appoints a partner he can slow down, and he'll only work normal office hours. The practice is remarkably busy and successful. When he decided to buy the practice from old doctor Kingsley three years ago, he was worried that he had over-extended himself with the bank and that the practice might proof to be a mistake. He smiles, he has done well for himself, very well. He paid the last installment on his bank loan seven months ago. He can afford a partner and he could do with some extra free time, especially now that he has a wonderful fiancé to spend his free time with. He has reason to celebrate tonight.

The long dinner table is set with a white tablecloth and white, elegant plates for twenty people. A large silver candle chandelier stands in the middle of the table and the candlelight bounces off the crystal wine glasses, painting small sparkles around the room like hundreds of little fireflies.

It would've been a fantastic fairy wonderland, Alice thinks somber, if tonight didn't weigh so heavily on her heart. How is she going to fake her happiness through this night, knowing that she and Norman are deceiving these people who are attending their dinner.

Alice smiles, everyone is seated around the dinner table, and she sees the contentment on Norman's face as he sits at the head of the table, having a conversation with the man on his right, and they laugh together. She doesn't know the man, Norman did introduce him to her when he and his wife arrived, but she can't recall his name. She doesn't know most of the guest tonight. She is grateful to have Miss Crompton, here. And, of course, Oliver, she is intensely aware of him sitting next to her on her left.

"Are you enjoying it, little Alice," he whispers close to her ear, making her pulse race.

"I'm enjoying every moment, Oliver," she whispers back, and smiles at him. "It feels as if I'm in a dream." She doesn't lie to him, it's the truth, this must be a dream. How else did she get herself into this situation? She looks into his eyes, and she sees the seriousness in those black- purple pools. If he only knew how desperately she wants to win his heart. If he should know that her heart already belongs to him. Yes, that he holds her heart and her dreams in his two hands.

"I see," he says calmly. "I just had to come and see this debacle for myself to actually believe it. So, you decided to marry a man you barely know. You are still very young, Alice. Believe me when I tell you that love will only hurt you. The only thing I learned from love is the power it gives someone over you."

She gasps softly. He has just told her very honestly that he isn't interested to ever be romantically involved with anyone. No, that he is not capable to be. He was never hers, but losing him here, now, breaks her heart. But she smiles and picks up her wine glass and takes a sip to swallow down the tears aching in her throat.

They are sitting at the table, eating, and talking, when they hear a car stop outside the house.

"Oh, I hope I'm not intruding?" They hear Matron Frances' voice from the foyer. Then she appears in the dining room door. Norman gets up from his chair.

"Matron Frances, what a surprise! Please, come join us. Have dinner with us." He waves his hand at his housekeeper. She quickly starts to clear a space on the table, but Frances stops her, "Thank you, dear, I'll just squeeze in here, if you don't mind," and she walks to Oliver's left-hand side. The young girl sets a plate and cutlery.

"Thank you, doctor Graham, but I've already had dinner. I was on my way to nurse Tyndall, when I saw all the cars outside and it looked like a social gathering." She says across the table. "And if Mohammed doesn't want to come to the mountain, then the mountain will come to Mohammed," she whispers with a smile to Oliver. Oliver frowns lightly. He pours some wine in her glass, she picks up her wine glass and she looks into Oliver's eyes and smiles. "Thank you, Oliver."

Oliver feels irritated with her presence here next to him. Does she not feel in the least embarrassed to arrive at an obvious private dinner party uninvited? Can the woman not feel she isn't welcome, he wonders, while she is talking non-stop and touching his arm every so often.

Alice forces herself to smile. Matron Frances obviously saw Oliver's car among all the others and decided to stop. She talks to Oliver as if she and he are the only two people at this table. Alice gets up and excuses herself to go and wash her hands.

Beatrice follows her. "What is the Matron doing here, Alice? It seems she wasn't invited."

"She wasn't, Miss Crompton. Maybe she'll stay only a little while. I'm so glad you are here tonight. I don't know any of these people, and I don't think it was necessary for Norman and I to have an engagement dinner so quickly."

"He is definitely very much in love with you, Alice. He can't keep his eyes off you. Luckily, the night is almost over, dear. Let's return to the dining room." says Beatrice calmingly.

Frances puts her empty glass down on the table as she gets up from her chair. "I am really enjoying our chat, Oliver, and I don't really want to leave now. But nurse Tyndall is also still expecting me. Will you walk me to my car, Oliver?" she asks, smiling at him, her hand resting on his arm.

Alice and Beatrice come out of the bathroom as Matron Frances and Oliver are about to walk out of the front door.

"Oh, there you are, Alice. Congratulations with your engagement to doctor Norman. I wish you both a wonderful future. It seems love is in the air in Arundel." She says, almost overly friendly, smiling up at Oliver.

"Thank you, Matron Frances. That is truly kind," accepts Alice, smiling.

"I have to, unfortunately leave now, I do have a prior appointment. Oliver is so kind to walk me to my car. Enjoy the rest of your evening."

"Good night, Matron." Alice and Beatrice remain in the door, they smile and wave back at Frances as she and Oliver reach her car. Frances turns to face Oliver.

"I have something urgent I need to discuss with you, Oliver. But I don't want to bother you with it now. We can discuss it another time when we can meet more privately."

She stands on her toes, her hand glides over his chest and she kisses him on his cheek, and then adds, "Thank you for the wine. I will phone you."

"Does it have anything to do with my uncle's care, Matron?" he asks alarmed.

"Oh, no, Oliver," she laughs softly, touching his arm. "No, you silly man. It's about us, you and I."

"I beg your pardon, Matron Frances. I think there is some misunderstanding, there is no "us" to discuss."

"Well, of course now is not the time or the place. I understand you want to keep your private life ... well, just that – private."

Oliver's eyes flash in hers.

"Hear me clearly, Matron, so we can prevent any further misunderstanding. There is no "us". There never was and there never will be. Do you understand me?"

She gasps softly. Goodness, the man is upset and outspoken. She only wanted him to know how much she cared for him.

"I understand, doctor Howard," she says quickly, looking at him hurt. "I apologise if I upset you. It's just...you will never know how I feel about you," she adds, close to tears.

He sighs, suddenly sorry for being so harsh towards her. He puts his strong hand on her shoulder, trying to calm her. She steps closer to him, almost standing in his arms.

"It's alright, no harm done," he says. "You must understand that we are also colleagues."

She looks at him with tears in her eyes, and says: "I totally understand that, Oliver. Precisely because I love you so much. I only wish you would realise that and that you won't reject my love. Don't you realise I would give my life to you? You mean everything to me."

He feels sorry for the young woman standing in front of him, but he is also losing his patience with her. "Listen, Matron, don't carry on with this, please. I don't love you. I am sorry for disappointing you, but nobody can dictate to their hearts. So... this is the last conversation you and I will have about this matter. Now you will have to excuse me, I have a dinner to attend. Good night, Matron." He immediately turns around and walks back to the house. He hears her sobs as she gets in her car, then she slams the door shut and drives away. He shakes his head, angry again. The woman is crazy, he thinks to himself. But he won't entertain whatever dream she is living in. He looks up and notices Beatrice in the foyer, a slight frown on her forehead.

"My apologies, Miss Crompton. I can't imagine how anyone barges in so uninvited. Where is Alice?" he asks when he notices her absence.

"She has returned to the dinner. Oliver, I don't want to interfere in your business, but feel free to take these words to heart: be very careful of Matron Frances Leighton." Beatrice warns, almost as if with a foreboding.

"What are you trying to say, Miss Crompton?" he asks angrily.

Beatrice looks at him fearless, and like a mother she says, "I don't know how much you know about women, but women like her grabs the whole arm when one offers only the pinkie. Frances knows how to spin a web and I can see she is busy spinning a web for you. A woman can see this in another woman. And for Beatrice Crompton it is very clear. Avoid Matron Frances, she is not the right woman for you, Oliver." Beatrice keeps rambling on as they walk back to the dining room.

Alice looks up and meets Oliver's eyes. She fights back her tears and looks away. The intimate scene she just witnessed a few minutes ago from the front door replays in her mind. The fact is that Matron Frances is an attractive woman. But she didn't expect to see her and Oliver standing so close to each other. And definitely not to see how Frances was touching Oliver and for him to allow it. It was obvious to her that he enjoyed it! And that upset her, especially because she had judged him to be quite the opposite, because she thought of him as much more private and discreet. She can see he is upset. He is probably upset because Matron Frances had left. They certainly seemed to be sharing an intimate moment outside in the dark. Oliver doesn't sit down again. He greets everyone, thanks Norman and herself for an enjoyable evening and then he leaves the house.

Beatrice stares out of the kitchen window into the darkness, a warm cup of tea forgotten in her hands. It was a lovely evening, she thinks to herself, until the wretched Matron Frances showed up uninvited. Alice handled it as if it were the most natural thing to happen. But since they got back to Stanton Manor, she isn't herself. And Beatrice can't figure out what is bothering the girl.

"Please excuse me, Miss Crompton," says Alice as she pushes her tea aside. "I have a slight headache. I think I'll take two tablets and go to bed. It was quite a busy evening."

"But, of course, child. I can see you don't feel yourself. I shall phone doctor Graham..."

"No, please don't, Miss Crompton!" She stops her. "It is nothing which two headache tablets won't sort out. No, luckily, I don't feel so bad that I need a doctor. I am only tired, and it's been an exciting day. And I quickly want to check in on Uncle William before I turn in."

She immediately excuses herself and walks out of the kitchen. Miss Crompton with her piercing eyes and questions will make it too difficult for her to hide her feelings much longer.

Her eyes burn from the tears suddenly welling up again. She should've known that other women would also find Oliver irresistible. He is probably one of the handsomest men she's ever seen. But what she never would've guessed is the fact that he would be so public with his affections. And as she again recalls the vision of Oliver and Matron Frances from earlier tonight, she becomes furious.

She takes her pillow and throws it across the floor with pure frustration. If this is how love makes one feel, she would rather live without it, she decides. Tears of powerlessness run down her cheeks. How could she have been so stupid to let a handsome, charming man like Oliver Howard into her heart? Did she not learn her lesson well enough the first time with Robert?

She feels angry at herself and sick to her stomach when she gets into her bed and switches off the bedside lamp. She'd be his if he only asked. She closes her eyes, and she prays that this love she feels for Oliver would disappear. Sometimes, your heart needs more time to accept what your mind already knows.

She turns onto her side and tries to calm down. Tomorrow she'll feel better, she thinks in the dark. Yes, tomorrow the sun will shine again. And then she will laugh at herself for being so silly to cry over a man!

Stanton Manor hasn't changed, Helen thinks to herself while she is walking up the stairs with Beatrice to Emily's private sitting room. She once was a welcome guest at Stanton Manor... once, when she was a shy young girl dreaming about Henry Howard. Henry... her love for him has outlasted time and space, which is why she could never love another man again. Even the knowledge that he would've married Annabelle could not change how she felt about him. And now he has long since passed away. Maybe it does give her some consolation that her first love has remained intact in her heart because Henry never married. It offers some comfort to dream about the possibility that he might have come to love her had he not died so young.

"It's best we walk a bit slower, Helen," warns Beatrice. "The help did say Emily asked we come to her private sitting room, but I know her: she would probably want to put on something nicer before we arrive."

"After all those jam tarts you ate it is probably better for your health if we walk a bit slower, Beatrice," teases Helen her.

"Food is good for one's health," says Beatrice obstinate. "Don't let the clever doctors tell you that fat makes people sick. just look at me: I have never been in a hospital, and when I get a cold, I eat myself healthy. but on the other hand: Emily only gets troublesome when I am sick, that is why I have to take good care of myself."

Together they walk down the broad passage and Beatrice wobbles to a stop in front of a door, she looks over her shoulder to Helen and says with a sly wink: "She is playing the role of the queen of Stanton Manor again. Let's put her in her place for a change."

"What do you mean, Beatrice?" asks Helen worried.

"You will see," she answers mysteriously, knocks on the door, opens it, and walks in.

Is much slimmer than she was in her youth, but she is still a beautiful woman, thinks Helen to herself and looks at Emily who is sitting on a gold-plated chair with dark red upholstery.

"Let me introduce you, Emily," says Beatrice formally.

"Professor doctor Helen Upton, meet Lady Howard."

"Beatrice!" Helen scolds her. " I have already met Emily in my youth."

"Professor?" Emily looks impressed. "I remember your father always bragged about his clever daughter when he did the house call in Chichester, Helen, but after his passing I never heard anything about you again."

"I became a lecturer in psychology and earned my doctor's degree, but I actually just retired. Hello, Emily," greets hidden with a charming smile and shakes Emily's hand.

"Welcome in Stanton Manor, Helen. I was so excited when I heard that you were nurse Browning's aunt. I didn't really have close girlfriends when I was still a girl, but I remember that you sometimes accompanied your father when he visited my parents."

"Mainly just to admire all your toys and beautiful room," smiles Helen and sits down on a chair opposite Emily. "And later your dresses. You always looked like a princess."

"My parents could afford it," says Emily noticeably flattered. She taps nervously with her fingers of her right hand on the armrest of her chair. "A woman of your class... I was wondering: do you not want to come and stay here in Stanton Manor? Eleanor isn't so young anymore and I doubt if she could succeed in making your vacation in Tortington very pleasant."

"You are gossiping now, Emily," reprimands Beatrice her. "There is nothing wrong with Eleanor's hands or mind."

"You won't understand, Beatrice," says Emily, and she lifts her chin haughtily. "Professor Upton is used to intellectual companionship and all the comforts money can buy." She looks at Helen.

"I understand you inherited quite a wealth after your father's passing away, Helen?"

"I inherited somewhat. But I enjoy my vacation in Tortington, Emily. Aunt Eleanor goes out of her way to make my stay as pleasant as possible. I would unnecessarily offend her if I should come to stay here," says Helen decidedly.

Beatrice sniffs upset through her stubby nose. "Some people don't take their wealth too seriously, Emily. they know their manners," she says crossly.

Emily ignores her and frowns. "Please, don't misunderstand me, Helen. I don't have anything against Eleanor, but I am aware of Oliver's presence in Tortington. For sixteen years I tried to give him a decent upbringing, but once a foundling child, always a foundling child. Does his boorish attitude not bother you?"

"On the contrary, Oliver and I get along just splendidly. As a matter of fact, he is also my cardiologist. I can't say anything about him but to sing his praises," answers Helen evenly.

"A chameleon, which is what he is," says Emily dismayed. "But I don't trust him. He conspired with my mother-in-law and made sure he inherited Tortington. I am warning you, Helen, he is probably also after your money."

"I appreciate your warning, but Alice is already my sole heir," Helen informs her with an undisturbed smile.

Emily sits up straighter, a greedy glow in her dark eyes. "Alice? Nurse Browning?" she asks surprised.

"Yes, Emily. Alice lost her mother when she was five years old. Clara was my only sibling. That is why she asked me to take care of Alice. Alice, of course, has her father and three brothers but a young girl needs a mother figure, as well. After Clara's passing, I filled the role as a mother in her life, she is to me like my own daughter - the daughter I never had."

Beatrice sniffs emotionally. "Oh, that I have misjudged you so, Helen. Imagine, I thought you were an educated woman with a dictionary in the place where your heart should be, but now I must hear that you have a soft mother's heart, just like a normal person... it is so wonderful!"

"Hush, Beatrice," orders Emily upset, turns to Helen, and continues keenly: "If only I had known all of this earlier, Helen... for years I have been worrying myself about choosing Richard's future wife, but a girl of our class; not just someone from the workers class..."

"If you are referring to Alice, Emily: There is absolutely nothing wrong with her hands or mind and it is her choice to be useful to her fellow man as part of the working class, as you put it. But Alice has inherited quite a sum of money from her grandmother on her father's side. And then there are also the family farm and the family jewels. Alice works because it is her choice to do something meaningful with her life, not because she is a church mouse," Helen interrupts her with a tad of annoyance in her voice.

"But..." Emily stares upset at her. "Now I understand why doctor Graham was so eager to become engaged to your niece, Helen. He is still busy paying off his practice which he bought over from old doctor Kingsley. Of course, he is hoping to marry Alice so she can pay for his practice."

"If the children love each other..." says Helen indifferently.

"Love is not pertinent in this case. As I am saying: the doctor is only looking for a rich wife. You will have to act fast to end this engagement, Helen. I believe Richard is the proper groom for Alice," says Emily determined.

Helen surprises smile with effort. "I have come here with the purpose of talking to Alice about her engagement. Would it be convenient if I could talk to her now for a bit?"

"Obviously, Helen. But don't you want to have a cup of tea with me first? I forget my role as hostess..."

"The tea can wait, thank you, Emily. Where can I find Alice?"

"Beatrice will bring her here," says Emily and stands up from her chair. "I enjoyed your visit, Helen. let's do it again."

"I shall, thank you, Emily. Goodbye," greets Helen, a mysterious smile around her lips. There has always been gossip stories that Emily belonged in a mental clinic, but there was nothing wrong with Emily's conversation with her. did aunt Eleanor this try to bring her under a false impression of Emily? No… there was the incidents where Emily threatened to attack Oliver with a pair of scissors. Who is the real Emily, she wonders frowning?

In the passage Emily turns in triumph to Beatrice smiling wide. "What have you to say now, Beatrice? Did I behave well enough?"

"Not too bad," Beatrice has to admit, her eyes suspiciously on Emily. "But what nonsense was that about Richard having to marry Alice? Goodness, Emily, Richard is a man of twenty-eight. he is old enough to choose his own bride."

A sly glow burns in Emily's eyes. "Richard knows yields the scepter. If he doesn't do as I say, he will never inherit Stanton Estate."

"Maybe, but you cannot force Alice to fall in love with Richard. She's already engaged to doctor Graham," says Beatrice angry.

"What normal girl will choose the unattractive, poor doctor over my son?"

"A girl in love," answers Beatrice challenging and watches Emily distrustful. "And there is something else: Why are you suddenly so eager for Richard to marry Alice? All these years you prohibited the poor boy to bring any girl home, but now you can't wait to see him married to Alice."

"I didn't say they will get married immediately. Alice is still young. They can be engaged for a few years. Alice is a nurse. She can stay here in Stanton Manor and if we get along … You are not getting younger, Beatrice. Alice will be able to help me when you can't anymore."

Beatrice stops suddenly and bursts out insulted: "You selfish witch! You are not looking for a bride for Richard, but a slave for yourself. Aren't you ashamed of yourself, Emily Howard? Can you not think of anything except your own happiness?"

"I have to think of the future," says Emily with cold indifference. "Now go, go call Alice. Helen is waiting for her."

"Slier than a snake," mumbles Beatrice, and stomps off to the top of the stairs.

Richard kicks a cobblestone with the point of his riding boot. There is an annoyed expression on his face. "It doesn't make sense to me, Alice. Why did you have to get engaged to doctor Graham right now?"

"Would tomorrow or next week have suited you better?" she asks lighthearted.

He looks at her angry. "That's not what I'm saying. But you are my father's private nurse. Even doctor Graham doesn't know how long my father will still live, but as long as he does, he will need you. What becomes of him if you suddenly marry Norman?"

"There are other private nurses, Richard."

"Who? Old matrons with sour faces?"

"Does that matter? Whoever takes care of your father will be competent."

"But won't be company for me!" he bursts out.

She stares at him in surprise. "Goodness gracious, Richard, I didn't come here to keep you company. You are planning to marry Charlotte Hastings. If you are looking for female company, go visit her."

He presses his lips together. "You know my mother is watching me like a hawk. She knows the sound of my car's engine. I can't go anywhere unless I tell her beforehand. And then she even phones to see if I didn't perhaps lie to her."

"That is your own fault. You are twenty-eight. Why do you still listen to her?"

He looks at her in silence and doubt darkens his eyes.

"It's... It's not that simple. I don't even know if it is the truth but every time I oppose her she threatens that she will make sure Oliver inherits Stanton Estate."

Alice audibly catches her breath, her eyes big in disbelief. "But... can she do that? Stanton Estate belongs to your father, after all."

"In name only, but my mother has been ruling over us all for all these years. She says Oliver is my father's illegitimate son and..."

"What?" she interrupts him surprised.

"Please, Alice, don't discuss this matter with anyone else. I don't know if it is the truth, but if Oliver truly is my half-brother... He is two years older than I am. He is first in line to inherit Stanton

Estate."

"And you don't want to lose this old house and the estate?" she asks sympathetically.

Bitterness carves deep lines around Richard's mouth. "I hate this old house. But my mother inherited her family farm in Chichester from her father. If I am disowned... I don't mind confessing this: I am used to luxury. I made a total failure of my studies; I don't have any qualification. What do I do if I should be disowned? I don't see myself working on a fisher's boat or as a farm help for a meager salary."

"If Charlotte loves you... She inherited a farm from her late husband," Alice tries to console him.

"Never! I have my pride. I will not allow my rich wife to maintain me. That's why my mother has me jumping around like a puppet on a string, because she holds my entire future in her two hands."

"I wish I could help, Richard, but... I promise you I won't get married to Norman for as long as your father needs my help."

He smiles gratefully. "You are beautiful and sweet, Alice. If I did not love Charlotte, I would..." He coughs and blushes embarrassed. "Come ride with me," he changes the direction of their conversation.

"I can't. Your father is due for his next injection very soon and your mother... I'm not up for another argument."

"And you are now also engaged to be married," he says dejected, turns around and gets on his horse that's already been saddled. He waves with his horse-whip and rides away on a gallop.

Alice walks to the horse, Poppy, who Richard usually has saddled for her and feeds her a few sugar lumps. Poppy chews with gnashing teeth, sniffling, she searches for more sugar lumps and nuzzles Alice's neck.

"Maybe we can go for a ride this afternoon, Poppy. You and I... No!" she screams frightened as she is grabbed by the shoulders from behind and jerked around. Her shock turns into indignity as she faces Oliver's grim expression. "You idiot – " she bursts out loud.

"Hush!" he commands and lightly shakes her by her shoulders. "What is wrong with you, Alice? You had me under the impression that you were quite an intelligent girl, a graduated nurse, but you behave as irresponsible as a teenage lovesick puppy."

"Let me go, you rude bully! How can I talk if you shake me around so hard to make my teeth shudder?" she asks furious.

He drops his hands quickly. "Then talk. What is your explanation?"

"I was in the backyard when Richard came to the stables to go horseback riding. We..."

"Girl, do you want me to hang you from the nearest rafter?" He interrupts her in fury. "I want to know what came over you to get engaged to a complete stranger?"

He is upset about her engagement to Norman, she realises. Could he be just a little bit jealous, she wonders and smiles? Then she realises that she is smiling, and quickly puts on her pious face. Oliver looks like he could murder someone, so she will handle the situation with the utmost seriousness, she decides and says formally: "Doctor Graham asked me to marry him, and after serious consideration, I accepted."

"Nonsense! You don't know the man. You also don't love him. It was clear as daylight at your supposed engagement dinner."

"How would you know, doctor Howard? You don't even believe in love," she retaliates.

"Maybe not, but I do use my common sense. You have seen Norman once or twice, and now suddenly you are engaged to him. Why?" he asks brash.

"Because... e... because it is custom to first get engaged to a man before you marry him," she answers calmly.

"And because you are head over heels in love with him?"

She looks away and says adamantly: "I will never marry a man if I were not head over heels in love with him."

Oliver watches her closely through squinted eyes, he writes his fingers frustrated through his hair and asks unexpectedly: "Can you look me in my eyes and tell me that you love him?"

If he doesn't leave quickly, she is going to burst out in tears, she thinks and keeps her face turned away from him. How can any man be so blind? Can he not see how obviously she loves him with every cell of her being? She loves him with every breath she takes, with every beat of her heart, but he expects her to look him in the eyes and to admit that she loves someone else.

"You are not my father, Oliver. Stop behaving like a nosey old man. Norman and I are engaged and there is nothing you can do about it," she answers, her voice hoarse trying to withhold her tears.

His anger makes way for concern, and he looks at her worried. "Why, Alice? Do you have financial problems? Debt you cannot repay? Is that the reason why you are so eager to marry Norman?" His voice is calm and sympathetic.

Now she's going to cry like a baby, she thinks to herself. The tears burning behind her eyelids, and she bends her head down.

He takes her by her arms lightly and pulls her closer to him. "If it is finances or any other problem, little Alice: I will help you. Have you forgotten we are friends? It is not necessary for you to marry a complete stranger purely because you need money."

Her shoulders start shaking and he pulls her in his arms tight to his chest. She sobs heartbroken: crying with the devastated heart sore of a girl who realises her love is in vain.

"Alice... Alice," he says, his voice deep and comforting. "Nothing can be so bad that you should cry about it. Just tell me what I can do to help you."

I am ... I am crying because you are holding me so t-tight. You are s-smothering me," she sobs helpless.

He takes her by her shoulders and gently pushes her away from him. "Why do you not trust me, Alice? Why do you shy away from the truth? I know you don't love Norman."

She sniffs, wipes her hand over her eyes, takes the handkerchief he offers to her and dries her tears. "You said it yourself, you don't believe in undying love. Love is not going to make my marriage to Norman any happier. We have the same interests. We like each other. That is enough."

He swallows hard. "There is such a thing as love. You know there is. I ... e ... I was just talking... talking nonsense."

"No, you weren't. You believed yourself. If you are honest with yourself, you would admit that you still love Charlotte Hastings," she protests, she feels her eyes welling up again and quickly wipes her eyes with the handkerchief. She hates Charlotte Hastings, because she is the reason why Oliver will never love any other girl again, she thinks, even as she realises she is being unreasonable. Charlotte didn't ask her to fall in love with Oliver; she didn't even ask herself. Love is.

"Charlotte and I had a very interesting conversation earlier today," he says, sees the interest in her eyes and continues: "I can't believe that I once loved her."

"Exactly! Love is just a word. It is much more important to marry someone who shares your ideals and your interests... someone you can communicate with," she speaks her mind, but her heart screams another truth.

"If that is the truth then I – " he starts and bites off his words, the expression on his face suddenly unreadable. What is wrong with him, he thinks confused? Was he really just about to say to Alice he was willing to marry her? No... no, never! As long as his past remains a mystery, he will remain a stranger to love. And still... how can his heart ever accept Alice and Norman being married? But on the other hand: what does it matter if she marries Norman of all men? She has the right to live her own life, the right to her own happiness. But can he ever accept that she belongs to another man? Any other man? No, he is thinking like a madman, he admonishes himself.

"Why does my engagement to Norman bother you, doctor Howard? Do you mean for all of us to be so skeptical about love? Do you want all of us to remain so unhappy, just because you are?"

"Don't be your usual miss-know-it-all, Alice. I am only concerned about you because I care about you and I'm trying to be your friend, but nothing I say or do is good enough for you. And, in heaven's name, stop calling me doctor – you make me feel like a stranger in my own town."

"You keep bossing me around and telling me what to do with my own life as if are giving me orders like a doctor."

"Because you behave like a child. I have asked you several times to call me by my name. Do you find it so revolting?"

"No, but I don't like you. You've irritated me from the first moment I met you."

He stares at her in silence for a moment and feels the anger boiling up in him. "You are very opiniated, little miss, but you should know: you irritate me as much. I think you are a spoiled, real know-it-all little girl who needs a good hiding."

"You sound just like my father when his arthritis acts up, doctor Howard. Why don't you rather go find yourself some more pleasant company? I'm sure Matron Frances would be very eager to oblige."

"Matron Frances has nothing to do with our conversation! What I want to know is if you are planning to ever talk to me like an educated person? I came here to talk to you about your irrational decision to get engaged to a man you don't know at all, because I am concerned about you."

"Exactly. You are always pushing and pulling me around like a rag-doll and you scream at me as if I'm deaf! Do you treat everyone you supposedly care about like this, doctor Howard?"

She turns her head and the sunlight fall on her face; he sees the sparkling in her eyes.

"Are you enjoying your fights with me, Alice?" he asks, his voice now soft and controlled.

"From the very first moment, doctor Howard. It makes it so much easier to tell you exactly what I think. I think it is a sin to make a murderer's den of one's heart."

He unconsciously steps closer to her and looks down into her eyes, he sees the temptation of her full lips. "And you enjoy being so honest. I wonder..."

She realises too late what he is planning, his arms close around her and he kisses her hard on her lips. When he lets her go, she stumbles backward, her eyes big and bewildered on him.

He laughs muffled. "Why so quiet? Did I finally find a way to silence that sharp tongue of yours?"

Alice remains silent.

"Alright, little Alice, this is the deal: you behave yourself, and I will let you be. But if you try that tone of voice with me again, I will kiss you again even if it is in the main street on a busy Saturday morning."

Alice remains silent, staring wide-eyed at him.

"I have to leave Arundel tomorrow. I'll be back in a week," he says, now uncomfortable, turns around and disappears around the corner of the stables.

She remains standing next to Poppy's stable, and cries with the inconsolable heartbreak of a child, unaware of the tears streaming down her cheeks and dripping cold in her neck.

"My poor Alice-child!" Helen reaches her with a few steps and takes her in her arms. "If I hadn't gotten tired of waiting for you and hadn't looked out the sitting room's window, I would not... What did Oliver do to make you cry this hard, dear?" she asks concerned.

"N-Nothing," sobs Alice and cries with abandon whilst holding on to Helen.

"Nonsense, child! I have eyes in my head. I saw how he was shaking you around. Did he hurt you? Are you in pain?"

"T-Terrible pain," she sobs muffled.

"Where?" asks Helen sharply.

"Where my heart is." She looks up dejected. "Is it love, Aunt Helen? Is love the greatest pain in the world? Is it, Aunt Helen?"

Helen's eyes fill with sympathy as she looks at Alice's tearful face. "My poor Alice-child, did you get engaged to Norman Graham with the hope that you would forget about your feelings for Oliver?" she asks with sympathetic understanding.

"No, that is not what happened at all," denies Alice heftily. "Norman was only trying to help me when Lady Emily started with her insults again. Richard asked her if I could go horseback riding with him, then ... then she said that I would do anything to catch a rich husband like him." Her eyes flash, her sadness forgotten for a moment. "I was furious! Who does she think she is? Do I look like the type of girl who would marry a man just for his money?"

"Calm down, dear. Did you forget? I know you. But what happened then?"

"I told her, on the contrary, I was already engaged to someone else. She then wanted to know who the man was and … and then Norman helped me and said that it was him." She sighs disheartened. "I know it was wrong to lie, but at that moment there was nothing else I could do."

"Then it is only a fake engagement, Alice. Surely Norman realises that you don't love him?" says Helen relieved.

"I think Norman is in love with me," says Alice dejected.

"But you don't love him. You aren't seriously going to marry a man purely to put Emily in her place, child!"

Tears well up in Alice's eyes again and lays like a misty cloud between her and the reality of her pain. "What does it matter who I marry, Aunt Helen? Oliver…" she muffles a sob in Oliver's handkerchief and looks down.

Helen places her arm comforting around her shoulders and gives her a hug. "You can try, Alice-child, but you can't run away from love. If you are senseless enough, you will marry Norman, but you will never be happy. You don't choose love, it chooses you. It's got a little bit to do with destiny, fate, and what is written in the stars."

"I can never be any unhappier than what I am right at this moment, Aunt Helen. If Norman loves me – maybe I can learn to love him," she says heartbroken.

"You can learn good table manners, Alice, but not to love, because it is an inexplicable emotion born in the silent cervices of your heart. It would be a huge injustice to Norman if you marry him purely in the hope of forgetting about your feelings for Oliver," warns Helen.

Alice's eyes scream her desperation. "What am I to do, Aunt Helen? Oliver doesn't believe in love. He says it is merely a fairy tale. If he should ever guess how I feel about him, he would just laugh at me – or even worse, he would feel sorry for me." She grabs Helen's two hands in hers and pleads urgently: "Let's go back to London, Aunt Helen. I know I will forget about my foolish love if I don't see him every day."

"Do you believe yourself, Alice?" Helen asks softly.

Alice stares at her in silence and then bends her head down. "No... but I can hope."

"You have never been a coward, Alice. A hopeless love is also not a unique experience. More than thirty years ago I had to look into Henry Howard's eyes and laugh, and chat as if he were just another man, even though it felt like my heart was tearing in a million little pieces. You don't have less pride or inner strength than I do. You can also do it," says Helen with unwavering certainty.

"But if we leave...," Alice hesitates.

"You are a coward and I refuse to believe that. However difficult it may be act as usual towards Oliver. You can't forsake William now – in any case, not before you have found a good replacement. And that is another matter I want to discuss with you."

Alice looks at her questioningly.

"We came here for a vacation, Alice," Helen answers her silent question. "You became William's private nurse with the sole purpose to help Oliver. It is quite clear to me that you can't help him, therefor you have to come back to Tortington. You do still need me, dear!"

Alice sighs resolutely. "More than ever, Aunt Helen, because you understand. You will help me to be strong, Aunt Helen."

"No, Alice, I know people say you get over it, sooner or later. I would say it too, but I know it's not true. You will be happy again, that even I can ensure you. But you won't forget. You never forget. If you ever love again, it will be because something in the man reminds you of him. I can listen and be sympathetic, but you will have to learn how to live with your heartache by yourself."

"I know, but... The sooner Norman can find another nurse, the sooner we can end this charade of an engagement. And then I can go back to Tortington and... and show Oliver I feel nothing for him."

Helen flashes a smile. "That won't be necessary because he is unaware of how you feel about him. I miss our chats. Don't keep me waiting too long."

Alice flees to her room the moment Aunt Helen departs. She switches on the light and walks to the dresser mirror, her heart still pounding in her chest. She looks guiltily at her reflection, notices the deep red blush on her cheeks, the bright sparkling in her eyes, and covers her face with her hands.

No, it can't be true... And yet... just for a brief magical moment she was on a wave of ecstasy and experienced a passion she has never known before. Is this love?

The question shocks her, and she starts from the possibility.

She went to university for four years, she was surrounded by hundreds of handsome, charming men every day. She was engaged to one of these men. You see an attractive man, admire his physical beauty, feel the attraction, but tomorrow you've forgotten about it again. Desire was never love.

Is that what she feels for Oliver... desire? But he makes her so angry, and he is always laughing at her! He is so self-confident and proud and domineering and so aware of his success and how handsome he is. And to top it off, selfish and a bully – just look how he always treats her.

She knows what love is, doesn't she – she loved Robert for four years. Robert was always charming and polite. He would never have been so discourteous to kiss her like that, and even if he did... there was no magic in his kisses. Was she maybe never in love with him? She wás planning to marry him. She was content with him – well, until she wasn't. He was very self-centered, ambitious to the point of manipulation, and he did lie to her. Oliver is too straight-forward and proud to ever treat anyone so loathsome, he would rather just walk away than to use someone like that.

And if she had never met Oliver Howard... She doesn't want to admit it to herself, but if she really was honest with herself, she has no other choice.

Robert will never be Oliver. Robert fades away to someone small and insignificant next to the strong, domineering Oliver. Even if she forgets that he only wanted to marry her for her money, and if she recalls only his good characteristics, the times with him now seem so colourless and drab.

She knows it now: she never loved Robert, not with the kind of love a woman should have for a man. He was like a habit in her life, a safe pillar, but he wasn't the passionate, great love of her life.

Will Oliver be the great love of her life? She smiles bitter and sits down with a sigh on her bed. It will never be Oliver. Oliver prefers tall, manicured, formal women like Matron Frances, and a similar lackluster relationship with no magic, the same as she and Robert had. She realises it now, but Oliver doesn't want anything more than his predictable, boring relationship with Matron Frances.

If she returned to Tortington she can at least be close to Oliver again, even if it is just for the last few weeks before she and Aunt Helen return to London. If you repeat a word over and over it loses its meaning. How many more times must she repeat Oliver's name in the hope he will mean less to her with every breath she takes? What does it even matter if Oliver won't ever love her? Beggars of love are grateful for every little crumb which life sends their way: even if it is only the privilege to listen to the deep warmth of Oliver's voice.

Charlotte twists herself from Richard's passionate embrace, notices the surprise on his face, but turns her back to him.

"What's wrong, Charlotte? Aren't you happy about my surprise visit?" he asks concerned and moves closer to her.

"Happy?" she swings back to face him, discontent written over her face. "How can I be happy when, again, you make me feel like one of the poor little Jones's who were dependent on the scraps handed down by the rich and wealthy?"

"What makes you say something like that? Don't I always treat you with the greatest respect? Do I ever make you feel unworthy?" he asks puzzled.

"Not on purpose, no. But as long as you must keep your visits to me a secret… You are ashamed to introduce me to your family, right Richard? You can't forget that my father was the drunkard of Arundel," she says bitter.

"No!" he denies her accusation heftily and takes her in his arms. "You didn't choose your parent, Charlotte – as I didn't choose my mother. I have said it to you, if not once a hundred times: she believes I'm her personal property and if I don't dance to her tune, she will have me disowned."

"And your inheritance is more important that your love for me?" she asks accusingly.

"How can you even ask that, my darling? Nothing on earth is more important than you are. If you only knew how much I want to marry you," he answers with unveiled worship in his eyes.

"If you mean that: let's get married right now."

He takes a long breath. His expression in shock. "And my inheritance then? How can I give you whatever you want when I'm as poor as a church mouse?"

"Have you forgotten? I have inherited millions." Her expression is clear and lucid. "Once, I believed riches and wealth was everything I wanted, but now…" She falls silent and looks critically at Richard. He is one of the handsomest men she knows, but that is not why she had fallen in love with him. He overwhelmed her with the intensity of his love for her. Oliver… She was a fool to follow him the other day. Oliver has always been the man with the unshakable morals; a man of integrity. She should've expected his judgment of her to marry an old man for money.

"Do you expect me to be dependent on my rich wife's money?" Richard asks offended.

"Didn't you say you were interested in taking over the farm operations?"

"I did, and it is the truth. I hate Stanton Manor and the factory. If I should inherit my mother's family farm, I would make that my home. The manager of the factory can live in Stanton Estate, or perhaps someone else would want to buy it and convert it into a hotel," he answers uninterested.

"And if you are disowned?"

His expression hardens. "Then there is nothing left for me because you won't marry a poor man and I won't allow my rich wife to take care of me."

"No, Richard." She puts her arms around him and rests her cheek against his chest. "The farm is a huge piece of land, but absolutely useless to me. I can't manage the farm. If you love me enough to marry me despite your mother... You will be the head of the house even if I inherited the land."

"A farm manager can do the same job," he says gruffly.

"Maybe, but a farm manager can't love me unconditionally. I... I haven't forgotten where I have come from. Even if I could not love you, I would have married you if only out of gratefulness, because you never remind me of my background or resent me for marrying old Thomas Hastings for his money."

He looks at her in wonder. "How can I ever resent you for your marriage? You were good to your husband." He smiles boyishly. "I am a jealous man. I am glad you didn't love Thomas with all your heart."

"If you love me, then invite me to Stanton Manor to meet your parents," she demands.

Richard hesitates, and then smiles excited. "Why not? I will ask Alice to pretend you two are old friends."

"Alice? That is not perhaps the nurse taking care of your father?" She looks at him suspiciously. "I heard she was very beautiful."

"She is, but she is already engaged to doctor Norman Graham, so you don't have to be upset," he teases her and kisses her on her lips.

"Are you sure she will play along?"

"She will. Alice is just that type of girl: she is a trusted friend, and she knows how unreasonable my mother can be."

His laughter is clear and care-free. "We are going to outmaneuver my mother, Charlotte! And I already know: the moment my mother has met you, she won't be able but to love you."

She isn't looking for love, only acknowledgement, Charlotte thinks bitter. To be a guest at Stanton Manor – ten years ago she wouldn't even have dreamed of such a possibility. To be accepted by Emily Howard, would be a personal victory for herself, especially after her humiliating talk with the haughty Oliver.

Helen walks slowly along the riverbank, her gaze on Oliver who, as if he is part of the gray rock, is sitting fixed on the rock staring out over the flowing water. She takes place next to him and he remains silent, his gaze still on the river.

"You made my niece cry, Oliver," she is the first to break the silence between them.

"I'm sorry," he answers hoarse.

"Are you really?"

"He looks at her sharply. His eyes are purple-black pools with emotions she can't explain. "Alice didn't get engaged to Norman because she loves him, Aunt Helen. She hardly knows the man. How can she love him?"

"Did she deny that she loved him?" asks Helen calmly.

"She said love was just a word; that communication and shared interests were the only prerequisites for a happy marriage. Does that make any sense to you, Aunt Helen?"

"I would say the girl is being very practical," she answers approvingly.

"Practical!" He roars and looks embarrassed. "Sorry, I didn't want to lose my temper, Aunt Helen, but a few days ago little Alice... Alice spoke with such conviction of the importance of love. There must be another reason why she decided to marry Norman. Does she perhaps have financial problems?"

Helen suppresses a smile with effort. "Definitely not. Alice will never tell you herself, but she has inherited quite a bit of capital, shares, and treasured family jewels from her grandmother on her father's side. She sees the surprise on his face and smiles. "Alice is not a millionaire, but she surely doesn't have to marry any man for money."

"Oh. Then... then you believe she has fallen in love with Norman?"

"Of course not. I say this without bragging: I have an extremely beautiful niece. There have always been admirers in her life, but until now she has always followed her healthy intellect."

"And her healthy intellect made her decide that Norman would be her future husband?" He asks sarcastically.

"Yes, alright, you sound like a jealous lover – or an overprotective father, Oliver. Alice has basically been forced into the engagement with Norman because..."

"Forced!" He repeats his eyes in narrow slits of gleaming black coals. "If Norman touches Alice..." He becomes aware of Helen's amused expression on her face and explains mumbling: "Her father... her brothers aren't here to protect her. She is my guest. It is my responsibility to protect her."

"Not against Norman, he was only helping her when Emily made it clear to Richard that Alice wasn't good enough to go horseback riding with him. I know my niece: she is proud and impulsive, and that is the reason why she then told Emily that she was already engaged to someone else. Obviously, Emily then wanted to know who her fiancé was, and it is then that doctor Graham decided to help Alice." Helen falls silent and notices with satisfaction the expression of perplexity on Oliver's face.

"But..." He closes his mouth and frowns grimly. "Why didn't she just tell me it was only a fake engagement?"

"Did you give her a chance, Oliver? I was watching the two of you from the window in Emily's private sitting room. You stormed my niece and started shoving her around. Believe me, young man, if I had been in the vicinity, I would've put you in your place!"

His face colours in embarrassment. "Well, yes... perhaps I did act a little...e... untactful."

"Untactful, or jealous?" she asks straightforwardly.

He stares at her in silence. "Only overprotective, Aunt Helen. I consider Alice a friend, and she is in this situation to help me, so I feel obliged to keep a watchful eye over her."

"As long as you also feel obliged to apologise to her for your boorish behaviour then I have nothing more to say about the matter," says Helen, gets up and walks away without a further word.

Oliver watches her with a feeling of resentful powerlessness. Why are women so eager to think a man is jealous when he is merely acting like a gentleman? But his behaviour wasn't actually that of a gentleman, he admits to himself. He was furious – mad enough to commit murder – because Alice... Alice is too young to get married, he decides and feels strangely relieved. Marriage is a serious decision and therefore a girl must be much more mature before she can consider marriage. He will talk to Alice and explain the matter to her...when he returns next week. Hopefully, if this trip to Ireland goes well, he'll have all his answers he's been looking for his entire life, and Alice doesn't have to stay at Stanton Manor any longer or continue this fake engagement with Norman. And after that he and she can be friends again.

Chapter 9

The house is pitch-black and silent in a way that is fast becoming familiar in its miserableness. It has been a long, long time since any sort of party was hosted at Stanton Manor, and even longer since there was laughter echoing through the passages. Guests are strictly prohibited unless they're formerly invited by or approved by his haughty Aunt Emily. Aunt Emily has never handled stress very well, and Uncle William's illness has been pushing her straight to the edge, Oliver thinks to himself as he finds his way silently to the study. Not because she is at all heart-broken over Uncle William's fast deterioration but because she is so desperate to find and destroy the envelope and the documents which hold the answers to his past before Uncle William passes away, he thinks cynically.

Oliver hears a creak down the dark passage drifting through the passage of the first floor, and he stops, waiting, listening.

Was that just this old mansion and its moans and groans or is someone else also lurking around in the dark? Everyone should be asleep by now, it's just after midnight. Oliver waits a few minutes, when there's no sound again, he slowly makes his way to the study again.

It's been years since his aunt and Uncle had shared a bedroom. She had even moved to the opposite wing as her quarters. And now with Uncle William being so ill, it has also become a matter of convenience so doctor Norman Graham and the nursing staff could come and go whenever Uncle William needed anyone, and of course most importantly, to ensure that Aunt Emily's precious sleep wouldn't be disturbed.

The house feels so much darker these days since from what he can remember. Where the house once had a brightness to it, an openness even in the late nightly hours, now the shadows were oppressive and seemed to cling to every surface. Even though Oliver grew up in Stanton Manor, the passages have an almost ominous feeling to them now.

Well, one thing hasn't changed, he is still the intruder in this manor, he thinks with a smirk, and tonight also literally. The windows are kept firmly shut, so as not to let in too much of a chill, and the curtains are now almost always drawn closed here on the second floor. Miss Crompton had tried to argue with Aunt Emily that some sunlight and fresh air will do Uncle William the world of good, but his aunt had been firm on the matter. And everyone knows not to press any matter with Aunt Emily, lest one wants to unleash one of her mad outbursts. The drawn curtains and closed windows didn't truly have any bearing on anything, after all, save for the depressing atmosphere it creates. And having a dying man in the manor is certainly enough of a dimming force that they could not even blame it all on the closed windows or the now stuffy passages. But tonight, it suits him perfectly so he can pursue his nightly search unnoticed.

As he draws close to the study, Oliver hears voices coming from Uncle William's bedroom door which sits open just a crack. He can hear Aunt Emily's high-pitched voice and Uncle William's breathless groaning as their voices drift out to him in the dark. It sounds as if they're in the middle of a heated argument.

"I want him to know," says Uncle William. "All this time, all these years, the boy deserves it, and I don't have much time left to make things right with him."

Aunt Emily insists, "Stop talking, you old fool! You made a promise to me!"

"A promise I shouldn't have made." Uncle William counters, no small amount of bitterness in his words. "I'm dying, and we both know it. Oliver deserves to know the truth."

Aunt Emily sounds almost frantic when she says, "He's never going to know! You promised me that he would never know who his real parents are. I won't let that change, William. I won't!"

Oliver's interest is instantly piqued. He presses himself to the wall and carefully nudges the door open, just a touch more. He can only sort of see into the room from here; the dim bed lamp is switched on, the foot of his uncle's bed is visible, the blankets piled in a heap near the hardwood foot board. His Aunt's arm comes into view when she throws an arm out a moment later.

"You cannot go back on your promise," insists Aunt Emily. "Richard is the sole heir of Stanton Estate. I won't let you take that from my son, our son!"

"My darling Emily," says Uncle William in a soft faint voice.

"Oh, shut up William! Don't even start with your delirious mumbling! Tonight, you will tell me where you have hidden that envelope, or so help me..."

"What has happened to us? This lie has only brought us misery." Uncle William interrupts her in a mumble.

There's a long pause, and then Aunt Emily stands at the foot of the bed, facing towards Uncle William, clenching her hands in fists. Her black hair is in a mess and there are tears on her cheeks, but instead of looking like the grieving wife she seems devious Oliver thinks guiltily... but the guilt isn't enough to kill his curiosity.

His aunt and uncle have not ever spoken about Oliver's birth parents. They have always been very firm about the fact that his parents had died, and their identities were of no consequence. But the consequence to him of not knowing is that he has no identity. How can he have a future when he doesn't have a past? But this conversation between Uncle William and Aunt Emily makes it seem as if there's another layer to the reason why they never wanted to tell him the truth about his birth. Something deeper and darker than Oliver had originally realized. There's a tightness forming in his chest, a bundle of nerves and anticipation that keeps swelling up and up, flooding into him.

"I know that I promised to keep it a secret," says Uncle William.

Before he can continue, Aunt Emily shakes her head. "The only other person who could ever corroborate Oliver's lineage without those documents is Henry."

Oliver's late Uncle Henry left for Ireland nearly thirty years ago and died in World War Two. It caused a great shake up within the family. Uncle Henry was Uncle William's older brother and the sole heir to Stanton Estate and the transport business. But when he died, naturally Uncle William inherited everything. It isn't something that people like to discuss. In fact, Oliver's uncle and aunt very seldom brought up Uncle Henry's name, if ever. Up until now, Oliver has always presumed it was because there are simply too many bad memories attached to the man, but now he wonders if there might have been something more.

"I know," says Uncle William. "And if anyone else finds out that he's still alive, then this house of cards will come down on all of us. There are so many knots and twists in this lie, Emily. We've gotten ourselves so tangled up in it all, I can barely tell where one end starts anymore. But I do know, it is time to end this."

"William..." Aunt Emily trails off, her breath hitching.

He doesn't dare open the door up any wider, lest he risk getting caught. Instead, he closes his eyes and tries to focus on what they're saying, for his uncle's voice drops into a low whisper, "I know that he didn't want to come home scarred as he was... that he didn't want to face our parents... but I wish that I could see him. I wish I could see Henry just one more time. He always maintained that he was content with his position as a lecturer in economics at the University of Dublin, and I'm glad for that. But he's my older brother, and I miss him so terribly that it's almost an ailment in and of its own."

"It will never happen! Over my dead body!" sneers Aunt Emily.

"I have done what I have promised you. I have never breathed a word about Oliver's heritage, nor about Henry," says Uncle William. "But Emily, I am tired. I want to end all of these lies. I want to straighten my affairs. I need to fix what I have done."

Aunt Emily tells him, "I won't allow that, William. You made a promise to me, and I will make damn sure you keep it. I'm the one who has to stay behind and handle it all. Richard will be the sole heir to Stanton Estate, and that foundling child will never know any of this."

There's a long, long pause of silence.

"William! Do you hear me? Don't you dare fall asleep on me!" Aunt Emily shrieks.

But Uncle William doesn't respond. It's a clear dismissal if one has ever been given. Oliver is suddenly at risk of getting caught! Quickly Oliver peels away from the wall and silently makes his way down the dark passage. He makes sure to avoid the creaky floorboards and flings himself into the first open door that he comes across.

By a stroke of luck, it's the study. Oliver hurries over to a shelf and squeezes in between the shelf and the tall grandfather clock. He can hear his aunt move down the hall, and then keep going. She doesn't so much as pause outside the study door.

Relief washes over Oliver. He finds the secret shelf-door, he slips through it and starts to make his way down the stairs which will bring him out in the kitchen and then he can leave the manor through the back door.

Back in his car which he parked down the road behind some trees, Oliver lets his head fall back, pressing it hard against the headrest of the driver's seat, and stares up at the roof. The conversation that he just listened in on rolls through him like ocean waves, tumultuous and spinning.

Oliver isn't certain what's more of a shock. That Uncle William felt the need to make a promise to Aunt Emily to keep his lineage a secret – a promise that even Uncle William's death bed can't seem to break. Or the fact that his long dead Uncle Henry is still alive.

Why did Uncle Henry not want to come home after the war? He was the sole heir to the entire Estate and the transport business. Why would he have given that up to remain a lecturer at a university all these years? And if that were his choice, why then pretend to be dead?

Scarred and embarrassed, that's what Uncle William had just said. But could there be more to it? That surely there must have been, or else Uncle Henry wouldn't know where Oliver's parentage lay, and the whole thing wouldn't be a knotted mess of secrets, as Uncle William had called it, Oliver thinks to himself.

That, of course, leads into a new problem.

Oliver knows more about his birth now than he ever has before. There's someone out there who might be willing to answer his questions and tell him the truth of the matter. Uncle Henry, whom has been thought dead for many years, is truly alive and simply in another country.

And now Oliver must decide what he's going to do about it.

For three days and four nights, Oliver rolls things around in his head. It's on the fourth night that he comes to a final decision. If his uncle Henry is truly alive, and really does know the truth about Oliver's lineage, then Oliver must find him!

Before sunrise the next morning, Oliver pulls out his suitcase and then he packs with swift decisiveness. Oliver brings no frivolities with him. He keeps the suitcase light, it's going to be a quick flight over to Dublin, find his uncle, get his answers, and fly back. Two days at most. With little planning beyond that, he pulls on his shoes and his jacket, fetches his wallet, and heads for his car.

He hefts the suitcase up into his arms, carrying it down the stairs of the hotel. A few members of the hotel staff are already up and working, the sound of breakfast being prepared drifting out of the kitchen. Oliver nods at the house cleaner when he passes her, and then hurries through the front doors.

The porter is standing on the path directly in front of the front doors. Oliver freezes for a moment, and then remembers that his leaving isn't all suspicious. He told Alice he had to go back to London for a few days, everyone will assume it is for a patient who needs his attention. Feeling more confident in himself, he lets out a 'good morning' to the older man as he walks past him to where his car is parked. It's just over an hour's drive up the A283 to Heathrow Airport, so he'll be there at about seven o'clock this morning. The flight he booked last night to Dublin is only at ten past eleven this morning. He'll be at least four hours early, but he just couldn't wait one minute longer in that hotel room, he'll rather sit and wait at the airport. Then another hour and a bit to fly to Dublin. If all goes well, he'll be in Dublin by around one o'clock and then he's going to the University of Dublin to find Uncle Henry immediately.

There is no real fluff or grandness in arriving at Dublin. He rents himself a small room near the airport, checks into it, changes into something a bit more appropriate for meeting with a long-lost family member, and then heads out. The University of Dublin is large and sprawling. Oliver has to ask around quite a lot to find out which hall hosts the lectures on economics.

When he finally locates the right room, he finds that there's an older man within it, clearing chalk from the black board. At the sound of the door opening, the man turns and tells him, "The lecture is over for the day, I'm afraid. If you've missed it, you'll need to ask around and see if someone can lend out their notes." Oliver looks into the face of the middle-aged man with gray-blonde hair and an eyepatch over his right eye. A terrible scar runs from his right eye to his chin. The man is tall and thin, but broad-shouldered. His scarred face doesn't detract from the professionalism found in the rest of his stature; black slacks and a tidy looking suit jacket, complete with a dark green tie and a pale blue button up.

"I'm not one of your students, actually," says Oliver, stepping into the room. "You must be Professor John Milton. They told me that you were one of the lecturers in economics."

"Not a student?" The man puts down the eraser and claps his hands together a few times to try and wipe the dust from them, white puffs clouding up into the air. He moves around the desk and crosses the room with a limp in his walk to where Oliver is standing, looking him up and down.

"I dare say, you're much too young to be anyone looking to hire me for something, and I don't think you have the look about you for someone hoping to get an apprenticeship."

"I'm not here for either of those reasons," says Oliver, agreeably. "My name is Oliver, and I was hoping that you might be able to help me find someone."

Almost tartly, John says, "I don't disclose information about my students." And then, a touch more agreeable, "I think a person's private information is just that, private, if we're both being honest chaps about it. And besides that, I'm not sure I could be of much assistance in any case, I've got too many students who come in for a few classes and then change subjects when they realize economics does actually require one to attend class." He chuckles.

"It's not about a student," says Oliver. "I'm looking for someone else that's supposed to work here at the University, in this lecture hall. A man named Henry Howard is supposed to be a professor of economics here."

"Henry," echoes John, sounding almost mystified by the name. "Whatever could you want with Henry?"

"He's my uncle. I've come to give him important family news. It's about his brother," says Oliver, which isn't entirely a lie. The way that Uncle William had spoken about wanting to see his older brother one more time, it had cut a wound into Oliver's heart. He couldn't imagine what it must be like to know that you're dying, and to not even have the comfort of your family to draw on.

John purses his lips together but waves a hand as though to urge Oliver on.

Oliver tells him, "His brother is dying of cancer. And he wants to see Uncle Henry one last time, before he passes on."

A look that can only be called pure grief settles onto John's face. He shifts his balance to his left leg, and then leads Oliver by the shoulder over to one of the front row desks where the students sit. "Have a seat – Oliver, was it?"

Oliver nods and sits down. To his surprise, the professor sits down beside him, angled to face Oliver. He reaches out and gives an awkward pat to Oliver's knee, as if trying to comfort him.

Then John says, "I'm sorry, but it seems as if you've come out all this way for nothing."

"It isn't nothing," says Oliver. "Uncle William is my adoptive father. And if there's anything I can do to convince Uncle Henry to come back home, even for a little bit, I'll do it. I just need to know where to find him."

John shakes his head. "That is the problem, though. I don't know who told you that Henry was here, but they were wrong."

"He's a professor here," insists Oliver.

"Yes, he used to be," says John. "Henry and I were colleagues here at the university and we were both on the premises when the German bomb raid happened during the war. But that is about thirty years ago. I have never quite been able to put into words the horror of that day, and I sure am not able to magically find them now. The sounds. The heat." John closes his eyes and shakes his head, mouth pulled into a thin line. "Your uncle, he was right here with me."

Oliver has never spoken to anyone that was so thoroughly entrenched in the war. He's read about it, of course. Everyone has. They were taught the history in school. And they all knew someone who knew someone who had been in the war themselves or a family member who experienced the war.

But Uncle Henry was never around to talk with, and no one really likes discussing what it was like to be stuck in the middle of a seemingly endless war, let alone the hell of the bomb-raids that innocent civilians had not been expecting.

That tightness that has been building up in Oliver's chest since he first eavesdropped on his aunt and uncle's conversation swells up that much more, until it feels like he's about to choke on it.

John either doesn't notice Oliver's discomfort, too focused on his own, or he simply has no words of comfort to offer the younger man.

Instead, he continues, "He was a hero, your uncle. I would have died that day if it weren't for Henry. He helped me out of the rubble, made sure that I got free before the rest of the roof came tumbling down on me. You can obviously see I did not come away Scot-free from that attack." And he gestures with his hand to his face. "But I was still one of the lucky ones." He says bitterly.

Oliver glances up at the ceiling, as though half worried it might fall in a second time. Large parts of the University of Dublin had to be rebuilt in the wake of the war, though the construction crew tried their best not to make it jarringly obvious which parts were new and which ones had history to them. After a moment, where John offers up no more information, Oliver looks back at the older man and swallows hard.

He asks, "What happened to him, then? Uncle William said that Uncle Henry was here, that he was alive. I think there must have been a letter between them, though I'm not sure of that fact."

"There might have been," says John. "He made it to the hospital, I was told, and he lived for three days under the care of the doctors there. He might have had a nurse pen a letter for your Uncle William, he died in the hospital from his injuries."

A heaviness seems to settle in the air between them then, and Oliver swallows hard. "Is that true? You aren't lying?"

"I wouldn't have any reason to tell you anything that wasn't truthful," says John, with a shake of his head. "Henry died because he stayed and helped me, and I will carry that guilt with me for the rest of my life. Whatever letter your uncle got, I'm sorry to say that he's clung to a false hope all of these years."

Oliver thinks on that for a moment and can see how it might make a bit of sense. And yet there's something else that bothers him. After all, he only came seeking answers for his uncle as half the reality. The rest of it, well, that had been a wholly selfish reason. And… it's a wholly selfish reason that still very much motivated his travelling here to find his Uncle Henry.

"Alright," says Oliver. "I'll be sad to pass that news on to Uncle William. He had so been hoping to see his brother one last time. He really is extremely ill." A pause, and then, "Would there be someone else here I should inform about my uncle's failing health? Did Uncle Henry perhaps have a wife? Or a child?"

John thinks on it for a moment, and then gives a slow shake of his head. "I know that Henry was married, but they never had any children. And I don't think there would be a way to tell his wife. From what I know, she left Ireland after Henry's death. I wouldn't have any idea of how or where to find her."

That hits Oliver like a punch in his gut. It means that there's no way out here either for him to find out who his parents are, who he is, and Oliver can't come up with any other ways to find out the truth about his lineage.

He stands up, trying not to look too put out about the whole thing, and gives what he hopes is a respectful nod before holding out his hand. "I appreciate you taking the time to speak with me, professor Milton, thank you. I had best get going, though. If Uncle Henry isn't with us anymore, then I need to let his brother know."

John stands up and takes the offered hand, giving it a firm shake. "I hope that your flight home is safe, lad, and that your uncle might take a turn for the better. You never know when a miracle might occur."

Oliver had been hoping that this conversation would be his miracle. The fact that it isn't, well, he supposes that there's no changing it. Instead, he says his goodbyes to the man and heads back out into the passage of the university. He had gone across the seas looking for answers and is now forced to come to terms with the fact that he took this trip for nothing. Oliver doesn't waste time in Ireland. As soon as he realizes that there are no answers to be found, he sets about purchasing another flight ticket back to London.

Emily looks up angrily as Richard walks into the dining room with his riding clothes. "And now, Richard? You know we have lunch strictly at one o'clock. And why are you dressed in your riding clothes? Is that how I raised you?" she asks with cold disapproval.

"I went riding along the river and totally lost sense of time, Mother. I apologise. If you expect me to first go and change then I would rather grab a quick bite in town," he answers and looks at her fearlessly.

"Sit down, Richard," says Beatrice impatiently. "We are again eating leftovers today; cold meat and salad...Gmpf! My poor stomach cramps up with cold food, but in this house, nobody ever bothers to ask me what I would like to eat."

"How about a warm packet of fish and chips, Ms. Crompton?" asks Richard who is still standing behind his chair.

"Dear child, would you really..." Beatrice starts eagerly.

"Sit, Richard!" Emily interrupts her abruptly. "And you, Beatrice, can only benefit from following my healthy eating habits, before you eat yourself into an early grave."

"As if my death would bother you, now that you have decided that Alice will take care of you in the future," says Beatrice offended.

"Excuse me, Ms. Crompton?" asks Alice. She chokes on a piece of salad and starts to cough uncontrollable.

"Help nurse Browning, Beatrice," commands Emily. "And you, Richard, don't have to stand there like a salt pilar. Help the girl."

Alice takes a sip of water from the glass next to her plate and says a little hoarse: "Everything is fine, Lady Howard. I don't need any help."

"Why don't you call me Aunt Emily, Alice? Seeing that you are practically part of the family we don't have to remain so formal anymore," says Emily, and smiles friendly.

Thank heavens she doesn't have food in her mouth, or she would choke again, thinks Alice and stares at Emily speechless.

"Good heavens!" says Beatrice baffled. "Do you have a fever,

Emily?"

"I think my mother drinks in secret," grins Richard and sits down.

Emily looks at Richard suspiciously. "You are suddenly behaving quite rudely towards me, Richard. Have you not perhaps been drinking in secret?"

No, I only started to not fear my mother, Richard thinks to himself, but he doesn't answer her. Charlotte loves him. She will marry him, even if he doesn't inherit one cent. He knows deep in his heart that he doesn't want to lose his inheritance, but if that is the only way... He still has his self-respect. He will work like a mad-man on Charlotte's farm and double the business. If he has to be a slave for the rest of his live, then he prefers to belong to Charlotte.

"Leave the boy in peace, Emily. Aren't there more important matters you want to discuss?" asks Beatrice meaningful.

"Thank you for reminding me, Beatrice," says Emily smiling and looks at Alice. "I had the privilege of this morning of receiving a visit from an old friend, Alice: your aunt, professor doctor Helen Upton."

"I am aware of that, Lady Howard," answers Alice evenly, not trusting Emily's sudden over-friendliness.

"If you aren't rich, you have to be highly educated, or you aren't welcome in Stanton Manor, Alice," mocks Richard.

"Or you must work like a slave and eat left-overs," bemoans Beatrice. "When are you bringing the fish and chips, Richard?"

"Get in your car and go buy yourself fish and chips, Beatrice," says Emily furious. "You are interrupting an important conversation."

"Please, Emily, stop with your dramatics. Say what you want to say, so Richard can go and get the fish and chips," says Beatrice impatiently and pushes a tomato around with her fork in her plate.

Emily ignores her and resumes her conversation with Alice. "I am sorry you haven't told me right at the start that you are Helen's niece, Alice. As the Howard's of Stanton Estate, we have a certain standard to maintain, and we have to choose our friends carefully. But now that I have come to learn so much more about you... Why don't you take the rest of the day off? Beatrice can look after William and Richard can show you around. Richard, take Alice out for dinner tonight. Show her what Arundel has to offer."

Alice stares at Emily, looking for the right words to answer her, but Richard is first: "Did you forget Alice is engaged, Mother?"

Emily waves her hand in the air. "Who is Norman Graham really? A poor, struggling doctor who wants to marry a rich girl so he can use her money to pay off his practice." Her eyes search for those of the shocked Alice. "I consider it my obligation to warn you against Norman Graham, Alice. He is only interested in your inheritance. But should you marry Richard..." She smiles proudly. "The Howard's wealth is evident."

"If I marry who?" roars Richard and hits the table with his right fist.

Alice looks at him and bursts out laughing. He jerks his head in her direction and the anger leaves his eyes. He starts laughing, then throws his head back and roars with laughter.

"Can we now get the fish and chips, Richard?" asks Beatrice hopeful.

As an answer Richard and Alice laughs even louder.

Emily knocks with the handle of her knife on the table, her face twisted in anger. "How dare you laugh at me, Richard? Have you forgotten I have the power to disown you?"

Richard's laughter stops at once. He looks at Alice and asks seriously: "Would you want to marry me, Alice?"

"Just as much as you would want to marry me. We don't love each other," she answers honestly.

He turns to Emily. "There is your answer, Mother. Please excuse me. I'm going to get our fish and chips, Ms. Crompton," he says and gets up.

"Richard, wait! We have to seriously discuss... Richard, listen to me!" Emily screams, but he has already left the room.

Emily grabs the saltshaker and jerks her arm backwards.

"Don't, Emily!" Beatrice's command is calm, but unquestionable. "Throw that saltshaker, and my bags are packed."

For a moment it seems as if Emily is going to throw Beatrice with the saltshaker, but then the anger seeps out of her face, and she places the saltshaker back on the table. Her head bows down, something broken in the hanging of her shoulders.

"I am sorry for having to disappoint you, Lady Howard," says Alice remorseful, "but I don't love Richard. Excuse me, please."

Beatrice waits until Alice have left the room and puts her hand sympathetically on Emily's shoulder. "You have known it all of these years, Emily. Richard would grow up sooner or later. I must give it to you: you managed to keep him tied to you for an exceptionally long time, much longer than I thought, but he doesn't fear your threats anymore. Don't try to dictate to him any longer, or you will lose him for good."

"He is my son... mine! I am his mother. He will do as I say," says Emily, her voice low and muffled, her hands balled into fists."

"Did you let your parents dictate to you, Emily?"

Emily looks up. There is a frown on her forehead. "What are you trying to say, Beatrice?"

"Your parents always gave you whatever you wanted; they made you believe the universe revolved around you. You always took, you never gave."

"That isn't true! I have given Richard everything his eyes saw. I never denied him anything."

"Everything you could buy with money, yes. But do you love him enough to give him his freedom, Emily?"

"Freedom?" asks Emily incomprehensible. "Richard is free to come and go as he pleases."

"No, Emily. Richard must always report where he is going and what he is doing – and then you even phone him because you don't trust him. DO you call that love, or possessiveness?" asks Beatrice straightforward.

"I must protect him against gold diggers. Richard is a handsome man and the sole heir to Stanton Estate. If he marries the wrong woman..."

"Richard is a man of twenty-eight. Give him the opportunity to make his own mistakes, and to learn from those mistakes. It is his right."

A light of insanity starts flickering in the dark pools of Emily's eyes. "I have the upper hand, Beatrice. If Richard doesn't marry a woman of my choice…" She falls silent, gasping, her face contorted in hate.

"You will make sure William disowns him? Is that what you want to say, Emily?" asks Beatrice quietly.

Emily's lips pull into a taunting grin. "You are cleverer than you look, Beatrice Crompton. But you are correct: if Richard marries without my consent, he won't inherit one cent. I will make sure of that."

"Money can't buy everything," says Beatrice, and groaningly gets up from her chair. "And now you must excuse me. Talks like these just makes me hungry. I think there is still a box of chocolates in my room."

What does she do now, Emily wonders with a feeling of unknown powerlessness? She kan behave like a lunatic or pretend she is having a nervous breakdown, but Beatrice will know she was only faking it; Beatrice will pack her bags and leave without glancing back once. William… No, William won't help her. She rejected William years ago when he brough Oliver to Stanton Estate and he never tried to reconcile with her after that. Richard… She can't lose Richard's love. But she would have to do something drastic to ensure he doesn't also turn against her.

Alice listens to the storm wind of the southeastern pulling at the windows and moaning around the corners of the house. Then she sits up restless on her bed and switches on her bedside lamp. The unwelcome cold makes her shiver, and she gets out of her bed and pulls a tracksuit pant and sweater over her pajamas. She won't sleep tonight, she realises. She will sneak to the kitchen, make herself a hot chocolate to drink, and find a book to read in William's study. The more uninteresting the book, the better, it might lull her to sleep, she thinks and switched on her torch.

A moment later she closes her bedroom door soundlessly behind her, quickly glances up and down the dark passage and sneaks to the stairs. Thank the heavens for this stormy night, she thinks and smiles. Tonight, the stairs can creak because this wind makes the entire house creak.

She reaches the bottom of the stairs and sees a dim light down the passage to her right. She switches off her torch, waits a moment and then moves light-footedly to the passage door. The Passage is dark, but the study door is open, and the main light is switched on.

Is there someone else in Stanton Manor who can also not sleep tonight, she wonders and walks to the study. She audibly gasps for her breath when she sees Emily behind the large desk.

Emily quickly looks up, for a moment looking guilty like she was caught red-handed stealing and then smiles warmly. "You come as if you were sent, Alice. I need your help."

"Oh..." Alice swallows and walks closer uncertain. "I couldn't sleep. I wanted to look for a book to read."

"Don't make excuses. You are free to come and go as you please," says Emily friendly. Her gaze measures Alice. "But if you really can't sleep, then maybe you can help me searching..."

"I will help with the greatest pleasure. What are we looking for?" asks Alice in wonder.

"A packet of documents and letters. I... e ... I gave it to William years ago, but he can't remember where he has put them. If you could possibly find them – I would compensate you generously for your trouble."

Alice sees the sly expression on Emily's face and knows she doesn't have to ask why the documents and letters are so important to her. Oliver. The secret hiding place Uncle William referred to. Aunt Emily knows that the evidence to Oliver's lineage is hidden somewhere in the house but why is it necessary for her to search for it at night, while everyone else is sleeping?

"I don't want compensation, Lady Howard, but I will help you to look for it with pleasure," she says calmly.

"As you wish. The documents and letters were in a large brown envelope. I assume I don't have to ask you not to read the contents."

Alice keeps her face expressionless. "No, you don't."

"Then we understand each other but… there is something else. I don't want anyone else to know about this. Beatrice is a gossiper and William will only get upset that he isn't able to remember where he had put the envelope. Do you understand?"

"Completely, Lady Howard," answers Alice, and forces a smile.

"Then I will go to bed again. Beatrice has this habit of looking in on me announced or unannounced," says Emily, smiles in conspiracy and walks out of the study.

Alice walks to the desk and almost faint from fear as one of the sections of the bookcase, to her left, suddenly swings open and Oliver walks into the room.

"Close your mouth, girl, if you scream now, I will be forced to knock you out," he whispers and quickly walks towards her.

Chapter 10

How can she pretend to be upset with this tall, dark man walking towards her, when her heart wants to bounce out of her chest at the sight of him, wonders Alice with a powerless feeling? He was gone for a week, and she missed him. She doesn't want to argue with him; she wants to walk into his arms and plead with him to love her as she loves him. And then what? She still has her self-respect, and she won't humiliate herself like that. She will show him disdain – disdain because he doesn't love her, she decides and lifts her chin challenging.

"Why should I still protect you?" she asks resentful. "You aren't my friend but my enemy. You deny me the love of a wonderful man such as Norman Graham."

Oliver smiles lazily, tauntingly. "My dearest Alice, I wish for you all the love you can have. It is your incapacity to love a man which has me concerned."

"Look who's talking! Aren't you the all-knowing man who told me only recently that an undying love is merely a fairy tale?" she asks angrily.

"Touché. But we are now talking about you, little Alice. Women do believe in the wonder of love – adult women. You are still way too young to consider such a serious decision as marriage," he answers with a confidence which makes Alice's blood start to boil.

"You insulting nitwit! Who are you to dictate to me? My aunt Helen is very happy about my engagement to Norman," she says tauntingly.

He laughs muffled. "Oh, yes, I know ... I know. Aunt Helen is ecstatic and relieved that it is only a fake engagement."

Alice stares at him baffled and then her eyes flash like green bolts of lightning. "You... you miserable conniver! How dare you force my aunt to... to discuss personal information with you?"

"Belief me, that was not difficult at all," he answers, his voice warm with subdued laughter. "I have this irresistible charm that makes women just... well... trust me."

She doesn't have to pretend to hate Oliver Howard anymore, because at this very moment she has every reason to really hate him with every cell in her body. His eyes and his voice taunt her because he knows her secret. But this has always been the case: she only amuses him; even though she was foolish enough to had hoped that maybe one day she would see an expression of love in his eyes, she thinks bitter.

"I lied to aunt Helen about my engagement because I knew she wouldn't approve of such a sudden engagement," she tries unconvincingly.

He takes her by her shoulders and her body jerks involuntarily under his touch. He frowns concerned. "Are you scared of me, Alice? You surely must know I would never do anything to hurt you," he interprets her reaction wrongly.

"Your touch disgusts me," she says coldly, and prays she doesn't burst into tears again. He mustn't talk to her as if he cares for her, mustn't look at her as if she actually matters to him, because then she can't suppress her love for him, she thinks hopelessly.

He looks at her intensively, his expression inexorable. "Do you mean that Alice? Does my touch disgust you?"

She hesitates, staring speechless into the unreadable depths of his purple-blue eyes and then shakes her head. "No... not really, but the circumstances... As long as you can't accept that I'm more than capable to make my own decisions about my life, it would be better if we stay out of each other's way."

"And your promise to help me uncover the truth about my lineage?" he asks contemplating.

"E... yes. I will still help you. Aunt Emily asked me to look for a brown envelope with letters and documents. She said she gave the envelope to Uncle William years ago to keep safe but now he can't remember where he had put it." She forgets about her personal feelings and continues excitedly: "It can mean only one thing: Aunt Emily knows about the evidence about your past. She must have a serious reason why she would want to destroy it."

He frowns in disbelief. "Has aunt Emily made you her confidant?"

"More than just her confidant," she answers with a grim smile. "Aunt Emily is so impressed about the fact that I am the niece of professor doctor Helen Upton, that she is insisting Richard and I should be married."

"The snobbish old witch!" he explodes. "I hope you used your healthy mind and refused to give in to her wishes."

"I don't think my healthy mind had anything to do with it, but it just so happened that I'm already engaged, and I am very well aware of Richard's love for Charlotte Hastings," she answers moved.

"Thank heavens for small mercies." He looks at her intently. "What now, Alice? What are you going to do when you find that envelope?"

"It's your property, isn't it?"

He smiles relieved. "Thank you, little Alice. I realise I don't deserve your loyalty because I have behaved like a beast towards you. Will it mean anything if I said I'm truly sorry for ever making you cry?"

She swallows at the throbbing knob in her throat and avoids looking into his eyes. "I have already forgotten about it. I am more concerned about why it is so important to Aunt Emily to find those documents and letters about your lineage. I don't doubt for one second she wants to destroy it. The question is: Why?"

"Pure spitefulness. I have always been the despised foundling child to her. As long as I don't know who my real parents were, I will always remain the nameless foundling."

"No, Oliver. Richard told me he is obliged to do as Aunt Emily commands because if he doesn't, she will make sure you inherit Stanton Estate because you are his half-brother." She is unaware that she is holding his arm and shaking it lightly. "Do you realise what that means, Oliver? You are a Howard, even if you are an illegitimate child."

"He smiles cynically. There is a bitterness in his voice when he continues: "That is just another fairytale, Alice. When Uncle William brought me here twenty-nine years ago, all the town's people and residents of Stanton Estate were gossiping about the possibility that I was Uncle William's illegitimate son. But I'm not. Uncle William assured his mother, my grandmother Caroline, on her deathbed that I was definitively not his son. I know Uncle William. He wouldn't have lied to grandmother Caroline."

"Is there absolutely no other way to find the truth, Oliver?"

"For a brief moment I thought there was, that's why I left last week, but it was another dead-end."

She sighs disappointed. "Then Uncle William is our last chance. He must tell you the truth about your birth because he won't be here for always."

"Has his condition deteriorated?" asks Oliver alarmed.

"No... to the contrary. These days he is stronger, with a much keener interest in life. In the mornings he sits in his chair in front of the window looking at the gardeners. I also read to him often and then we discuss what I've read. I belief he is lonely, that is why he's given up on life."

"I can understand that. Aunt Emily has kept Ms. Crompton fully occupied. Richard and his father have never been friends. He probably felt he had no reason to hold on to life any longer – until you showed up."

"And you, Oliver. He often asks whether you have discovered the secret hiding place yet." She falls silent, a slight frown on her forehead. "I wonder... Uncle William is awake regularly during the night. Nobody will hear us sneaking up the stairs to his room in this storm. Shall we dare?" she asks with an excitement in her voice.

"Why not? Come, girl!" he orders, takes her hand and switches on his torch.

"I forgot to tell you: Uncle William is convinced that he has told you where the secret hiding place is," she says muffled as they move closer to the stairs.

"Maybe he has, but I probably was very young when he told me about it because I can't remember anything. Hush!" He warns and starts climbing the stairs with her.

They reach William's bedroom and Alice switches on the bedside lamp. "Uncle William? Oliver is here," she says softly and looks at Oliver disappointed. "He is asleep. Could you wait a while? I would hate to wake him."

"If we have no other choice... Let's just hope Aunt Emily..."

"Hell's bells!" curses Beatrice loudly and steamrolls into the bedroom. "Alice, if you want a secret lover can't you think of a better place to meet with him?"

"Softly, Ms. Crompton!" pleads Alice in a panic. "If Aunt Emily hears us there will be murder!"

"And what makes you think I won't commit a murder?" Beatrice asks angry. "There I am, dead quiet in my bed, wondering when this horrible wind will blow us down this cliff, and what do I hear? Footsteps sneaking around in the house... blood-thirsty murderers coming to slit my throat like a dump sheep. No, my dear, have you no heart? I may be fat, but don't let anyone tell you I have muscles..."

"Beatrice! Beatrice, where are you?" yells Emily's shrill voice suddenly down the passage.

Beatrice doesn't think twice, grabs Oliver by his neck and whispers: "Get down on all fours. Quick!"

Oliver obeys, too worried to argue. Beatrice plucks the bedspread off William's bed and throws it over the awed Oliver. He groans audibly as Beatrice sits on his back and prays that his torture won't last too long.

Emily appears in William's bedroom door and Beatrice grabs her stomach and groans loudly.

"What is the matter with you, Beatrice?" asks Emily concerned and walks closer.

"I have the most excruciating stomach cramps, Emily," and Beatrice bends over and groans loudly. "No, don't come closer! It's that new virus and it's extremely contagious... and fatal. Alice will help me... will take care of me until my last breath."

Alice muffles a laugh behind her hand and pretends to be sobbing. "I will stay with you until the very end, Ms. Crompton," she promises solemnly.

"Contagious, Beatrice?" asks Emily worried and quickly retreats back to the door. "Should I phone Doctor Graham?"

"Umph!" groans Oliver under the bedspread, his arms shaking with the effort under Beatrice's weight.

Beatrice moans louder. "Just go, Emily. Alice already phoned. I don't want to drag you with me to an early grave. Oh...oh, ouch, heavens...Hold my hand, Alice, I can feel the end is approaching fast now."

Emily flees from the bedroom and moments later they hear her bedroom door slamming close.

"Lie and deceive!" Beatrice starts and lands legs in the air as Oliver collapses under her. "Blimey, young man! Tomorrow I'll be all bruises thanks to you. Why are you so light in the pants?" she says upset, totally unaware of Alice kneeling next to William's bed, trying to muffle her laughter in his linen.

"My entire spine is distorted. You are heavier than a house, Ms. Crompton," says Oliver resentful and helps her to get up. "Why did you have to sit on top of me? I could've crawled under Uncle William's bed," he says angrily.

"Sinners should be punished," says Beatrice pious. "Yes, Alice, and what are you kneeling there at William's bed, as if you're praying? I can see you're laughing. Throw William's bedspread over his bed again. I will get rid of this man," she says upset, grabs Oliver's hand and pulls him with her towards the bedroom door.

William's muffled laughter makes Alice stand up quickly. "Were you awake all of this time, Uncle William?" she asks confused.

"Who can sleep with Beatrice's bleating in your ears?" he asks and sits up against his pillows. "The poor Oliver. After tonight he is a broken man," he continues, and laughs with his shoulders shaking.

"It is good to hear you laugh, Uncle William," says Alice contend. "I am sorry we woke you. Oliver wanted to talk to you, but he doesn't dare to come here during the day."

"Has the boy still not remembered where the secret hiding place is?" he asks concerned.

"No, Uncle William. And now Aunt Emily is also looking for the letters and documents. I found her in the study tonight when I wanted a book to read. Luckily, she has confided in me and asked me to help her in her search."

"Did she tell you the letter s and documents are in connection with Oliver's birth?" he asks tensely.

"No. She said it was documents and letters she had asked you to keep safe for her but now you could not remember where you had placed them. And now that she knows that Aunt Helen Upton is my aunt, she considers me important enough to be her confidant and to help her with her search."

William's lips contort in a bitter smile. "How typical of Emily... She has always been so aware of her position as a Howard, and she considers all other people below her class." He smiles at Alice. "I was glad when you told me about Helen, girl, and if Helen wouldn't mind, I would very much appreciate a visit from her."

"Aunt Helen would love that, but are you strong enough to receive visitors, Uncle William?" Alice asks concerned.

The clear light in his eyes speak of renewed determination to hold on to life. "Stanton Manor is once again a house filled with life and laughter... and young people. I can't avoid my last breath but perhaps I could postpone it, at least until I have fulfilled my obligation. Will you stay here to help me, Alice?"

"With pleasure, Uncle William." She falls silent and hesitantly starts: "If you aren't too tired..."

"I'm not. What do you want to tell me?"

"After Aunt Helen's visit Aunt Emily decided Richard and I should be married."

He laughs muffled and shakes his head. "The poor, foolish woman. Just because Richard does everything she demands, she believes sha can also dictate to you. You aren't going to marry a mommy's boy, are you, Alice?"

"Richard and I are good friends, but we don't love each other. Richard loves Charlotte Hastings and wants to marry her, but ..."

"Charlotte? Isn't she the girl who married Thomas Hastings?" he interrupts her.

"Yes, Uncle William. She is now a widow and I believe Richard truly loves her. Are you against their marriage, Uncle William?"

He looks at her with a patience borne from pain. "Does anyone have the right to withhold anyone else's happiness from them? If Richard and Charlotte love each other I will not stand in their way."

"I am so happy, Uncle William! But Aunt Emily threatened to disown Richard if he should marry Charlotte. Can she do that?"

He looks down and strokes the sheet covering his legs. "It is a little complicated, Alice. Emily inherited her family farm and the money from her parents. I... I own shares in the transport business, some other shares, and an amount of money. If Richard has the courage to decide his own future, tell him to come talk to me."

"Are you willing to help him, Uncle William?" she asks eagerly.

"I will decide that once I have spoken to him." He closes his eyes and mumbles: "It will be a strange triumph if Richard and I can finally become allies. But he is my son… my only son."

His breathing slows down, and Alice realises he has fallen asleep again. She switches off his bedside lamp and quietly walks out of his bedroom.

Stanton Manor has become her home, she realises. She isn't afraid of Emily who'll just appear out of nowhere in her long, white nightdress and her wild hair, anymore. Uncle William, Richard, and Miss Crompton are her friends… her new family. She won't go back to Tortington, there she will only be met with heartbreak and impossible dreams.

Richard walks over to Alice who is cutting roses and putting it in a basket for William's room. "Busy, little Alice. Are you now also doing the housekeepers job for her?" he teases.

"No, but your father likes flowers. He sits hours on end in front of his bedroom window looking out over the garden."

"Sits?" He stares at her astonished. "I thought my father was a hopeless invalid who could scarcely lift his head."

She warns him with her eyes. "He wás a helpless invalid before I came here, because all of you just left him all alone in his room waiting for him to die as soon as possible."

"That is a low blow," he says guiltily.

"No, it is the truth, Richard. I don't deny it: your father is a sick man, but with the right care he won't be dying tomorrow or the day after. He is still very interested in what is happening in Stanton Estate. We talk for hours on end; I must be careful that he doesn't get exhausted. He wants to talk to you."

"Excuse me?"

"You heard me. I told him about you and Charlotte and …"

"How could you, Alice?" he interrupts her upset. "My father is an even bigger snob than my mother. He would never allow me to marry Charlotte."

"That is how little you know your father, nitwit. He expressly said he has no right to stand in the way of anyone's happiness. If you really love Charlotte, he wouldn't stand in your way."

Richard stares at her speechless, shakes his head in total disbelief and then gives her a hard slap on her shoulder. "You wonderful girl! You, beautiful Alice, deserve a kiss!" he bursts out laughing.

"And you deserve a slap, because you just broke my shoulder," she says angrily, but smiles despite her throbbing shoulder. "Your father is your friend, Richard. I believe he truly missed having his own son."

"All these years my mother made me believe he preferred Oliver over me," he confesses.

"Your father is well aware of that, but nothing has to prevent the two of you to now mend your fences."

No, but – I wanted to ask you a favor."

"I'm listening," she says and looks at him expectantly.

"I want to invite Charlotte to Stanton Manor. If you could pretend to be old friends or maybe family… Will you please help me, Alice?"

She shakes her head. "Not family or old friends, because if that were the case, I would've mentioned her long ago." She frowns in thought. "Did Charlotte and her late husband ever go to London?"

"Yes… yes, they have friends in London."

"Fantastic. Charlotte and I met each other once or twice at John and Amy Carlisle's house. We visited there together. We liked each other and that is why I decided to invite her over for a visit here." She smiles mischievous. "Does my lie sound convincing?"

"You are an angel," he laughs, bends closer and gives her a kiss on her cheek. "I am leaving right now. Maybe I can bring Charlotte today still."

"Do that," she answers, quickly cuts a few more roses and jogs back to the house.

Alice storms into the kitchen, she sees Miss Crompton moving to the kitchen window with a stiff left leg and asks worried: "What happened to your leg, Miss Crompton?"

She plants her hands on her hips and breaths out angrily: "Don't even ask, dear. I tell you, Alice, that miserable young man lay down on purpose so I should trip over him and nearly break my neck. And here I am now, literally one-legged like a heron in a duckpond. If that Oliver ever again sticks as much as his nose inside my backdoor, I will hit him with a pan over his head!"

"I will help you, Miss Crompton, but I will also need your help in return," says Alice secretively.

"To do what?" asks Miss Crompton mistrustingly.

"It has to do with Richard and Charlotte, Miss Crompton. I am going to pretend that I have met Charlotte before at mutual friends' house in London and that I've invited her to come over to visit me here. If you could now help me to ...e... control Aunt Emily... Oh, you know what I mean, Miss Crompton."

Beatrice stares at her upset, but there is a warm glittering in her eyes. "No, but that is what I like to hear! Imagine, child, Charlotte could've been one of us six little Crompton's, she also grew up on charity. She was just much prettier and cleverer that I ever was, at least she had sense to marry a rich, old man."

"Then you will help me, Miss Crompton?"

"Of course, child, but please wait until tomorrow. I am in pain, dear, I am in pain. My knee refuses to bend and with this foul weather gather so quickly outside, my arthritis won't be far behind either." Beatrice looks upset right from the start. "Oliver is just like my fat: a cross and a test. I tell you this right now: if my leg wasn't killing me right now, I would've been after that nitwit right now and..." She stops mid-sentence as the backdoor swings open and Oliver steps into the kitchen.

"You, you... scoundrel! How dare you –"

"A cream cake and a large box of chocolates for Miss Beatrice Crompton!" interrupts Oliver her tirade and holds out the white cakebox and a huge box of chocolates. "Or are you in too much pain to eat it, Miss Crompton?" he asks concerned.

"I did almost swallow my false teeth but seeing that I didn't..." Miss Crompton smiles radiantly, forgets about her sore knee and waggles closer at an amazing speed. "Get us some tea, Alice. I am hungry," she continues, already busy taking the cream cake out of its box.

"I am very sorry I made you fall, Miss Crompton," says Oliver pious and glares at Alice snickering.

"Oh, dear child, I am also not a dainty feather," Beatrice gives up. "It's just: there is nothing better to heal my arthritis than a dozen Lemon Blueberry Scones. Two dozen works even better."

"It is going to rain very soon, Miss Crompton. The clouds are dark-gray, and the wind is blowing downwards," answers Oliver and looks through the window at the stormy weather outside.

"Then you better make haste, child! Do you really want me to be up the entire night with my arthritis pains?" She asks angrily.

He sighs and heads for the door. "Would you perhaps want to come with me, Alice?"

She hesitates only a moment and then walks towards him. "Why not? I need a few things from the town," she answers and slips through the door before Beatrice can stop her.

"Take me to The Swan Hotel, please. Arundel. In Highstreet on the left."

The driver looks at his older passenger when he starts the car. The man's hat is pulled low over his eyes. It is obvious he doesn't want people to look at his face.

"There are some other hotels much closer to us and more modern, Sir. The Arun View Inn is right on the river, and the Premier Inn Hotel..."

"I know, but take me to The Swan Hotel, please. I prefer it."

"Alright, Sir, as you wish." The driver shrugs his shoulders, lets the clutch go, and leaves the port of Littlehampton on Ferry Road to the A259, he turns right onto Ford Road which leads around the traffic circle to Maltravers Street to High Street. A quick twenty-minute drive straight to The Swan Hotel in the heart of Arundel. The entire way runs parallel along the River Arun.

"I knew the place years ago," the passenger explains to the taxi driver, making some polite conversation, as he drifts away in his memories while gazing out the car window at the river flowing by. "Even lived here for a while. And us humans have this knack to remain sentimental, always going back to somewhere to see if it had remained the same. Nothing, of course, ever remains the same, especially not after thirty years. But alas – one can also not stay away."

The driver nods his head in silent agreement.

"No, I just thought, Sir, if you had wanted to stroll around the town tonight then something more central..."

"I will find my way, thank you." The old man falls silent again. These young men have it in their heads that once you hit sixty it is old age and a wheelchair waiting. Well, wasn't there a time when he shared that same opinion? And that was only yesterday. The hotel on the corner of High Street was built in 1759 and remains a well-known beacon in the heart of Arundel.

"It's that building there," says the older man excited. "Grand, isn't it?"

The older man directs the driver to park in a courtyard at the rear of the building which used to be stabling for horses and coaches.

"Where are you headed now?" he asks the driver as they unload his suitcase from the boot of the taxi.

"Back to Littlehampton, Sir. Back to the missus of twenty years."

"You have one of the good ones then." He says looking up at Stanton Manor on top of the cliff. "This old Manor... I could never decide if it looked stately or ominous looking up at it from down here," he says, mumbling to himself. "Well," he shakes his head as if coming back to the present, "Thank you, and drive back safely." The older man hands the driver a five-pound note, and a drizzle of rain starts again.

The driver takes the suitcase to the hotel entrance then greets the older man and runs to his car, pulling his jacket collar over his head.

The old man enters the warm hotel with the porter bringing in his suitcase.

"Feels like I have never left," says the old man, and he pull his raincoat-collar up and pulls his hat lower over his face. "I've known it for years. Good morning, Mam. I have a room reservation for one, please."

"Certainly, Sir."

The woman behind the reception counter is small and in her mid-forties. She looks drab and tired. The hotel seems to be empty. He looks around. The general appearance dates back to the early century, but to him it is clear that the glory of those years is still captured in the décor. Old, luxurious, and opulent, not cheap at all.

"Name, please?" the woman asks while she pulls the register closer.

"John Milton."

She looks up. "Have you visited Arundel before, Mr. Milton." She asks.

"Yes. Yes, I have, a very long time ago."

"Welcome back, Sir. You know what they say: the more things change, the more they stay the same… I'm sure you will find that also here in Arundel."

He clears his throat. "Mam, is room twenty-eight available by any chance, please?"

"Yes." She answers without consulting her register and seems a bit surprised. "Certainly."

"I would appreciate it. I once stayed in it. The view towards the cliff and Stanton Manor is magnificent."

"Very well, Sir. The room is yours."

The porter helps to carry the suitcase to room twenty-eight on the second floor. There are no lifts in the hotel. The room is a nice, updated surprise. Spacious and comfortable with a large, soft double bed, thick carpets, and the original large window he remembers so well with its view towards the cliff and Stanton Manor. The capricious weather has allowed some sun through the rainclouds, and the cliff and the Manor on the left and the river to his right glistens in the sunlight. The window frames the Manor on the cliff like an antique oil painting.

"Nice, just as I remember it," John says to the porter as he walks in behind him, he sits down on the bed with a sigh, rubbing his left leg. "I was here when World War Two started, in this same room. Of course, it's been quite a while, but time also flies by so fast... The town has changed a lot. It has been a wish of mine for a long time now to come back just one more time to walk in the streets of Arundel, in the winter, in the rain. To see all the old, familiar places again. Well, here I am, back at The Swan Hotel after thirty-two years, and here it hasn't changed much, at least."

He sounds excited, like a schoolboy on his first holiday.

"If there is nothing else, Sir..." the porter says as he walks out of the room, holding the doorknob in his hand to close the door.

John gets up with a groan, takes a five-pound note out of his wallet and hands it to the porter. "Thank you," he says as the porter closes the door.

Oliver and Alice try to dodge the rain by staying under the shop canopies making their way back to his car, they laugh in each other's eyes and then start to jog.

"I feel and look like a drowned chicken," says Alice as they reach the car, and he opens the door for her.

"You look like a mermaid who got stranded on the beach," he teases smilingly and swings around as someone taps him on his shoulder.

"Hallo Oliver," says the man, "Mr. Milton. John Milton. From Ireland."

"Yes, I remember quite well." Says Oliver gruffly. "What brings you to Arundel, Mr. Milton?"

"I have come here to visit aunt Eleanor Wallace. I saw you come out of the grocery store. Is there any possibility if I could ask to drive up with you, please?"

Oliver hesitates, but Alice says spontaneously: "Aunt Eleanor would be happy to receive a visitor. Open the door, Oliver, so I can put down all these bags before everything is soaking wet."

"Sorry," says Oliver brusque and helps Alice into the car. He closes her door and looks at John Milton suspiciously. "Aunt Eleanor doesn't live at Stanton Manor, Mister Milton."

"I'm aware of that, but Tortington isn't far from the old mansion on the cliff." He looks Oliver squarely in his eyes. "If you have doubts, you can confirm with the receptionist at The Swan Hotel that I have a reservation there."

"No... that won't be necessary." Oliver walks around the car, unlocks his door, and opens the passenger door in the back. "Please, get in, Mister Milton."

"I know I look like a pirate, I'm not one," says the man and climbs into the car.

Alice becomes aware of the tension in Oliver, realizing it must be difficult to drive in these stormy conditions and heavy rain. She looks over her shoulder at the quiet Mister Milton. "Are you family of Aunt Eleanor's, Mister Milton?"

"No, he's not." Answers Oliver rudely.

"No, just a very old friend, Miss."

"I'm Alice Browning. Please call me Alice, Mister Milton," she says with a friendly smile, feeling sorry for the man with the scars on his face. Luckily, she is a nurse, she has learned to look at unlucky people like Mister Milton without shock or disgust, she thinks thankfully.

"Thank you, Alice. I am uncle John. I'm an old family friend of the Howards," he replies more at ease. There is now a small smile around his mouth.

"I will drop you at Stanton Manor and then I'll take Mister Milton to Aunt Eleanor, Alice," says Oliver matter-of-factly.

"That won't be necessary," says John quickly. "I prefer to walk."

A frown forms between Oliver's brows. "I apologise if I came across impolite, but the walk could be quite taxing on your leg, Mister Milton. Do you not prefer that I drive you to aunt Eleanor?"

"My left leg is amputated just below the knee, but I've had years of getting used to my artificial leg. That is why I prefer to walk." He explains looking at Oliver in the rear-view mirror.

"As you wish," says Oliver and brings the car to a stop at the turn-off. "You can walk from here. That is Tortington there on the hill."

"Thank you for the lift, Oliver" says John and opens his door.

"Goodbye, Alice. We will see each other again; I'm planning on staying here for a while."

The car door closes behind him and Oliver pulls away with screeching wheels.

"What is wrong, Oliver? Why don't you like Mister Milton?" asks Alice baffled.

He tries to smile. "I don't know. He makes me uncomfortable, that's all. We shall phone aunt Eleanor from Stanton Manor and warn her that John Milton is on his way... just in case," he says and then concentrates on the road again.

Helen hears someone knocking on the back door, she gets up from her chair and stays standing still as the back door opens, a strange man walks in and closes the door behind him.

He strokes his hands through his wet hair, sees Helen standing next to the kitchen table and asks uncertainly: "Does aunt Eleanor Wallace not live here anymore?"

Helen stares at him in silence, her eyes on the black eyepatch and the crude scar which is now a purple red colour due to the cold.

He turns his head a little to the right, so his profile and the unblemished left side of his face is in her view. "I apologise for my appearance. It usually takes a moment before people adjust to it," he says muffled.

"I apologise for staring at you, Mister..."

"John Milton. And you are?"

"Helen Upton."

He keeps his face turned away. "Nice to make your acquittance. Is aunt Eleanor home?"

"Not at this moment. Miss Beatrice Crompton phoned to say she wasn't feeling too well, so aunt Eleanor quickly drove over to Stanton Manor. Unfortunately, this storm just started. I expect her to return once the rain has subsided somewhat."

"Oh... do you mind if I should wait here for her?"

"Not at all. Take off your wet raincoat and hang it behind the door. There are some warm crumpets, and I just made a pot of fresh tea. Would you like to have a cup with me?" Asks Helen hospitable.

He moves with a slight limp in his step to the kitchen table and looks intensely at Helen. "Your hospitality surprises me. My appearance usually has quite the opposite effect on people."

"Because they don't know you." Helen smiles slowly. "I know you are supposed to be dead, but you are Henry Howard, aren't you?"

Chapter 11

Helen notices how her visitor presses his lips together in a thin line while a cold animosity hardens the expression on his face. "You are mistaken, Miss Upton. I'm John Milton," he says clearly.

She smiles brightly. "How do you know I'm Miss Upton if you hadn't known me since my youth, Henry? If I hadn't recognised your profile and your eyes, I would certainly have recognised your voice. And your hands. I remember the half-moon scar on your hand because you got that injury in a rugby match."

"My eyes?" He asks with a smile of self-loathing.

Helen smiles impatiently. "My goodness, do you expect me to refer to your eye every time? I'm a woman of fifty-five, but I still refer to my face, not my wrinkled face."

He stares at her speechless, his gaze intense. "You are three years younger than I am, but I remember the Helen Upton from my youth: highly intelligent, very attractive, but an outspoken little twit I tried to avoid."

"Did you avoid me on purpose?" asks Helen, caught off-guard.

His smile makes her forget about his eyepatch and the scar on his face. "What else? You always treated me with a measure of contempt, almost as if you tried to say that I was the heir to Stanton Estate only per chance birth, but your intelligence made you part of the real elite."

"If you thought that then you are dumb, Henry," she reacts angrily, and then smiles unwillingly. "You will probably not try to deny that you are Henry Howard now anymore."

Henry shrugs his shoulders. "Will it be of any use? For the people of Arundel, I died more than thirty years ago in a bomb-raid in Ireland. Maybe I should've remained dead, but William's silence has lasted long enough."

"Does William know that you are still alive?" she asks shocked.

He nods sternly. "Someone had to know. After the bomb-raid I wasn't able to work for more than a year. I needed money for the plastic surgery and ..." He looks down. "And for my artificial leg, because the surgeon had to amputate my left leg just below the knee."

"But your poor parents... How could you do that to them, Henry?" she asks resentful.

"I was only twenty-seven then, in the peak of my youth. I don't think of myself as being vain, but I do realise I used to be attractive to women. You didn't see me right after the incident, Helen. I looked like a monster – a cripple, one eyed monster. And there was the woman I loved. I couldn't go back to her just to see the look of disgust and fear on her face."

"Are you referring to Annabelle?" she asks muffled and relives the half-forgotten feeling of powerlessness and unfulfilled longing, because Henry could never love her.

He laughs bitterly. "The moment I realised Annabelle was in love with Grayson, I forgot about her." He sees the disbelief on her face and continues: "I don't deny it: there was I time I was head over heels in love with Annabelle, but her treacherous affair ended all feelings I had for her. She always had demands and dreams, but she could never make any comprise to anyone else – her life was all about her, as was the case with both the Montgomery sisters."

Then there was another woman in Henry's life, Helen thinks to herself with a feeling of loss and quickly gets up as the phone starts ringing in the passage. "I'll be back right now, excuse me, please," she says calmly and walks out of the kitchen.

Henry stares at her with admiration in his eyes. Helen has made a friend with age, she possesses a calm, softer beauty and a calmness that puts him at ease. It is strange that she never married, because even at school she was admired by most of the boys.

"It was Beatrice Crompton," says Helen as she enters the kitchen again a few moments later. "Oliver is apparently concerned about my safety, which is why she phoned. You didn't tell me you already met Oliver Howard, Henry."

"I met Oliver a week ago when he came to Ireland looking for Henry," he shrugs his shoulders. "I told him then that I was John Milton, an old colleague of Henry's, and that Henry did in fact die after the bomb-raid. He believed me. I met Alice Browning today, she was with Oliver in town."

"Alice is my niece," explains Helen and pours two cups of tea. "Oliver is William's and Emily's oldest son. Come sit and have some tea. Or would you prefer that we sit in the lounge?"

Henry takes a seat at the kitchen table, a frown of confusion between his brows. "I prefer the kitchen, thank you, Helen. But Oliver ... William had me under the impression that he and Emily had only one son, Richard."

"Only one own son, yes," explains Helen while she puts out two plates with crumpets. "William and Emily adopted Oliver." She falls silent and then she continues hesitantly: "Maybe it's for the better if you understood the real situation. Oliver has never been welcome in Stanton Manor. William has always maintained that Oliver is the son of two of his old student friends, but in the beginning, everyone was wondering if he wasn't William's illegitimate son."

"Isn't he?" asks Henry brusquely.

"No. Aunt Eleanor told me that William assured your mother on her deathbed that Oliver wasn't his son. But your mother loved Oliver, and that is why she had left Tortington to him."

Henry chuckles muffled. "I can just imagine what Emily's reaction was to that. Tortington is part of the Stanton Estate."

"Emily has never forgiven your mother, in her eyes Oliver has always been a foundling-child." Helen takes a sip of her tea, wishes she didn't feel obliged to be hospitable, but then forces herself to continue: "The woman you met... Don't you want to phone her?"

A smile plays around his mouth, but his expression remains enigmatic. "Even if I had wanted to, I can't. She was a girl from Italy, Giuliana Agosto. We were married for only a few months when the bomb-raid happened. She died. I don't know much, I was in a coma, and when I eventually recovered enough to make sense of my world, I was told that she had passed away while I was in the hospital."

"I am very sorry," she says with sincere sympathy.

"I'm not, because Giuliana... I don't believe she would've been able to live with the wreck of me who survived after that day."

"If she loved you..."

"Well, we'll never know. All for the best if you ask me."

"I understand," says Helen without looking at him. "Another cup of tea, Henry?"

"I would like that..." Henry begins and then falls silent when they hear the engine of a car approaching. He gets up and walks over to the window. "Aunt Eleanor decided to brave the storm. At least it has calmed down a bit."

Helen hears the car door slamming shut and opens the back door. "Why didn't you wait for the storm to pass, Aunt Eleanor? I assured you I was perfectly safe and no reason for any concern," she says as Eleanor enters the kitchen.

"That fat woman will still be the cause of me going crazy at my age," Eleanor starts angrily while taking off her raincoat. "There is absolutely nothing wrong with the woman, except that she..." Her sentence fades into silence when she sees the strange raincoat hanging behind the kitchen door. "I forgot about our visitor.

Where is he?"

Henry moves away from the window. "Hallo, Aunt Eleanor," he greets, and smiles uncertainly.

Eleanor squints her eyes and tilts her head a bit to the side. "Speak again, son. It is as if I want to recall your voice, but with the eyepatch and that ugly scar on your face – "

"I don't look like the boy you raised anymore, aunt Eleanor," he says with a bitterness and self-loathing in his voice which fills Helen with a feeling of protest and sympathy.

"Henry?" says Eleanor breathless, her face pale and her eyes wide. She grabs her chest and succumbs in the nearest chair. She breaths fast, her eyes nailed to Henry's scarred face. "How... How is this possible, child? All these years... All the sadness..."

"I have forgotten you aren't young anymore, Aunt Eleanor," he says repentant. "I'm sorry I didn't first write to let you know I would be coming back." He looks at Helen, worried. "Should we phone the doctor?"

"Leave the doctor, Helen," commands Eleanor feisty. "A cup of tea will do the trick, but before I drink it: don't think that I will ever forgive you for the heartbreak you caused your mother and myself, Henry. If you had written just one letter your mother would've have died peacefully."

"I had good reason why I wanted everyone to think I had died, Aunt Eleanor. And after the bomb attack... Maybe I had hoped I would actually die, because my appearance even filled the nurses with disgust and fear. I can't even recall how many surgeries I had to undergo to regain just a semblance of being an actual man," he explains. His voice cold and bitter.

"We are your family, Henry. We would've accepted you," says Eleanor resentful.

He stares at her in silence. "Maybe. I don't know. Maybe I was being selfish because to me you weren't dead. William wrote a few times – never more than once a year."

"Did you know about your parents' deaths?" asks Eleanor sternly.

"Yes, Aunt Eleanor. But William's letters about their funerals reached me long after it had happened. I was a lecturer in economics at the University of Dublin and during holidays I travelled all over the world. I had a… a new face and a new life. I couldn't come back to Arundel to be pitied by everyone who knew me from my youth."

"Vain, that is what you are, Henry Howard. Vain and selfish," says Eleanor heartbroken.

He smiles regretful. "I realise that now, Aunt Eleanor, but it has taken me thirty years. When I was younger, William and Emily moved into Stanton Manor with my parents. William successfully managed the transport company in my absence. They were normal, happy people. Stanton Estate didn't need me."

"But we did," Eleanor maintains.

"Have some tea, Aunt Eleanor," Helen tries to calm her.

"Thank you, Helen." She finishes her tea and turns to Henry again. "Why did you come back now, Henry? For William?"

"I haven't received any letters from him in over two years. I tried to phone him at Stanton Manor a few times, but Miss Crompton answered the phone every time. I couldn't figure out what was going on, and so I decided to come back." He takes a slow, deep breath and asks hesitantly: "William…"

Eleanor nods silently. "He is alive, but he has stomach cancer."

"No!"

Eleanor sees the shock and pain on his face and forgets about her sadness and resentment. "He is doing so much better since Helen's niece, Alice, has been taking care of him. But I'm grateful you have come back, Henry. Your brother needs you."

"Then you forgive me, Aunt Eleanor?"

She smiles unwillingly. "You are alive, Henry, and that is all that matters. Welcome back, my child."

Henry bends over her, gives her a hug and a kiss on her cheek. "Thank you, Aunt Eleanor. Do you still bake those delicious jam tarts?"

"I should say so, child. And now I'm going to brew a pot of strong coffee. You and I have thirty years to catch up on," says Eleanor and gets up from her chair.

Oliver flips a half-baked pancake in the air, catches it in the pan and places the pan back on the stove. He turns with a triumphant smile to Beatrice who is looking at him angrily. "What did I tell you, Miss Crompton? Aunt Eleanor taught me this little trick because you always kicked me out of the kitchen."

"You know Emily said the children weren't allowed in the kitchen," says Beatrice angrily. "But don't imagine yourself a master chef, child. If my arms weren't so short, I could also easily flip a pancake like that."

"Of course. I have forgotten about your short arms, Miss Crompton," he says sternly and winks at Alice who is trying to stuff a dishcloth into her mouth, so she doesn't burst out laughing.

"You have always been a little know-it-all, Oliver. Move away from my stove. I'm baking the pancakes, not you," says Beatrice defensive and elbows him out of her way.

"And here I am just trying to help a fallen, old lady with a sore knee and arthritis," he teases.

"You are looking for a slap, child! A fallen woman is … is bad, I'm an old lady with some bodily pains." She glares at him furious. "And don't tell me you didn't know that, Oliver."

"No, but you certainly fell last night, Miss Crompton, which is why…"

"Out, devil's child, out! You said you felt unsure about that strange John Milton you picked up in the town How do you know the man hasn't already slit Helen's or old Eleanor's throats?" Beatrice realises the seriousness of her own words and stares at him with wide eyes. "Oh, goodness, Oliver, maybe the two women are laying in their own blood and…"

"Miss Crompton!" Alice interrupts her abruptly. "Uncle John was very embarrassed about his scarred face, but he is definitely not a murderer. And you have already phoned aunt Helen, and she assured you they were perfectly safe."

"How do we know she wasn't forced to lie to me? Maybe this man held a gun to her head and told her what to say to me," Beatrice continues.

Oliver frowns worried. Maybe he was too at ease – or maybe he is just enjoying the time here with Alice. He frowns deeper. How long can you keep running from a truth that has already taken hold of your heart? He really likes this girl with the long, blonde hair and the soulful green eyes. He knows the fine perfection of her nose and the allure of her full lips with their wordless invitation. He looks at her and every movement of her slender body mesmerizes him. Is it possible that he has fallen in love with her, he asks himself?

He is a foundling-child… a thrown-away child. How can he ever expect a girl like Alice to love him? Sometimes he gets the idea that she does like him, but Norman Graham has got the lead on him: Norman knows who his parents are, who he is. Howard is not his real surname. How can he ever ask Alice to be part of this fraud; to take a surname that isn't even his own?

"Stop frowning, Oliver," says Alice, elated about his visit. "I'll quickly phone aunt Helen again."

She quickly walks out of the kitchen, and he looks at her until the passage door closes behind her.

"Sick to death," says Beatrice in front of the stove and sniffs loudly.

"Do you have a cold, Miss Crompton?" he asks with forced interest.

"I'm talking about you, you poor soul," says Beatrice, her expression all-knowing. "It's not because of the pancakes that you decided to challenge Emily in being in this house, dear. You look like a love-sick puppy whenever Alice is in the vicinity."

"Nonsense! I'm a man of thirty, not a love-sick teenager, Miss Crompton."

Beatrice's chuckled laugh is taunting. "That is why you look sick to death, child. But that is your own fault. If you weren't so stubborn to admit your feelings, then doctor Norman wouldn't have managed to snatch the sweet Alice from right under your nose."

"I don't have any marriage plans, Miss Crompton. And you know why. How can I ask Alice to become Mrs. Howard when I myself don't have any right to the surname?"

"Oh, please, so much nonsense I haven't heard in a very long time. You have been a Howard for twenty-nine years. And Alice isn't marrying your surname. The question is: does she love you enough to break her engagement to marry you?" asks Beatrice practically.

"We will never know that, because I refuse to ask her as long as my lineage remains a secret," he answers gruffly.

"Go back to London then, child, because you will just find your own heartbreak here if you ..." Beatrice breaks off her sentence as Alice enters the kitchen. "What did Helen say, dear?"

Alice smiles assuring. "Aunt Eleanor got home safe. She and uncle John are chatting up a storm in the kitchen." She looks at Oliver. "I know my aunt, Oliver. She didn't lie to me. Let's make some coffee and eat pancakes."

"You didn't perhaps want to invite Norman over?" asks Oliver, his back turned to her as he is taking out plates from the cupboard.

"Now, that is a good plan," says Beatrice with a smile. "Phone him and tell him he is very welcome, Alice."

Alice licks her lips, stares with intense concentration at the kettle and says: "Norman phoned early this morning to hear how uncle William was doing. He doesn't know if he'll be able to come over today because he has a delivery scheduled for today."

"Oh, that's disappointing. You get to spend so little time with your fiancé, poor girl. You haven't even had time to look for an engagement ring," says Beatrice sympathetically.

"We aren't going to look for an engagement ring, Miss Crompton," says Alice quickly. "Uncle William is eager to meet Charlotte and aunt Emily knows now that Richard and I are only friends. I told Norman we don't have to lie about our fake engagement any longer."

"No, but that is how I like it!" says Beatrice happy. She glances at Oliver who is looking at het expressionless and continues: "If doctor Norman doesn't know how to capture a young girl's heart, then he deserves to lose you, Alice. I can only hope not all men are so hopeless."

"How long are we still going to wait for the pancakes, Miss Crompton?" asks Oliver impatiently and walks to the stove. "Suddenly, I am as hungry as a lion."

"It's nerves, child. I remember the time I was in love with…" Beatrice's mouth stays open midsentence as the back door opens and Richard and Charlotte Hastings walks into the kitchen. "For goodness' sake! How many more wet chickens are still going to trample my clean kitchen floor with mud?" she asks angrily.

"It's not your kitchen, Miss Crompton. I would also bet anything that the cook is stuck in her room again after being kicked out of the kitchen by you," answers Richard and helps Charlotte to take off her wet raincoat. "Come, Charlotte. Alice has been looking forward to your visit for days now."

Charlotte Hastings – the girl Oliver once loved, Alice thinks and quickly glances at him. He, however, continues undisturbed to take out knives and forks from the drawer and setting it on the table.

Maybe Oliver is ignoring Charlotte because he still loves her, Alice thinks, and she feels a little sting of jealousy. Charlotte is undoubtedly a beautiful woman with her auburn hair and her brown eyes. She knows Charlotte is two years older than Richard, but her appearance definitely doesn't show her age.

"Hallo, Alice," Charlotte greets shyly.

Charlotte is tense and feels unwelcome in Stanton Manor, realises Alice, and she feels sorry for her. She smiles welcoming, quickly walks over to Charlotte, and gives her a kiss on her cheek.

"My goodness, it is good to see you again, Charlotte! And you are as beautiful as always. Actually, even more beautiful, but that must be thanks to Richard."

"It is," answers Charlotte, her smile grateful and relieved.

"Welcome in Stanton Manor, Charlotte," says Beatrice welcoming. "I know about yours and Alice's friendship and I am so glad you could be persuaded to come over to visit her. The poor child, Alice only has old people and sick people to keep her company."

"Do you know Charlotte?" asks Oliver, his gaze suspiciously on

Alice. "Why didn't you tell me?"

"Why did she have to tell you?" asks Beatrice angrily. "Alice also has two crowns in her mouth, but I'm sure you don't know about those either."

Charlotte sees the frown on Oliver's forehead, and she explains nervously: "Alice is just helping me. Lady Howard would never have allowed Richard to invite me over to Stanton Manor."

"You aren't going to reveal our secret, Oliver... When two people love each other... It is our duty to help them," pleads Alice.

"Do they love each other?" asks Oliver skeptically, with his eyes coldly fixed on Charlotte's face.

She meets his eyes fearless. "I do love Richard – and sentiment doesn't play a role," she answers calmly.

Then her little chat with him was purely sentiment, thinks Oliver, and subdues a smile with effort. But he knows Charlotte: she couldn't get a young, rich man to marry her, so she married an old, rich man; she had hoped he was still interested to marry her, but when it turned out he wasn't, she decided Richard would make a good substitute. Charlotte never loses, but he will give her one credit: she will be loyal to Richard as she was to her first husband.

"In that case: let's drink a cup of coffee and eat some warm pancakes on your future together," says Oliver carefree and takes two more plates out of the cupboard.

They all take place at the kitchen table, making jokes back and forth, and listening with only half an ear to Beatrice's complaints about her sore knee. Oliver forces himself to keep watch over the passage door, intensely aware of Alice sitting next to him. He sees how Richard and Charlotte looks into each other's eyes and he bends over to Alice.

"What is the real reason for your ended engagement, little Alice? I thought you and Norman shared the same interests?" he says in a low voice.

"Have you ever heard about love, nitwit?" she whispers and glares at him.

He smiles broadly. "Clever girl. You are too pretty and too young to be as sinical as I am. Welcome back to your fairy tale story, little Alice."

"What are you two whispering – " Beatrice starts to ask and then swallows half a pancake as the passage door bursts open and Emily appears in front of them.

Emily's quickly glances over the scene in front of her and her head jerks back. There is a mask of haughty superiority on her face.

"Thank heavens you aren't wearing your nightgown, Emily," says Beatrice before Emily can say a word. "Your daughter-in-law to be doesn't know about your antics yet, and first impressions are so important. Charlotte, dear, this is your soon to be mother-in-law, Aunt Emily. Emily, meet Charlotte Hastings."

Charlotte clings to Richard's hand under the table, too scared to say a word, and pleadingly looking at Alice.

"Charlotte and I have met each other a few times in London, Lady Howard," says Alice innocently. "I invited her over for a visit."

Emily's right-hand shoots forward, pointing a t the back door. "Out! Get out of my house, Charlotte Hastings. And you, Oliver, you are also not welcome under my roof."

Richard jumps up from his chair, his dark eyes gleaming in those of Emily's. "If you chase out Charlotte, mother, then I am going with her – and I won't be coming back," he says with a grim finality.

Emily seems caught off guard for a moment, but then anger wins over her sober thoughts. "You dare to challenge me, Richard? Do you understand that you won't have an inheritance if you marry that … that woman?"

He looks at her fearless. "Yes, mother. And Charlotte knows it too."

Emily laughs tauntingly. "You poor idiot! Charlotte Jones married Thomas Hastings only for his money. If I disown you, she will discard you like a used up old rag."

"No, I won't, Lady Howard, because Richard and I love each other," says Charlotte and gets up from her chair to stand next to Richard. "You don't have to pack any clothes, Richard. We can afford to buy anything you will need."

"Sit, children, sit!" roars Beatrice from the table. "Who did I bake all these pancakes for? Who did you actually come to visit, Charlotte? No. you sit, eat your pancake and chat with Alice." She turns to Emily, furious. "And you, you poor soul, you may have a cup of coffee and a pancake if you promise to behave yourself."

She has lost Richard; Emily thinks to herself in panic. Everyone is colluding behind her back. No…no, there is only one person responsible for all the misfortune and heartbreak that has followed her all these years: the foundling-child, Oliver.

"He must leave! Now!" she screams and points her finger at Oliver. "I have banned him from my house years ago."

"If Oliver goes, I go with him," says Alice unexpectedly and wishes the next moment she could bite off her tongue. How could she say something like that? What must Oliver think of her? That she is in love with him, she wonders and wishes the floor would open up and swallow her whole.

"That's correct, Aunt Emily. If you don't care about uncle William's health, then Alice and I will get married and return to London," says Oliver firmly.

Emily glares at Oliver and Alice, rests her gaze on Richard and says in an ice-cold voice: "We will talk later, Richard." She walks out of the kitchen and slams the door shut behind her with a loud noise.

"Oh, my word!" bemoans Beatrice and wipes the sweat from her forehead with her fine lace handkerchief. "I'm so nervous now I could probably devour all these pancakes all by myself. It's just…" She holds her hand in front of her mouth. "I think I ate something that must've been off – maybe it was the cream cake, or maybe the scones. I should lie down a while."

"Stomach pain at least doesn't kill, Miss Crompton," Oliver tries to calm her. His eyes dancing with laughter.

""You've never had my stomach or my pain, child. I feel like I am dying," she moans as she waggles out of the kitchen.

"We've won the first round, Charlotte!" says Richard impressed.

"How about some more pancake?"

She smiles half-heartedly. "I've lost my appetite. Let's rather go, Richard. The quicker you have that talk with your mother, the quicker we will know what to do next."

"Also true," he answers, and helps her to put on her raincoat.

"Thank you for your help, Alice. I hope one day we can truly be friends," says Charlotte sincerely.

"After today we are friends. See you, Charlotte," greets Alice.

Oliver waits until the back door closes behind them and then looks at Alice teasingly who is staring intently at her plate in front of her. "Are you upset with the pancake or with yourself, little Alice?"

Her eyes flash in his. "If you must know I spoke without thinking. Or...or maybe I just wanted to put aunt Emily in her place."

"Or maybe you felt sorry for me?" he teases.

She looks at him and says impulsively: "I could never feel sorry for you. You are too self-satisfied. You don't need anyone."

His lips forms unspoken words and then he quickly gets up. " I do need your friendship. Goodbye, Alice." He greets her, his voice muffled, and he walks out the back door.

Friendship. She hates that word. But she hates Oliver Howard even more, because he is the reason she is sitting here crying about a senseless love, she thinks to herself. She pushes her plate away and sobbingly rests her head on her arms.

Richard walks into his father's bedroom, sees him sitting in front of the window and remains standing in the middle of the room.

"Come in, Richard," William invites his son without looking away from the window.

"How did you know it was me, father?" he asks and walks closer. William turns to him with a smile. "After twenty-eight years I know my only son's footsteps."

"Oh." He clears his throat. "Alice said you wanted to talk with me. E... she said you know I want to marry Charlotte, father."

"I know, yes, and I'm very grateful that at last you have plans to be married. I can only pray that I should be alive long enough to see my first grandchild, but even if that doesn't happen... As long as I know that you are happy, that is all that is important to me."

"Thank you, father. It's just... Mother is threatening to disown me if I should marry Charlotte."

William nods. "And she will because she owns her family farm. I have some shares in the transport company, some other shares, and some capital. You won't be a beggar, my son."

"And Stanton Estate? The transport company? Is it true what mother says? Is Oliver going to inherit everything because he is your oldest son?"

"No, Richard. I have only one son, you. Stanton Estate and the transport company belongs to my brother and after my death, he will decide what to do with it all."

Chapter 12

Richard stares speechless at William. He takes a deep breath and then asks in clear disbelief: "Did I hear you clearly, Father? Did you say that Stanton Estate and the transport company both belong to your brother?"

"That is right, yes," answers William.

"But... but Uncle Henry passed away before I was born! Mother has told me through all these years that I was the sole heir to Stanton Estate. Why did you lie to me?" asks Richard with strained anger.

"I never said that you would inherit Stanton Estate. I certainly had hoped you would, seeing as Henry..." William sighs deeply, slight dismay on his face. "Henry didn't die all those years ago, but he did lose an eye and a leg and sustained serious wounds to his head and face. He was in a coma for several months. He looked like a monster – and I am quoting his own words. He had also lost his new wife, which he only learned about once he came to. He felt like only half a human. He didn't want to live anymore, and that is why he asked me to tell our parents that he had died. I went to Ireland to arrange his fake funeral; and then he and I also agreed that I would continue to manage the transport company on his behalf."

"All these years," Richard almost says to himself, shaking his head. "Mother blackmailed me emotionally, taught me to hate Oliver because she had me believed he was your oldest son, your illegitimate son, but your oldest son and he could take everything away from me. In the meantime, my so-called inheritance belonged to another man!"

"Is… is Stanton Estate so important to you, Richard?" asks William hoarse.

Richard paces tensely to the bedroom door and back again. There is an expression of bitterness and rebelliousness on his face. "No, Father. I take after my grandfather Montgomery – I have always wanted to have my own farm and work on my own land. But my own mother has been the cause that I grew up from a very young age with contempt for my own father for bringing my illegitimate brother to Stanton Estate. Why you and I never had a particularly good relationship. If you only knew, Father… I've always felt so sorry for my mother because she had to raise your lover's child – and all this time it has all been only lies!"

"Don't judge her too harshly, Richard," says William with a tolerance borne only from pain and deceit. "I'm not innocent, I was part of the fraud. But I had to make certain concessions – remain silent about certain facts – it was your mother's conditions for her to raise Oliver as her own child."

"Don't make me laugh, Father! Aunt Eleanor and grandmother Caroline, and Miss Crompton raised Oliver because mother always treated him like an intruder and a foundling-child." His lips pull into a bitter sneer. "And I certainly didn't treat him any better. I was still very small when I learned that Mother would do anything for me or buy anything for me as long as I treated Oliver with disdain and contempt. I was the sole heir, and he was the slave…as I were Mother's slave."

"Your mother's entire reason for being centers around you, Richard. Don't resent her for loving you." William pleads in his eyes. "We all make mistakes. I realise today I was a coward for giving in to your mother's demands, but thirty years ago... I just couldn't handle the constant arguments anymore, and so I acted against my own better judgement."

"As long as Mother stays out of my way..." Richard looks at the thin, old man and places his hand on his shoulder. "Thank you, Father, that you are willing to accept Charlotte as your daughter-in-law... and that you are not also threatening to disown me."

"Would Charlotte refuse to marry you if you were to be disowned?" asks William concerned.

"No, Father. Charlotte loves me. We will live on her farm, I will work on the farm, but if I knew I wasn't a penniless church-mouse... A man doesn't want to feel he is financially dependent on his rich wife."

William smiles reassuringly. "I'm not a poor man, my son. Get married as soon as possible, and go and live your live on the farm, but don't forget about me. I have longed for so long to be your father and friend."

Richard takes his father's skeletal hand in his own. "You are more than that, Father. I feel for the first time I have a father... a father who trusts me and treats me like a man. Thank you, Father." He smiles at his father, turns around and walks out of the bedroom overtaken by his father tears streaming down his hollow cheeks.

Oliver closes the kitchen door of Tortington behind him, he sees Henry and Aunt Eleanor sitting at the kitchen table and feels the hair in his neck stand on end. Something about John Milton just doesn't sit right with him, he thinks, aware of the unexplainable feeling of animosity and suspicion rising within him. This stranger is sitting in his house and his talking to his Aunt Eleanor as if he has all the right in the world to be here.

"Do you know Mister Milton, Aunt Eleanor?" he asks bluntly, takes off his raincoat and hangs it behind the kitchen door.

"Goodness, Oliver, did Beatrice's tough pancakes give you a stomachache?" teases Eleanor. "How many times must I still warn you, child? Everything Beatrice bakes is tough and dripping with syrup."

Oliver ignores her, his eyes suspiciously on Henry who is looking at him with open interest. "Who told you about Aunt Eleanor and Tortington, Mister Milton?" he asks brusquely.

Henry's face remains calm, but his eyes glisten with laughter. "Aunt Eleanor has been here from the moment I gave my first baby-cry coming into this world, but Tortington was built when I had marriage plans."

Oliver frowns in anger and looks questioningly at Aunt Eleanor. "Oh, child, let me relief you of your suffering. Mister Milton isn't Mister Milton. He is Henry Howard, your Uncle William's older brother. Henry, meet Oliver Howard, William's adopted son," she introduces them with a bright smile.

"Henry... Henry Howard?" asks Oliver. His voice is hoarse, as if it is choking with shock. "But when I met with you in Dublin you were adamant that you were a friend and colleague of uncle Henry's. So, you lied to me? And now you are here? I don't understand." Says Oliver confused.

"Last week in Dublin?" asks aunt Eleanor now also confused.

"Yes, aunt Eleanor, that's where I went last week to look for uncle William's brother, Henry."

"Uncle Henry, son," Henry helps him correct. "I'm sorry for lying to you at the time. You are a stranger, and I have maintained to be dead to my own family for more than thirty years. I was definitely not telling a complete stranger who I really was. But then you told me about William's deteriorating health, and, well..."

"Apologies. But Uncle Henry, if you grew up with Uncle William..." Oliver looks at Aunt Eleanor, a bright light of excitement in his eyes. "Uncle Henry, you would then know about the secret hiding place Uncle William talks about. Right, Aunt Eleanor?" He suddenly frowns suspiciously. "That is to say, if you really are Uncle Henry Howard, because we all know he died years ago in Ireland."

"Let's rather say: I wánted to die because the bomb-raid not only maimed my body but also my spirit," says Henry, and Oliver can hear in his voice a measure of the pain he must've gone through. "That is now over with, Henry," says Aunt Eleanor calmly. "I know I was upset with you for having deceived myself and your poor parents but how can I judge you when I haven't walked even two miles in your shoes?"

He looks at her gratefully, gets up and holds his hand out to Oliver. "Nice to meet you, Oliver. Do you belief me now, or should I keep my reservation at The Swan Hotel in town?"

Embarrassment paints Oliver's face a bright red. "Aunt Eleanor and grandmother Caroline are the only two people who didn't reject me as a child, now I am overprotective over Aunt Eleanor. I apologise for my initial suspicion," he says and shakes Henry's hand. "Nice to meet you too, Uncle Henry."

"Henry, you can help Oliver," says aunt Eleanor enthusiastically. "I already told you: William suffers from stomach cancer. I believe he has remorse for never telling Oliver who his real parents were. William realises his time is getting short, and so he told Oliver there is an envelope with letters and documents hidden in a secret hiding place which would give him all the answers he is looking for. I remember you and William had a secret hiding place as children. Can you still remember where this place was?"

Henry frowns as he tries to recall his youth while Oliver watches him intensely. He smiles slowly. "William and I had several secret hiding places, but usually the staff would find our hidden treasures sooner or later and would then take it back to our rooms or throw it in the rubbish."

"Isn't there then a secret hiding place?" asks Oliver with a feeling that he just lost everything in his life.

"There was one hiding place which no-one had ever discovered. But whether it is still there – I would have to go to Stanton Manor to show you, Oliver."

"Could we possibly go there right now, Uncle Henry?" he asks eagerly.

Henry chuckles cynically. "Have you forgotten about my face, young man? And what about my so-called death? Beatrice and Emily would have to be fore-warned that I am still alive, and William...I would appreciate it if I could have a talk with William's nurse before I visit him. He is a sick man. The shock of seeing me again could be detrimental to his health."

"That is so thoughtful, Henry," says Aunt Eleanor approvingly.

"I'll drive back to Stanton Manor right away to get Alice," says Oliver and walks to the back door.

"Oliver, wait!" Henry holds his hand up in the air. "I've had a very long journey and it's getting late. Tomorrow is another day."

Oliver takes a step closer to him, his blue eyes almost purple-black with emotion wanting to scream like a madman about the unfairness life has dealt him, and now he is so close to the answers he's been looking for his entire life. "Uncle Henry, do you know how long twenty-nine years are? Every day of my life I've wondered: who am I? Where do I come from? Who my parents were? I'm not a Howard, Uncle Henry. I am Uncle William's and Aunt Emily's foundling-child – a nameless, illegitimate child, who could never be part of the wonderful Howards. I have no name. I have no lineage. I am no-one. I am a supposed adopted child, but I was never even afforded the right to call my adoptive parents Father and Mother. Aunt Emily made sure that I never forgot, not for even one minute of one day, that I was merely an extra mouth to feed, humiliated, treated with disdain, always a burden – and now you ask me to wait one more day, Uncle Henry?"

Henry gazes at him in silence, his face expressionless. "Aunt Eleanor tells me you are a successful cardiologist, but still unmarried. Your namelessness has crippled you from the inside."

"If you understand, Uncle Henry, why must I wait until tomorrow to bring Alice here to you?" asks Oliver, his voice hoarse with tense emotion.

Henry sighs tired and covers his face with his hands.

"You are being unreasonable, Oliver. Henry is dead tired," says Aunt Eleanor quietly.

Henry looks up and smiles at her. "No, I'm just being a coward,

Aunt Eleanor. There are matters William and I have to discuss – matters I would prefer to postpone. But the man is right: why wait until tomorrow?" He looks at Oliver. "Bring William's nurse here, Oliver. I will talk with her. And warn Beatrice that I am still part of the living."

"I shall do that, Uncle Henry – and thank you very much," answers Oliver and storms out of the back door without his raincoat.

"Thank you, Henry. You have no idea what it would mean to the boy to, at long last, know who his parents were," says Aunt Eleanor sincerely.

Henry laughs humorless. "I wouldn't know, but to see William and Emily and Beatrice again with my scar-ridden face ... If I could, I would've permanently postponed my visit to Stanton Estate."

"Now you are just talking nonsense, child," Aunt Eleanor chides. "Look in the mirror again: you look like an attractive pirate. Your face didn't shock me, only the fact that you weren't dead. And Helen treats you like always. When a woman loves..." She abruptly breaks of her sentence and clamps her hand over her mouth, her eyes wide on Henry.

"Say that again, Aunt Eleanor, did you say -"

"I spoke without thinking," she interrupts him angrily. "But it happens when one gets to the age of seventy-eight. You become senile overnight."

"Or perhaps just honest?" he asks. She remains quiet and he leans closer over the table and says urgently: "Should I rather ask Helen if you were speaking the truth, Aunt Eleanor?"

Eleanor looks at him resentful, sees the seriousness on his face and sighs impatiently. "I am now committing a sin, Henry, because Helen confided in me in confidence. You see, already as a young girl, she had fallen in love with you, but you were three years older than she was and you were in love with Annabelle. She realised you would never love her."

"I don't believe it! Helen always treated me with a measure of contempt, as if she wanted to make it clear I didn't deserve to inherit Stanton Estate," he answers in disbelieve.

"A girl with pride and self-respect uses all methods to hide her true feelings, Henry. But I know why Helen never married. Only a few days ago she was sitting right in the very spot where you are now, and she told me about the only man she had ever loved: Henry Howard."

Henry remains silent for so long that Eleanor assumes he is not going to answer her. "I should probably not have told you, child, but now you know," she says repentant.

"I am not the same man Helen once loved, Aunt Eleanor. My scarred face – "

"Yes, all right, you aren't busy buttering me up, Henry. Helen lives under this very same roof as you do. Ask her if her love which made her a spinster is strong enough to make her forget that you aren't young and handsome anymore," she interrupts him angrily, upset, and guilty because the betrayed Helen's trust.

"I don't dare, Aunt Eleanor! How can I ever expect a beautiful woman like Helen – " His voice slams shut in his throat as the passage door swings open and Helen walks into the kitchen.

She smiles confused. "Did I interrupt something? Should I have knocked?" she asks teasingly.

"You come as if you were sent, Helen." Says Aunt Eleanor calmly. "Henry wants to know if you could love a man with a scarred face and an artificial leg."

"Aunt Eleanor!" Henry jumps up from his chair. "I can certainly still speak for myself. I haven't lost my voice."

"Only your self-confidence, dear, so I shall help a little bit," says aunt Eleanor innocently.

Henry frowns angrily and glances shyly at Helen, who has a red blush on her cheeks and looking like a trapped rabbit. "I apologise for Aunt Eleanor's straightforwardness, Helen. You and I will have our chats – to really get to know each other. Who knows, maybe... maybe you wouldn't want to go back to London."

"Henry is trying to say that he would like to marry you, Helen." Aunt Helen translates again.

Helen smiles calmly. "Thank you, Aunt Eleanor, but I agree with Henry: we would like to get to know each other better."

Eleanor sniffs loudly. "At my age there is no time to wait. I'll let you two alone. Get to know each other. Fast," she says impatiently and walks out of the kitchen.

Henry and Helen look at each other and then start laughing with the carefree joy of two people who know that time is no factor in the wonder of their newly found love and a life together.

Beatrice steams into the kitchen with Alice in tow right behind her. She stops right in front of Oliver, heaving for breath. "Here she is, Oliver but I warn you: if I die of stomachache my death will be on your head. But that is how it goes with fat people: they receive absolutely no mercy from others. No, because we are all gluttons who – "

"For goodness' sake, Miss Crompton, be quiet for one second and listen to me," Oliver interrupts her irritate. "I have very important news to tell you, news about uncle Henry Howard."

"Oh, my word, dear. Why must you speak about the dead right now at this moment when it feels I could die from my stomach?" she asks resentful and moans in pain as she clutches her stomach.

"Who said I wanted to speak about the dead, Miss Crompton? Sometimes it so happens one hears of the death of another and then it is only a story."

Beatrice's eyes widen in her suddenly pale face. "Blimey, child, you aren't trying to tell me that the news about Henry's death and funeral was purely a story?"

"That is exactly what I'm trying to tell you, Miss Crompton." He looks at Alice who is now also staring at him wide eyed. "The man, John Milton, whom we picked up this morning... Well, I already met him last week in Ireland. That's where I went. But then he told me that he was a friend and colleague of uncle Henry's at the University of Dublin, and he assured me that uncle Henry did indeed succumb to his injuries after the German bomb-raid. He decided to come back to Arundel after I told him that uncle

William has stomach cancer and doesn't have much time left. He told me this morning that Uncle Henry Howard never died. He is, in fact, uncle Henry and aunt Eleanor and aunt Helen confirmed his identity. He is very eager to talk to you, Alice. Are you free to come with me?"

"If Miss Crompton would keep an eye on Uncle William. He is sleeping now, but in case he should wake before I'm back," answers Alice, and forces herself to not sound too eager.

"Wait, Oliver. First tell me exactly what this John Milton..." Beatrice starts curious.

"There isn't time now, Miss Crompton. Don't tell everyone the news just yet, Uncle Henry wants to handle this in his own way," he warns, takes Alice by the arm and steers her out the back door.

Alice sits on the end of the kitchen chair and listens to Henry, her eyes bright with happiness which she can't begin to express in words. John Milton is Henry Howard – and Henry Howard will know where the secret hiding place is which has kept the secret of Oliver's lineage hidden for so long, she thinks ecstatically to herself.

"Only you would know whether William has the strength for a meeting with me, Alice. Does he not have any heart problems?" Henry asks concerned.

Alice smiles reassuringly. "No, uncle Henry, there is nothing wrong with his heart. And ever since he and Richard mended their relationship, his is also in much better spirits. But I'll warn him first that you are coming to visit him."

"Let's go then," says Oliver, his expression drawn and unnaturally pale. "While you talk to Uncle William, Uncle Henry can show me where the secret hiding place is." He turns to Henry, "Please, Uncle Henry?"

"Patience isn't one of your virtues, is it, young man?" says Henry with a slight smile, but he gets up from his chair.

Emily sits on her gold-plated chair looking haughtily at Richard entering her private sitting room, and without even glancing at her, sits down on the couch opposite from her.

"I didn't give you permission to sit, Richard," Emily says coldly.

"You also didn't give me permission to breath, Mother, but yet I'm doing it. I'm on my way to Charlotte, Mother. What did you want to discuss with me?" he asks fearless.

"There is nothing left to discuss," she snarls, her eyes glowing with a barely controlled anger. "You taunted me openly today, in front of total strangers... You, the son I sacrificed everything for. But you made your choice. Marry that gold digger but remember: you won't inherit one penny."

"Maybe not from you, Mother. But my father already promised me that I will remain his heir,"

Richard retorts calmly.

The blood drains from Emily's face and makes her eyes seem black against her white skin. "So, now your father and you are conniving against me behind my back." She says in a hysterical voice.

He smiles slightly. "Who has been conniving all these years, Mother? Stanton Estate and the transport company belong to Uncle Henry."

"No! That is a lie! Henry is dead!" she shrieks upset.

"Uncle Henry isn't dead, and you know it, Mother. But my father isn't a poor church mouse. I am grateful to him, because I don't want to be the poor man who marries a rich wife"

"You can be a million... a multi-millionaire if you don't marry that woman. I will leave the Montgomery farm and all my investments to you. You could pick and choose from all the girls in England," Emily plays her Ace.

Richard rises from his chair. His expression determined. "I already chose, Mother. I'm marrying Charlotte. Now you have to choose: if you still want a son then accept Charlotte as your daughter-in-law."

"I would rather die!" Emily screams hysterically. " You will not get one penny from me! I will leave everything to Oliver!"

"Do that, Mother. I've always wondered whose illegitimate son

Oliver really is, but now I know," says Richard with a smile and walks out of the room.

Alice holds William's hand in hers and smiles compassionately in his eyes. "You look so much better after your nap, Uncle William. Is the pain bearable?"

"A pretty face like yours makes me forget about the pain, child," says William and squeezes her hand lovingly. "Ever since you came to me… It's as if I have given a new chance on life. Richard is getting married, and who knows, I might even get to see my first grandchild." He smiles. "Even a dying man can still have dreams, Alice."

"We all die one day, Uncle William. Forget about that word. You want to live, and that is all that is important." She falls silent, uncertain how to give him the news about Henry.

"You can speak, child. What is bothering you?" He asks, as if he can read her mind.

"I… I know Uncle Henry isn't dead," she says softly.

He smiles. "Did Richard tell you?"

"No, Uncle William. Uncle Henry was worried because he hasn't heard from you in almost two years. He tried to phone but Miss Crompton answered the phone every time. Uncle Henry couldn't risk talking to her, and so he decided to come here."

William sits up in his bed, an expression of relief and joy on his face. "Henry is here? My dear child, if that is the truth…"

"Just don't get upset, Uncle William. You don't have to talk to Uncle Henry if you don't want to," says Alice concerned.

"No… no…you are concerned for no reason." His eyes start to swim in his tears. "It is the answer to all my prayers… I have to talk to Henry, Alice. Ask him to come to me."

"I'm already here, William." Says Henry from the open bedroom door and walks quickly over to the bed. He holds his hand out to William. "Hallo, my brother. If I had known you were sick, I would've have come much sooner."

William grabs his hand in both of his. "You are here, Henry, which is all that matters now." He looks at Henry's scarred face, a ghost of his youth in his smile. "You still win, right Henry? You are still more attractive than I am."

"I've always wanted to be a pirate," says Henry grim and sits down on the chair next to the bed. He looks at William intensely. "How are you really doing, William?"

"I'm good... really good. Because at last I have the opportunity to confess my guilt," says William hoarse.

"Your guilt?" asks Henry confused.

"Giuliana... I did as you said: after my visit with you in the hospital in Dublin I went looking for her. I found her living with one of her friends."

"Yes, I remember Louisa, they lived together when I met..."

"Let me finish, Henry. I told Giuliana that you had died, and I invited her to come back to England with me. When we arrived back, I booked her into a hotel in London, and then I came back to Stanton Manor."

Henry smiles. "Giuliana never knew I was the heir to an Estate or the transport company. Was she surprised to see Stanton Estate?"

William shakes his head, a silent plea for forgiveness in his eyes. "I didn't account for Emily. She believed you had died; that she was now the owner of Stanton Estate. She insisted that I kept quiet about Giuliana, or she would leave me. I... I was too weak to refuse her anything."

"Then our parents never met Giuliana?" asks Henry restrained.

"Let me go, Beatrice!" shrieks Emily from the passage. "I want to know who is with William!"

"I will lock you in your room, Emily Howard!" roars Beatrice and comes heaving for breath into the room behind Emily.

Henry looks up irritated. "Hallo, Emily. I see you still behave like a spoiled little brat." He smiles slightly as he looks at Beatrice. "Hallo, Beatrice. Am I seeing double? Or have you gotten fatter?"

"My goodness gracious..." Beatrice stares at him in shock and then she smiles as brightly as the summer sun. "Henry! Lo and behold! Emily, it's our very own Henry!"

Emily audibly gasps for breath, stares at Henry as if she is seeing a ghost, and then pulls her lips in a sneer. "That's funny," she says, and starts laughing, softly at first and then louder until her hysterical laughter has her clinging to the bedroom door.

Beatrice hesitates for just a moment, walks to her, and gives her a slap in the face.

"Ouch!" Emily pushes Emily away from her. "You idiot! I'm not hysterical! I'm laughing because of Henry's stupidity to ever have trusted William." She looks at Henry, a light of madness in her eyes. "Has he told you about Giuliana, Henry? Your wife stayed in that hotel room for seven months and then she died giving birth to your son."

"My son?" asks Henry, his voice a hoarse whisper of shock.

"That is what I wanted to tell you, Henry," says William guiltily. "I wrote to you that Giuliana was too sick to return to Italy, but… but she was pregnant. She died giving birth to your son."

Alice notices the scar on Henry's face turning purple, and realises how deeply upset he must be, but she knows that no-one can console him.

"Was… was my child buried with Giuliana?" asks Henry softly.

"No, Uncle Henry," says Oliver from the door and he enters the room with a brown envelope and some letters in his hands. "I looked in the old grandfather's clock, I removed the false bottom, and I found all the evidence about my past which I've been looking for so long."

"How dare you, you cursed foundling-child?" Emily screams and tries to grab the envelope in Oliver's hand. "It's mine! It's mine to destroy! Stanton Estate belongs to me!"

"Not anymore, Aunt Emily," says Oliver gruffly. "I am Henry and Giuliana Howard's son. I am not an illegitimate foundling-child, my dear aunt, my parents were married. But you knew this all these years, right, Aunt Emily? You could humiliate and curse me to your heart's content, while I had more right to Stanton Estate than anyone else here, except for my father."

"Oh, dear, just look at me bawling now," sniffs Beatrice, and takes out her little lace handkerchief to wipe her eyes. "And you too, Alice-child. Oh, dear child, all this time the foundling-child is the sole heir to Stanton Estate."

"Henry..." William's voice is hardly audible. "I could never refuse Emily anything, because I... I once loved her."

Henry takes his hand in his. "I understand, William, and I know what you did for my son without Emily's knowing. We'll discuss everything." He gets up, walks with a slight limp to Oliver, and puts his hands on his shoulders. "Your name should've been Henry," he says, hardly audible, a tremble in his voice.

"I am Oliver Henry Howard. Does that sound better, Uncle Henry?"

Henry smiles slowly. "It would sound even better if you would call me Father."

"I think I could manage that... Father."

They smile wordless at each other and then Henry turns to Beatrice. "Please remove this venomous woman from William's room, Beatrice, and make sure that she remains in her suite from now on, or she can return to the Montgomery farm in Chichester."

Emily head jerks up. "Come pack my bags, Beatrice. I have never in my life been a lodger. I shall return to the Montgomery farm," she demands haughtily and turns to walk out of the room.

"Hold it right there, your highness!" says Beatrice angry, her hands on her wide hips. "I warned you, Emily: when I pack my bags it is to go straight to my own family. I'm staying right here, and you are staying with me, or you can return to the spiderwebs and bats at the Montgomery farm all on your own. Do you understand me?"

Emily's face falls. She has lost William's love a very long time ago because she demanded from him to keep quiet about Oliver's lineage. Richard has already rejected her; only Beatrice, her loyal Beatrice, has remained. "I don't feel too well, Beatrice. Please, come sit with me for a while," she says meekly.

Oliver holds his hand out to Alice. "I am certain Uncle... e ... my father and Uncle William want a few moments alone. Let me show you where the secret hiding place was, Alice."

Alice looks at William concerned. "Do you need me, Uncle William?"

A smile pulls at Williams lips. "Not as much as Oliver, dear. Go with him."

Oliver's big hand closes around hers and they walk out of the room.

"It is time you and I had a serious talk," he says as they walk down the passage towards the stairs.

Alice nods. "I understand. Matron Frances is not willing to marry you while I live here. I will pack my bags immediately and return to Tortington. I understand if you want to appoint another nurse to take care of Uncle William. I don't want to be the cause of any unpleasantness between you and Matron Frances."

"That is very kind of you, Alice. But seeing that Frances and I aren't on speaking terms, not on any personal level in any case, I also don't see how you could cause any unpleasantness between us."

"Oh…" She looks at him uncertainly. "But that night at Norman's dinner party… I thought you were in a relationship."

He frowns angrily and says upset: "No, but if you insist, I will go fetch her. What is the matter with everyone? Will no-one allow me to decide for myself who I want to be with? I don't rub your nose in the whole Norman debacle, do I?"

"But…" Hope flickers like a small candlelight in a dark room. "But don't you love her?"

"Love? Have I ever said that? Alright, I was an idiot, I told you I didn't believe in love, but that is over now – for good. I now know what real love is. When you love someone, but you are nobody and you have nothing to offer this girl…When you don't even have a name to offer, then it is safer to believe love doesn't exist."

Alice shakes her head, back in the darkness of her broken heart. "No, that isn't true. But I hope this girl you speak of will also learn to love you one day, Oliver, because a futile love… Excuse me, please."

"Oh, no, not this time, Alice."

He unexpectedly stops on the stair landing, his big hands on her shoulders.

"I am old enough to get married. And I am more than in love to get married. And this past month with you has been more time than I needed to know I can't, I won't, live without you. Could you love me just a little bit, Alice?" Love glows in his eyes as he waits anxiously for the answer he so desperately longs to hear.

"You, Oliver, you believe in love?"

His smile is shy. "I've always thought it is a fairy-tale…" He falls silent and frowns angrily when he notices the sparkle in her eyes. "If you are teasing me, Alice, I shall pull you over my lap! Why don't you answer me?"

"Aren't you going to show me the secret hiding place?" she asks, embarrassed about her fast breathing and the blush on her cheeks.

"I first want to show you your hiding place, little Alice," he says with an unknown tenderness in his voice.

"My hiding place?" she asks, and it feels as if her heart stops as she holds her breath waiting for his answer.

"Yes. Tight in my arms, here in my heart." He pulls her close to him, his fingers stroking her cheek, a caress, a touch of love. "I like your fairy-tale land, my little Alice, because you taught me what love is, my beautiful beloved. Can you ever love me as much as I love you? Maybe even agree one day to be my bride?"

She bites her lower lip. "You… you are now the sole heir to Stanton Estate. Nobody will know that I have loved you long before… e… I mean…"

"You have loved me long before, my little Alice?" he asks, and laughs softly. "Oh, you lovely, beautiful girl! You are my whole life. You captured my heart that very first day in the parking lot…and I thought I loved you then. You can call me a chauvinist, a bully, an insolent nitwit, but just always love me!"

His lips find hers and then reality disappears, and they are carried away on the wings of their passion to a magical world of their undying love.

About The Author

Chrisna Kruger

"I've come here with no expectations, only to profess, now that I am at liberty to do so, that my heart is, and always will be, yours."
— Edward Ferrars, Sense and Sensibility (1995 screenplay)

From Jane Austen to Toni Morrison, one can find the most romantic and beautiful literary quotes in their classic romance novels. I am sure classic literature quotes about love will never be old-fashioned! The ultimate dream is to also be quoted alongside these remarkable writers.

I grew up in a time when everything explicit was highly censored and love was still sweet and dreamy, romantic - I prefer it that way. I have always dreamed of writing but always lacked the courage (I became a nurse, it was the "sensible" thing to do). Now I am taking that leap, at last, for the first time!

The old classic romances still make us all believe in, or at least dream of, true everlasting love. I hope to write classic romance novels for the 21st century. And what is a romance novel without an element of magic to it or if it can't take one to another world or time, whether real or imaginary?